SOUL OF A MOUNTAIN MAN

LOGAN MOUNTAIN MAN SERIES - BOOK 1

DONALD L. ROBERTSON

CM Publishing

COPYRIGHT

SOUL OF A MOUNTAIN MAN

Copyright © 2020 Donald L. Robertson
CM Publishing

All rights reserved. No part of this publication may be reproduced, distributed or transmitted in any form or by any means, including photocopying, recording, or other electronic or mechanical methods, without the prior written permission of the publisher, except in the case of brief quotations embodied in critical reviews and certain other noncommercial uses permitted by copyright law.

Publisher's Note: This is a work of fiction. Names, characters, and incidents are a product of the author's imagination. Locales and public names are sometimes used for atmospheric purposes. Any resemblance to actual people, living or dead, or to businesses, companies, or events, is completely coincidental. For information contact:

Books@DonaldLRobertson.com

❦ Created with Vellum

LOGAN FAMILY GENEALOGY

Ethan William Logan, 1779
    Married
    Rose Isabel Tilman, 1780
CHILDREN
Matthew Christopher Logan, 1797
Mark Adair Logan, 1798
Nathaniel Grant Logan, 1803
Owen Lewis Logan, 1803
Jennifer (Jenny) Isabel Logan, 1812
Floyd Horatio Logan, 1814
Martha Ann Logan, 1816

Matthew Christopher Logan, 1797
    Married
    Rebecca (Becky) Nicole Doherty, 1810
CHILDREN
William Wallace Logan, 1834
Callum Jeremiah Logan, 1836
Joshua Matthew Logan, 1840
Katherine (Kate) Logan, 1851
Bret Hamilton Logan, 1852
Colin Alexander Logan, 1854

1

August 1, 1830, Limerick, Tennessee

The tall young man stepped up to the line and looked at the rag tied on a stick two hundred yards in front of him. It would stand at attention, indicating a stiff breeze, and then fall limp. The wind had been unpredictable all morning. *Of course,* he thought, *it's like that every day in these hills.*

The crowd behind him had fallen quiet, waiting. As soon as the rag dropped, in a smooth motion, he brought the .54-caliber Virginia 2nd Model Flintlock Rifle to his shoulder while thumbing the hammer to full cock.

A large section of the wood chip that was tacked to the stump disappeared behind his thin blade front sight. The wood chip sizes had decreased with each round of competition. This one was a two-inch square. The competition had started with forty competitors and a six-inch chip, but it was now down to five shooters.

The long thirty-nine-inch barrel settled, steady in the sixteen-year-old boy's big hands. If watching him from behind, a stranger would have seen a full-grown man.

He was already reaching for six feet, and his slim hips only accentuated the wide shoulders that supported thickening biceps and forearms.

As the front sight settled on the wood chip, the boy released half of the air he had inhaled and held it for only a moment. His eyes took in the rag as it fluttered. He caressed the trigger. The quiet was split, first by an earth-shaking sneeze, then the powder in the flintlock's pan ignited in a small white cloud, followed by the crack from the controlled explosion inside the rifle. A cloud of smoke chased the two-hundred-and-thirty-grain lead ball from the barrel.

He held his sight picture, though nothing was visible through the dense cloud of burned powder, then lowered his rifle and stepped to the side, out of the smoke cloud.

The county judge walked out to the stump, bent over to examine the hit or miss, straightened up, removed his black top hat, and waved it back and forth over his head. Faintly, the crowd heard, "Dead center."

From behind him, the same man who had sneezed said, "Damn!"

The boy's pa whipped around and confronted the man. In a low but threatening voice, he said, "You're a stranger here, mister. I'll thank you to reserve your gutter language for the saloon. There are ladies and children present."

The boy spun around at the man's exclamation. His pa looked at him, nodded his head, and said, "Good shooting, Floyd."

Floyd returned the nod and stepped off the firing line. He had been the final shooter. Now they would nail up a one-inch chip. Floyd grinned to himself. *It's going to be mighty interesting.* With his keen eyesight, he was able to see the sharp outline of the chip against the stump, and even the small nail in the center securing it.

He glanced back at the man behind him, who now said nothing but glared at first his pa and then him.

Mr. Jedidiah T. Webley, the owner of the Feed and Seed store, was in charge of the shooting competition at the fair this year. His involvement was nothing new, since he ran it every year. Floyd watched as Mr. Webley strode over to the man who had cursed. "Mister, you stand well back from the firing line when you're not shooting. You don't need to be disturbin' the shooters with your sneezin'."

The man growled something so low that Floyd was unable to hear him, but Webley did. "I don't care if it was an accident. We don't need that kind of accident when a body's shooting. If it happens again, you'll be disqualified. You understand me?" Without waiting for the man's response, he turned back to the firing line and waved for the judge to tack the next chip onto the stump.

The judge shouted back, "It's already there."

Webley took out his glasses and slipped them over his nose, stared downrange, and waved back to the judge. "All right, folks," he said, "we'll be getting this next round going. Men, you'll fire in the same order, though I'd be surprised if any of you hit that little bitty thing."

"I cain't even see it," someone shouted from the crowd.

"Zeke," another member of the crowd said, "you done drank so much corn likker, you cain't see yore feet." Loud laughter burst from the crowd.

"All right now," Webley said, holding his hands up. "I ain't lettin' these fellers shoot until you all settle down, so let's have some quiet."

The crowd quieted, eager to continue the contest.

It had been raining off and on all day, but Floyd had enjoyed the county fair. Friends he hadn't seen since last year came into town from miles away, and this was the first time they allowed him to shoot with the men. He knew most of the competitors, but the man who had cursed he didn't know. While Mr. Willis was getting ready to shoot, he examined the stranger.

The man was bigger than average. Unruly, dirty black hair

jutted out from under the man's beat-up flop hat. He reminded Floyd of a bear, with little beady eyes. A beard covered almost all of his face. His chin hairs were stained from food and coffee and no telling what else, and he wore a greasy buckskin shirt and trousers. The crowd had given him and his partners a wide berth, especially on the downwind side.

Floyd shrugged. He didn't need to know the man, he just needed to beat him and the other three. The white chip against the dark stump stood out clearly. *Little bit smaller than a turkey's neck,* he thought.

The first man, Mr. Willis, who always bragged about his shooting, toed the line, loaded, and fired. Clean miss. Shaking his head and mumbling about the crosswind, he turned and walked away from the firing line. Neither of the next two men came close to the target.

The stranger stepped to the line, and before he began loading, he made a big production of looking at the trees near the shooting line, then checking around the target area. The grimy man rubbed his chin whiskers and appeared to calculate. Then he gave a decisive nod and at once began reloading. His rifle cradled in his left arm, he first opened the pan, poured in a dash of powder, and clicked it closed. Then he placed the butt of the rifle on the ground and, with the barrel near vertical, poured powder down the barrel from a horn. After finishing, he held the powder horn in the air and announced to the crowd, "Buffalo I killed on the plains."

Next he placed a patch of cloth on the muzzle, set the ball in it, and, using the ball-starter, drove the ball almost six inches down the barrel. He dropped the starter back into his fringed bag and pulled the long ramrod from its housing beneath the barrel. With one smooth motion, he drove the round ball down until it was tight against the powder.

The man brought the rifle to his shoulder and waited. Floyd watched the muzzle, solid at first, start swaying, drawing tiny circles. The man continued to aim at the chip, and with each passing second the sway became more pronounced. Just when Floyd expected the man to bring the rifle down, rest, and start over, there was a flash, and the rifle fired. At the same time, from deep in the crowd, there was another big sneeze. Floyd grinned. He recognized his good friend, Ezra.

Mr. Webley spun around, eyes searching through the crowd, his lower jaw thrust out like a bulldog.

Floyd realized he was holding his breath, waiting for the judge's call. This time, the judge's hat stayed on his head, and he yelled one word. "Miss."

The man charged up to Webley, yelling about being distracted because of the sneeze. Floyd eyed the target flag and the target. He didn't want to lose his concentration, even though it was almost impossible to keep from laughing. The man finally stomped by, glaring at Floyd. He leaned near and said, "Don't cross me, boy. You'd best miss. Those pistols are mine." Floyd ignored him and stepped up to the line.

While waiting to fire, he had run a dry patch through his barrel to pick up any loose burned powder that might affect the flight of his bullet. He primed and loaded his rifle, pulled the hammer to full cock, and glanced at the makeshift flag, which was now standing straight. The wind had picked up and was steady. He'd have to hold the width of the chip to the left.

The rifle had no sooner settled into his shoulder than he fired. The shot felt good. This time the smoke cleared quickly because of the wind, providing Floyd a clear look at the judge waving his hat and yelling, "Dead center!"

The crowd erupted in cheers. It was a dream come true. The entry fee had been expensive, five dollars, but he had saved for it, and now he had won. He had won that brace of US Harpers Ferry Model 1805 Flintlock pistols. They were .54 caliber, the same as his rifle. With the addition of the handguns, his supplies were complete. He was ready. Hopefully he would be able to persuade

Pa and especially Ma into letting him go. He'd be off to the shining mountains.

He might have looked like a man from the back, but from the front, with his enormous grin, his was the face of a sixteen-year-old boy.

Pa stepped up and squeezed his son's shoulder. "Floyd, that was some fine shooting. I was a mite concerned when the wind picked up like that, but I shouldn't have been."

Even at his near six-foot height, he had to look up as he grinned into the dark gray eyes of his pa. "Thanks. I just did what you taught me."

"Son, I taught you all I know, but that kind of shooting comes from an inborn skill. Don't let it go to your head, but you've got the touch. Now, let's go get those pistols."

"Not before I give my boy a hug, you don't." A woman, almost as tall as Floyd, elbowed her way past the crowd to step up and encircle him in her long arms.

He hugged her for a moment, then pushed against her arms. "Ma, we're in public," the embarrassed teenager said.

"Hang the public," she said, but released him. "Look at you. Why, you're not yet grown and shooting better than all these men." She waved her arm around to emphasize her remark.

One stepped up and stuck out his hand to Floyd. "Rose Isabel, don't you be embarrassing my nephew."

"Good shootin', Floyd. I 'spect if these old eyes were what they used to be, I could've given you a right smart challenge."

Floyd's pa responded quickly to his brother. "Paul, you've never seen the day you shot like that." He turned to Floyd. "Let's go, son. You've got some pistols to pick up."

Floyd's ma patted her brother-in-law on the arm. "That wasn't the smartest statement I've ever heard you utter."

"Well, I ain't never been much at not sayin' a thing when it's passin' through my head."

Rose stared at her brother-in-law. She shook her head, took him by the arm, and said, "Come on, let's go see those pistols."

"You did it, Floyd," a boy shouted. "I knew you would." He was about Floyd's age, not quite as big.

"Thanks, Ezra. Come on. We're headed after the pistols." He looked at his pa. "That's all right, isn't it, Pa?"

"Sure, join us, Ezra."

The pistols were on display at the Feed and Seed store. As the five of them stepped off the boardwalk to cross the street to the store next to the livery, four horsemen, led by the losing mountain man, pulled up in front of them. With the wind blowing from them to the Logan family, they smelled like something had crawled inside those buckskins and died.

The man tipped his hat to Ma, then turned his hard gaze on Floyd. "I told you to miss, boy."

Though only sixteen, Floyd laid his cold blue eyes on the man. "Mister, my pa tells me what to do. You don't and never will."

One of the man's gang leaned over and spit between Floyd's boots, then in a whiny voice said, "Boy, it ain't smart to talk back to Trace Porter. He's killed more men than you are old."

Floyd felt heat flush his neck. His pa and older brothers had taught him to back down from no man, and now his temper was rising. He held his rifle in his hands, and though it was unloaded, it made an excellent club. Training had prepared him in the use of the heavy long gun should there be no time to reload. His face remained expressionless as his muscles tensed to bring the butt of the rifle around and into the chest of the man leaning over the saddle. His father's hand tightened on his shoulder, and he tried to relax, but his temper continued to flame.

Pa gently pushed Ma back, and he and Paul stepped up on either side of Floyd. Ezra joined them.

"You'd best be riding out of town," Pa said. "You threaten my son, you threaten me. I don't take kindly to threats."

Porter, if that was his name, locked eyes with Floyd's pa.

The whiny-voiced miscreant moved his hand to the pistol that rested behind his sash, and said, "You farmers are biting off more than you can chew."

Floyd's pa shook his head and, in a low voice, said, "Go ahead, son."

The words hadn't cleared his mouth before the butt of Floyd's rifle started its arc. Floyd, his left hand on the forearm and his right on the small of the stock, released the tension in his shoulders and back, much like releasing a compressed spring. Speeding up as it moved through its deadly arc, the butt of the stock didn't stop when it came in contact with the whiner's oversized belly. The power of the blow lifted the man from his saddle and drove him over the rear of his horse, slamming him to the ground flat on his back, his feet sticking straight up. With the impact of his body on the ground, the air surged from his lungs, leaving him gasping for air, lips popping like a beached catfish.

Meanwhile the other three men, after getting their horses under control, reached for their weapons, but halted at the sound of at least forty rifle hammers clicking to full cock.

The man on the ground regained his breath and struggled to his feet, his face twisted into an evil grimace. "You shouldn't oughta done that, boy."

"Get on your horse while you still can," Uncle Paul said, his rifle muzzle centered on the man's belly.

The constable stepped forward. "Now's the time for you boys to ride out of here and keep going. We don't want to interrupt our fair today to bury four strangers."

While his friend climbed back on his horse, Porter looked around at the rifles pointed at them. He leaned over toward Floyd. "Don't come west of the Mississippi, boy. If you do, I'll hang your guts on a cottonwood tree for the magpies to eat." He straightened up, kicked his horse, and the men raced out of town, leaving only a cloud of dust as a reminder of their presence.

Floyd boiled with anger. His pa's calming hand on his shoulder restrained him. He looked around the street. They were backed up by neighbors and friends, some merely acquaintances, but people who had lived a life of defending what was theirs. There were some still around who had fought in the Revolutionary War, many who had fought in the second war of independence, or what the Brits called the War of 1812. Almost all had defended their homes against Indians. They wouldn't stand for a bunch of brigands hurrahing their town.

Ethan, Floyd's pa, made eye contact with most of those there and waved. "Thanks, folks." He turned to the constable and extended his hand. "Thank you, David."

"Think nothing of it, Ethan. Now, why don't you folks go get Floyd's pistols."

Floyd, the anger already passing, grinned at the constable, and with Ezra by his side, continued across the street. He nodded his thanks to the people he passed, as everyone went back to enjoying the fair. He walked around a big covered wagon with the six-mule team parked in front of the Feed and Seed store. Once inside the store, he saw Mr. Webley motion to him, and went straight to the glass counter where the pistols were prominently displayed.

"Congratulations, Floyd," Webley said as he opened the back of the counter.

"Thank you, sir," Floyd said, his blue eyes glued to the hands of the storekeeper pulling the two shiny weapons from the display case.

Webley lifted a pistol from the leather-covered, silk-lined display box where they both rested. He held it up to the light, the sunlight bringing out the warm glow of the polished wood. "These are fine pistols, Floyd. What's a boy like you going to do with a set like this?"

"I've got a plan, Mr. Webley."

"Well, my boy, I'd like to buy them from you. Say twenty dollars?"

Floyd picked up the remaining pistol. *Twenty dollars,* he thought as he tried the balance of the weapon. *That's a lot of money, but I need these pistols.* "No, sir, I'll be keepin' 'em."

"You need powder and lead, Floyd?" Mr. Webley asked, placing the pistol he was holding back in the box.

"No, sir, I've got plenty." He took a moment to load the pistol he had been holding, then shoved it behind his waistband, picked up the other pistol, loaded it, put it back, and closed the display box. After picking up the box, he turned to start toward his pa, only to find a stranger standing next to him.

The man, wide shouldered, with a ruddy complexion, was about his height and Pa's age. His trousers, held up by a set of wide red galluses, were tucked into calf-high black boots.

"That was some fine shooting, young fella, fine shooting. Name's Hugh Brennan," the man said and extended his hand.

"Thank you, Mr. Brennan." Floyd took the extended hand, noting the powerful grip.

"You won yourself a fine set of pistols. I imagine if you take good care of them, they'll come in handy sometime.

"Hope you don't think me too nosy, but it was impossible not to overhear you turn down Jedidiah's twenty-dollar offer. It whetted my curiosity. If you don't mind my askin', what's a boy like you plan on doing with a brace of pistols such as those in a small town like Limerick?"

If asked, Floyd would be unable to say why, but he had taken a liking to the red-faced stranger. He looked around. Ma and the girls were across the store, examining a bolt of blue material. They had called Pa over to show him, and he was nodding. The storekeeper had left the counter to help another customer.

Floyd lowered his voice to a conspiratorial tone and said, "I aim to go west, Mr. Brennan."

The man turned his head to look toward Ma and Pa, then said, "Call me Hugh. Do your folks know?"

Floyd shook his head. "I haven't told them yet, but I think Pa suspects. I tend to wander on my hunting trips. Sometimes I'm away for several days."

Hugh also lowered his voice. "This presents an interesting situation. I'm headed to Santa Fe de Nuevo México, by way of Independence, Missouri. I came back to see my family in Georgia, and I'm now returning to Santa Fe. I've known Jedidiah for many years and wanted to visit him for what will probably be the last time. Fortunate I was indeed to be here during the fair and see you shoot."

Floyd's heartbeat increased. He tried not to get excited, but he knew something important in his life was happening. He looked over at Ma and Pa and the girls, and they were still talking. Ezra was at the end of the counter, trying to decide what kind of hard candy to buy, and here this Mr. Brennan was talking about going west—*to him.*

"Anyway," Hugh continued, "I need someone to help me with the mules, hunt, and quite honestly, I feel more comfortable with an extra gun around."

"I can do it," Floyd blurted out.

Hugh held up his hand. "Now wait, Floyd. Don't be hasty. It looks like you haven't even told your folks of your desire to go west. I was planning on just saying howdy to Jedidiah and headin' on out. If you're interested, I can give you some time to talk to your folks. I can wait and leave in the morning, but it has to be early."

Hugh stopped and chuckled. "Son, you ain't even asked me how much I'm willing to pay you."

Floyd's eyes got bigger. "You're payin' me?"

"Reckon so. I can't have word get around that Hugh E. Brennan takes advantage of folks. How does driving mules, workin' from can to cain't, huntin' and scoutin' new country, and thirty dollars a month sound to you?"

Floyd, his deep blue eyes flashing with excitement, thought, *I'm going west. I'll see those tall mountains and trap beaver in no time.* Then his vision shifted to his folks. They had both stopped talking and were staring at him.

2

"Mr. Brennan, I need to tell my folks, and you should meet them."

"Why, that'd be a pleasure, Floyd." He turned to Pa and Ma as Floyd waved them over.

"Ma, Pa, this is Mr. Hugh Brennan."

"Mr. Brennan, I'm Ethan Logan, and this is my wife, Rose." Pa extended his hand.

Floyd watched Hugh tip his hat to Ma and take Pa's hand, meeting the couple with an open gaze.

"I'm pleased to meet you. Your son is quite a marksman."

Ma's smile was friendly but cool. "Mr. Brennan, our son can shoot quite well, but he is much more than a marksman."

The only sign of Pa's humor was a slight crinkling at the corners of his eyes. "But you're right, he is quite a marksman." The pride was clear in his voice.

Ma threw Pa a sharp glance and said, more a statement than a question, "You are not from around here, Mr. Brennan."

"Please, ma'am, call me Hugh. No, I'm not. My last living relatives back east are in Georgia. I came out to see them, probably for the last time, but I live out west, with the rest of my family."

"Oh." Ma nodded, now looking at Floyd. "You are on your way back home?"

"Yes, ma'am, I sure am. I'm a trader, mostly in beaver, and I'm headed back to my home in Santa Fe de Nuevo, México. I know Jedidiah from way back and wanted to swing by Limerick to see him. Lucky for me, your fair is going on."

"Well, it's nice to meet you, Mr. Brennan. I hope you have a safe trip." She turned to call over her shoulder, "Martha, Jennifer, let's go. We'll stop back by the store when we return from the fair." Turning back to Hugh, she nodded—"Mr. Brennan"—and herded the girls toward the door. Pa remained.

"Aren't you and Floyd coming, Ethan?" Ma said, pausing as she reached for the door latch.

Pa cast a knowing glance at Floyd and said, "Go along, Rose. Save me some pecan pie. I'll be along in a while."

The door closed behind Ma and the girls, and Pa turned back to Floyd. "What's going on, son?"

The moment had arrived. Both Ma and Pa were aware that Floyd had itchy feet. He came by them honestly, from both sides of the family.

Floyd tilted his head back to see his pa's eyes and said, "Pa, Hugh, Mr. Brennan, has offered me a job." He paused for a moment, took a deep breath and stated, "I plan on taking it."

The silence was heavy. Pa stared at his youngest son, who was not yet seventeen, for a long moment. He turned to Hugh. "Why would you offer my boy a job? You made it this far without a hand. Why do you need one now?"

"Did you see your boy shoot, Mr. Logan? You must realize there are few grown men who can shoot that well. I'll admit, watching him shoot, I would have sworn he was older. Look at him. From behind he looks like a full-grown man, and I watched how he handled Grif Pike." He gave a terse laugh. "Pike will never live that down."

"You know those men?" Pa asked.

"I do. They are poor representatives of mountain men. They're mean and lazy. I have no idea why someone hasn't shot them before now."

Pa shook his head. "Mr. Brennan—"

"Call me Hugh. May I call you Ethan?"

Pa nodded.

"Good. Ethan, I'm an excellent judge of mules, horses, and men. As I mentioned, I trade in beaver pelts. The trappers, mountain men, sell to me, and I transport the pelts to Independence or St. Louis. There I market them to the big buyers from the east coast and London. My business depends on my judgment of men, and my word. I choose not to trade with Trace Porter or any of the trash that rides with him."

"Good for you," Pa said. "I'm just not ready to turn my son loose yet. He's not even seventeen."

"Pa, I'm almost. I'll be seventeen in January."

"But you're not seventeen now, and what will your ma say? Have you considered her feelings or your sister Martha? And though you two aren't as close, what about your older sister Jennifer? It'll hurt all of them something fierce."

Floyd looked at the floor, then raised his head. "Pa, they'd be hurt no matter when I leave. I belong out west. It's on my mind all the time, and I'm set on going."

"Ethan," Hugh said, "I've spent many years in those mountains. I've crossed the plains more than most. Your son needs training, what to look for, which Indians are friendly and which aren't, how to read mountain weather. I can teach him that and more, and in turn he can help me. I'm not the spring chicken I used to be. Those mules can tire a man. I'll watch after him and teach him as long as he's with me. My family and I will welcome him in our home just like a son."

Floyd waited while his pa deliberated. The silence was heavy. Now, in a more conciliatory tone, he said, "Pa, Matt was only sixteen when he went to New Orleans to fight the English with you and General Jackson."

Pa shook his head. "That was different, son. Our country was being attacked. Now, I can tell you're restless. That's why I never said much when you were gone so long on your hunts. I figure, like most of the Logans and your ma's folks, you've got the wanderlust. But when you leave, we may never see you again."

Through all of his thoughts of his western adventure and planning, the possibility of saying goodbye to his family for the last time had failed to register with him. He had traveled far, for a lad, and had always returned. But now he recognized the truth in what his pa was saying. Standing here, right now, the way he figured, he was at least three months from the mountains. That would be a six-month round trip. How often could he travel half a year to see Ma and Pa, his brothers and sisters, and especially his little sister Martha, who so depended on him?

His eyes started to tear up, and he coughed, trying to hide the emotion. He whipped his head around to see if anyone else noticed.

Ezra had bought some hard candy and was amusing himself by looking at the rifles on the wall behind the counter. He turned, observed Floyd looking at him, and motioned his head toward the door. Floyd held up a finger, relieved that Ezra didn't seem to have noticed. He turned back to his pa.

"I never considered that, Pa. To be truthful, it makes me ache a bit, but the whole world is out there. You know my skills are pretty good, and I can learn. Deep down I know I'm meant for big things, and those things are out west. It's difficult to explain, but those mountains have a pull on me, and I've got a chance to go with a man who knows them. This just seems like it's supposed to be."

Hugh nodded his head. "I ain't for gangin' up on you, Ethan. But the boy speaks the truth. I had no other reason to be here today except to visit Jedediah, and I stopped at the shoot and watched your son with his rifle. I will not say that's providence, but it is, for sure, a powerful coincidence."

Pa looked out the window at the wagon. "When are you planning on leaving?"

"Winter's pressing me to get back home, and those plains are miserable when the snow flies. But I told Floyd here that I'd put up at the boardinghouse and leave in the morning if he's planning to come along."

Floyd knew when to be quiet. He could see Pa was ruminating on the decision.

The patriarch of the family turned back to his son. "I knew this day would come. I was just hoping it would be later by a couple of years." Then Pa's tone became hard and cold. "Mr. Brennan, I'm also an excellent judge of men, and Jedidiah is a friend. I figure you for an honest man, but if I'm wrong, and I ever hear you didn't do right by my boy, I'll be coming after you along with the entire Logan clan."

Pa raised his right hand and extended his index finger, his hand now a fist except for the long finger leveled in Brennan's face. The hand emphasized each of the next four words before dropping to his side. "Now, under those conditions, if you can still hire my son and teach him what he needs to learn and survive out there, then here's my hand on it."

Floyd watched Hugh meet the older Logan's hard gaze, then reach out and take his hand. "I'd not expect anything less. I can't guarantee his safety, but I can dang sure guarantee my efforts."

The two men shook hands and the solemn moment passed. Pa clapped Floyd on the shoulder and said, "Son, it looks like you're going to get your wish. Now get Ezra before he fidgets himself to death, and you two go shoot those pistols, but make it quick. When you're done, get yourself back to the fair. You need to be spending the scant time you have left with your family. It's gonna hurt them bad enough this evening when we have to explain what's happening."

"Thanks, Pa." Somehow the joy of winning and now shooting the pistols had vaporized. In its place was a deep, hollow ache, though tempered with the excitement of a new adventure.

Floyd turned to Brennan. "I'll be there before sunrise, Mr. Brennan. You won't have to wait on me."

"You do that, Floyd. Bring only the clothes and gear that you need. I'll provide the riding stock and grub. Now git."

Floyd strode to the counter and picked up the box containing the other .54-caliber US Harpers Ferry Model. "Let's go, Ezra."

The two boys hurried to the door. Before reaching for the latch, Floyd waved to Pa and Brennan, then turned to the storekeeper. "Thanks again, Mr. Webley."

Webley waved to him and said, "You earned 'em, Floyd. May they keep you safe for many years to come."

Maybe they will, Floyd thought. For now he wanted to find out how good he was with a pistol, let Ezra try it, and tell him about the coming departure.

THE PISTOL SHOOTING was enjoyed by both Floyd and Ezra, but the amusement ended when he informed Ezra he was leaving. Floyd understood his friend's disappointment. They had been friends since each was a toddler. Over the years, they had planned their grand adventure to the western mountains.

Though Ezra had given lip service to the trip, the recent years gave Floyd doubts whether Ezra's heart was truly in it. In fact, Floyd knew a young lady who lived just down the lane from the Masons' place had captured Ezra's heart. Here recently, Ezra Mason would get almighty tongue-tied when he talked to the pert Elizabeth Graham, known to her friends as Liza. Ma had said they were perfect for each other, and each time she mentioned them she would stare at Floyd with a raised eyebrow. He always ignored the gaze.

Also, Ezra had never gone on one of Floyd's long hunts. He always had an excuse. It had become obvious that Ezra would die right here in Limerick, Tennessee. *Well,* thought Floyd, *not me.*

At first Ezra's anger burst out, and he accused his friend of thinking only of himself, but soon relented.

Floyd saw the relief in Ezra's eyes when he realized he wouldn't have to make the decision.

"Shoot," Floyd said, "by the time I get back, you and Liza will be married with a slew of kids."

Ezra hit him on the shoulder. "Hush up. Ain't no one around here getting married any time soon."

Floyd rubbed his shoulder, grinning. "Bet you."

"A man's not supposed to gamble."

Floyd rolled his eyes. "I'll bet you one of these pistols that when I get back, you'll be hitched. Not only hitched, but hitched to Liza."

This time Ezra grinned back. "That's my plan if she'll have me."

Now Floyd whooped. "I knew it. All that west talk was just talk. You've had your eyes on her since we were in short pants."

Brow wrinkled, Ezra fixed Floyd in what was supposed to be a hard glare, but was more humorous than menacing. Finally, looking up at a squirrel that had come out after the shooting had calmed down and was now sitting on the end of a limb, barking at them, he said, "I've always liked her."

"Yes, you have." Floyd glanced at the sun working its way down the western sky. "I've got to be getting back to the fair."

Floyd opened the box, and Ezra laid the empty weapon into the silk-lined cutout space that gripped the pistol. "These are nice pistols, Floyd."

"Yes, they are. I'll clean 'em tonight when I get home." He closed the box and shoved the remaining pistol behind his waistband. "You going back to the fair?"

Ezra looked down and kicked a crawdad mound over, then

glanced at the nearby stream. "No. I don't think so. Liza was going home early from the fair. Think I'll wander by her place."

He looked up, eyes big. Floyd blinked twice and thrust out his hand. "Ezra, you've been a good friend. I'll miss you."

Ezra took his hand. The boys stood like statues. The squirrel ceased barking, spun, and raced to a hole in the tree. A bullfrog bellowed in the stream, while a fish splashed. Ezra blurted out, "Be careful in those mountains." He jerked his hand away and, with his rifle in his left hand, dashed down the road.

Floyd watched Ezra grow smaller in the distance, little clouds of dust rising from where his feet struck the dirt road. Ezra disappeared around a bend in the road. Loss weighed on Floyd's large frame like an anvil strapped to his shoulders. He stood, watching where his friend had been. He looked up at the hole where the cat squirrel had disappeared.

Floyd shook his head, took a deep breath, and picked up his rifle, turning to head in the opposite direction from Ezra's departure. He needed to get back to town and the fair. He took two steps toward the road.

"Hold it right there, boy!" Three of the mountain men stepped from the brush, their rifles leveled at Floyd's middle.

Floyd's thoughts flashed to the pistol in his waistband, but he had not reloaded after shooting it. He had planned on cleaning it later today. *Pa always said keep your weapons loaded, no matter what,* he thought with disgust.

"Heh, heh, heh. Look at him thinkin', Trace. I swear he wants to pull that pistol and shoot us."

Trace Porter, his eyes beady, and his lips pursed so tight Floyd hardly saw them under the filthy beard, lifted the muzzle of his long-barreled rifle until it was pointed into Floyd's face. "I'm itchin', boy, don't tempt me. It's been a week or two since I kilt me a white man. It'd be a fine pleasure to do it now. Nobody'd suspect nothing, what with all the shootin' you've been doin' and what's goin' on at the fair. Now lay that there rifle on the ground nice and easy."

Floyd gingerly laid his rifle on the ground, keeping his eyes on the three men.

Porter, using the muzzle of his rifle, pointed toward the box Floyd carried in his right hand. "You can hand my pistol box on over to the rightful owner." He extended his left hand, holding his rifle in his right like a pistol.

Floyd blew a blast of air between his lips and said, "I am the rightful owner. I beat you fair and square."

Porter looked at Grif Pike, the man Floyd had knocked from his horse, and nodded. Pike, right hand on the grip of his rifle and left on the forearm, stepped forward and, before Floyd could move, hit him with a horizontal butt stroke.

The slap of the polished wood striking Floyd's cheek cracked like a whip. The blow staggered him, but he remained on his feet. His cheek burned like he had thrust his head in a bed of hot coals, and his vision turned into brilliant stars for a few moments. He shook his head and tasted blood in his mouth. With his returning vision, he glared at Pike.

"Don't look at him, boy," Porter said. "I'm the one you're a-needin' to worry about. Now gimme that box afore I drop you where you stand."

Floyd felt the rage inside him. All he thought about was getting his hands on Porter and Pike. But reason kept interfering with his anger. He knew they'd kill him without a second thought. In fact, they still might. The pistols weren't worth dying over. Against his every desire, he extended the box toward Porter.

The older man grabbed it from him. "Keep him covered," he said to his two men, leaned his rifle against the tree, and opened the box. The other pistol nestled in its red silk case. He grinned, showing two missing teeth. Those remaining were dark, some broken.

Looking up at Floyd, Porter extended his left hand. "Gimme, but make it nice and gentle. I know Pike'd like to gutshoot you."

Floyd pulled the remaining pistol from his waistband, handing it to Porter.

Porter pulled the hammer back, exposed the pan, and laughed. "What were you going to do, boy, throw it at us? Ain't you growed enough to know you reload after you shoot? Why, I swear, you're just a babe in the woods. If I don't kill you, and I still might, you'd best never go west. 'Cause babies that don't reload their guns die quick." He guffawed at his last remark, slipping the pistol into its slot in the box and closing it. His gang members joined in.

Floyd's face burned from the gun butt, but also from embarrassment and anger. "I'll go west, and I'll find you. If you're smart, you'll leave those pistols right here, but if you take them, I'll find you, and when I do, I'll kill you."

Boswell, the third man, who had been quiet up to now, said, "We'd better kill him, boss. He means it. Look at them eyes."

Porter quit laughing and stared at Floyd. "Mather, you may be right. I don't like the looks of this young feller, not at all. Why, look what he did to Pike. He knocked him clean off his horse, and Pike not botherin' him at all.

"Are you serious, boy? You gonna come west and kill us?"

Floyd tried to hold his peace. His death sentence might be signed right now, but he couldn't stop. In a low menacing growl, never heard from him before, he said, "Every danged one of you."

Porter watched Floyd for a moment longer, then looked at Boswell. "Why, Mather, I think you're right. Look at this boy. He looks downright mean. Whatcha think we oughta do?"

"Finish him right now, boss."

Porter turned back to Floyd and stared at him.

"Nah, not now. Did you boys see all those folks back in town? We kill him, and we'll never get out of this country alive. Those fellers what was with him looked like they'd be mighty contentious should we harm their family.

"We'll just take these pistols, and because this here boy has been so unfriendly, we'll take his rifle too. How 'bout that, boy? You like us takin' yore rifle?" He turned to Boswell. "Pick up his rifle, Mather."

Floyd's mind raced. *How can I go west without a rifle? I can get by without the pistols, but I need a rifle.* "Mister, you can't take a man's rifle."

Porter, his biceps bulging through his filthy deerskin shirt, handed the pistol box to Pike and stepped closer to Floyd. "What's yore name, boy? I want a handle for who's huntin' me."

Floyd glared at the cold-eyed brute. "My name's Floyd Horatio Logan, and you'd best remember it, for I'll find you, and I'll—"

Though big, Porter was quick. Floyd had no hint of the coming sucker punch. The right haymaker landed solidly just in front of his left ear. The big fist split the skin at the edge of Floyd's eye, and the signet ring Trace Porter was wearing cut deep into his temple. He collapsed in a heap.

3

Someone was calling him. He finally recognized his ma's voice. He was in a well, but he could hear her yelling for him to wake up. *That's a funny thing to be saying. She ought to tell me to climb out. I hear her, but I can't see her.*

He strained to open his eyes. They were so heavy, like wet leaves sticking together. The right one opened and his ma was bending over him, wiping his face with a cool, but bloody wet cloth. The question he had was *who is hurt?*

"Floyd," his ma said, "can you hear me? Can you understand me?"

His right eye focused on her face, but it was almost impossible to get the left one open. What he could see out of his left eye was blurry. His eye and head hurt like crazy, but he still smiled up at his ma. "You sure are pretty, Ma. Everybody says so."

At that, she blushed and wiped his face a moment longer. "It sounds like you were knocked silly. Now stop with the foolish talk and tell me what happened."

A soft, small hand held his right hand. It was his sister Martha. He could see where tears had coursed down her round cheeks. He lifted his hand and, with the back of it, gently wiped the tears away. "Why have you been crying, Martha?"

"Floyd, we were so worried. Pa said you'd be back to the fair after you and Ezra went to shoot your new pistols, and you didn't show up for the longest. I got worried and mentioned it to Ma. She and Pa had been talking about something, and I could tell it was serious, from her face, and she looked around and called to Pa. He said it wasn't like you, and—"

Ma stepped in. "Slow down, Martha. You make me feel out of breath just listening to you. Anyway, Floyd, we went looking for you and found you in the grove. Your pa, uncle, and brothers, along with the constable and many of the townspeople, are out looking for the ruffians who did this to you."

"It was the mountain men, Ma. Porter wanted my pistols." He found it difficult to open his left eye wider than just a crack. He reached up to touch it. Ma took his hand in hers, pulling it down to the bed.

"Leave that eye alone for now. It's swollen and tender. It looks like they must have hit you with a club."

"The butt of a rifle. It was that Pike. The guy I knocked off the horse. I guess he wanted a little payback."

Ma's brows wrinkled with concern and anger. "Did he have something inset in the stock? Because you have a deep, circular cut just above your jawbone? You'll have a scar from it, no doubt."

He tried to shake his head, and it was like a load of gunpowder had gone off—all lights and pain. After long moments of recovering, he said, "I'm sure he didn't. I would have noticed it."

Floyd considered for a moment, started to nod his head but caught himself, and holding his head motionless, answered, "I was talking to Porter. He was close. Then I remember nothing." He was quiet, eyes closed, his mind churning. He remembered, just before he blacked out, a blur of motion—a fist. Floyd jerked his eye open, anger flooding in again. "Ma, he sucker-punched me! I never saw it coming. I owe him."

His ma placed her hand on his shoulder. "Relax, son, get some sleep. We'll talk about it in the morning."

He leaned back, relaxing into the bed, restful sleep blanketing him in its comforting warmth.

He jerked awake. This time, the left eye cracked open along with the right and fixed his ma with a steady gaze. "Ma?"

With sad eyes, she looked down at her youngest son. "Yes, Floyd."

"Pa told you, didn't he?"

She raised her head and looked out the window, watching the sun disappear, coloring the few clouds first gold, then orange, followed by purple and, the last few moments just before darkness, gray.

Rose Logan looked down at her youngest son. "Yes, Floyd. He told me."

"I've got to go, Ma. The Far West is out there calling me. I belong out there, and Mr. Brennan will take me and teach me."

Martha looked into Floyd's face, her eyes wide with surprise. Her lips started trembling. Tears again escaped her eyes to cascade down the plump, soft cheeks. "Ma? What's he talking about? He can't leave. Especially not now. How can he travel hurt like this?" Then she looked at her brother. "Why do you want to leave, Floyd? We have everything here. Your family is here. I'm here. I'll miss you."

Ma shook her head. "Son, in all the excitement, we hadn't yet told the girls. You can't leave now. Not hurt like you are. You must rest."

Floyd turned to his sisters. Even Jenny, now eighteen and well aware of his desire to head west, had tears in her eyes. He looked at his youngest sister. "Martha, I've always wanted to head to the Far West, the shining mountains. They pull me every day, every hour. You mean all the world to me, but one of these days you'll meet a young man. He'll take you away to build your own family. This is something I have to do. I ache to go."

Through the tears she stared at her brother. Then she threw his hand down on the bed and dashed from the room.

Jenny patted his shoulder. "She'll be all right. It'll just take time. You're her big brother. She's losing her protector. Let her cry it out." She turned and left the room, following her sister.

Floyd turned to his ma. He didn't know anyone tougher than her. She had plenty of suffering in her life. By the time she had labored to bring him into the world, she'd had two miscarriages, lost three children in childbirth, and a fall had killed his older brother Mark. Now he was leaving, maybe never to see them again. Guilt invaded his soul. But he couldn't turn away from the pull of the mountains.

He looked into her eyes. "Ma, I can't rest long tonight, only two hours at the most. Mr. Brennan wants to leave early, and I've got to get my gear ready."

The acceptance of an irresistible force washed over her countenance. Patting his strong hand, she smiled. "Yes, son. This day has been expected since you started disappearing in the forest. My regret is that it has come much too soon. You rest now. I'll wake you in a few hours. Don't worry about anything. There will be plenty of time for you to meet Mr. Brennan. Now get some rest."

Floyd watched her rise and walk over to the window. She stood looking at the darkness, as if searching for hope in the gloom. Long moments passed. Then she pulled the curtains together, turned, and walked from the room.

He relaxed back into the bed. Something nagged at him, but his head throbbed like ten smashed thumbs. It would come back when he woke. Floyd closed his eyes, enjoying the last soft bed for many months to come.

∼

His right eye opened, followed slowly by his still swollen left. Shock coursed through his body. He could see a brightening blue sky to the west. *Oh no, they didn't wake me. Mr. Brennan said before daylight. What have I done?* He leaped out of bed and grabbed the clean clothes that lay on the back of the chair. Once dressed, he yanked his boots on, jerked open the door, and dashed into the common area. He slid to a stop.

People filled the common room, which included a sitting space around the fireplace, kitchen, and long dining table. Ma stood at the wood-burning stove with Jenny and Martha. Pa was at the table, joined by Floyd's uncle Paul, older brothers Matthew, Nathan, and Owen, along with, and now his swollen left eye widened, Mr. Webley and, to his even greater surprise, Mr. Brennan.

Mr. Brennan is still here! he thought.

Now the smell of Ma's cooking registered. He watched Martha picking up the empty breakfast plates from in front of the men at the table. She walked to the washtub, where Jenny was washing the dishes, and slipped them into the water.

The low conversation had halted when he stepped into the room.

"Come on over and have a seat," Pa said, indicating the chair between him and Brennan. "How are you feeling, son?"

Bewildered, rubbing his jaw, Floyd walked over to the chair and sat.

"I'm not sure, Pa." He looked around the table at the men. "Jaw's a little sore, and my left eye's a little blurry—" He pivoted to Brennan, who was sitting on his right. "But my shooting eye is my right eye, Mr. Brennan, and I'll be fine before long."

Brennan laughed and clapped Floyd on his back. "I'm sure you will, boy. You're a lot tougher than Porter and his worthless bunch give you credit for. Your pa told me what happened. Why, I've seen that filthy sidewinder break the jaw of a full-grown man with his right fist. Reckon that's what he figured to do." Brennan laughed again. "But you showed him." He gave Floyd a good once-over. "Though it looks like you got pounded good."

Ma turned from the stove, wiping her hands on the long apron she was wearing. "I'll tell you what, Mr. Brennan, if I had known what that man would do to my boy, I would have shot him down in the street like the cur he is."

"Ma'am." Brennan nodded. "I have no doubt of your willingness or ability to back up what you say. I'm only sorry when he was born, his mother didn't put him in a tow sack with a big rock and drop him in the creek. That would have saved quite a few people the grief he's brought."

Ma loaded a plate of fresh ham, eggs, and grits and gave it to Martha. She brought the plate and a glass of cool milk to Floyd. She placed them in front of Floyd, leaned into his left ear and whispered, "I'm so sorry for acting silly. It was because I was surprised, and I'll miss you."

Floyd turned his battered face so he could see his sister with his good eye. "I'll miss you too, but I'll be back."

Martha looked unsure, but Pa spoke. "Martha, you don't have to worry. Floyd's a Logan. He *will* be back."

Brennan waited until Floyd finished eating and had emptied his glass of milk. Then he cleared his throat and said, "Mrs. Logan, thank you for asking me to this wonderful breakfast. Can't say I've enjoyed a meal as much as this since I left nome."

She smiled and started to answer, but he continued.

"But we've got to be on our way. There's a lot of country to cross, and I want to get home before winter sets in." He turned to Floyd sitting to his left. "Do you still want to go? Porter and his bunch are heading for the mountains too."

"Mr. Brennan, I ain't changed my mind, not one bit." He caught the frown on his mother's face. She couldn't stand *ain't* and always said it was a crutch for lazy people. He continued, hoping she wouldn't say anything. "Also, I'm not afraid of Porter or any of his bunch. I want to find him, now. We've got some settling to do."

"Good." Brennan shoved back from the table. "Then we'd best be on our way."

With shock, Floyd realized what he had been trying to think of last night just before he fell asleep. Before speaking again, the thought ran through his mind, *I don't have my guns, not even my rifle.*

His face fell. "Mr. Brennan, I've been so excited, I forgot. I don't have a pistol or rifle to my name." He turned to the storekeeper. "Mr. Webley, I've got my poke I've saved over the past three years. It has all my trapping money in it. There should be enough there to buy me a rifle, powder, and ball."

"Your pa told me you'd say that. You'd best talk to him."

Pa, as he was pulling Floyd's poke out of his pocket, said, "You're all packed, son. Your ma and the girls packed you up last night while you were sleeping. As far as your poke . . ." He dropped it on the table in front of Floyd. "I'd suggest you hang onto that for emergencies, for they always come along."

"But, Pa, my rifle, my pistols—they're gone."

"Yes, they are, but you've got family and friends here." He turned to his oldest son. "Matthew?"

Matt reached to the floor behind his chair and lifted the twin to Floyd's stolen rifle. "I bought this rifle new before you were born. You've shot it, you're familiar with it, and it shoots as true as yours did. I want you to take it." He watched Floyd prepare to object and held up his hand. "Hold on, brother. I have two other rifles, both good ones. I want to be sure you're protected by a good firearm. Take it." He stood, brought it around the table with a possibles bag and a powder horn. He grabbed Floyd by the right shoulder and squeezed, while handing him the bag and rifle.

"Thanks, Matt. I'll take good care of it."

Matt grinned at him as he walked back to his place at the

table. "You'd better, or I'll have to whip up on you when you come back."

"Your turn, Nathan," Pa said.

Nathan stood. "Well, it might surprise you, but we've known you were going to leave for quite a while. We just weren't sure when. On my last trip to Nashville, I stopped in at that well-known knife maker. I had him make you this, and I made the scabbard."

He reached behind his back and pulled a long, sheathed knife from out of his waistband. Gripping the hard leather sheath, he drew the knife into view.

Floyd gasped. He couldn't take his eyes from the long blade. At least eleven inches long, with a hefty brass hand guard in front of a thick antler handle. The antler had been polished and then lightly scoured to provide a secure grip.

Nathan handed it across the table to his young brother. Floyd took the knife in his left hand and grasped his brother's right. The two men held the grip, stretched across the long table. They released their grip, and while Floyd stood admiring the knife and sheath, Nathan straightened, with a satisfied smile on his face.

Floyd ran his thumb along the sharp edge and sensed a faint nick in the first layer of skin. He looked up and said, "It's beautiful."

Owen, his remaining brother, pulled a belt from his bag and tossed it to Floyd. It was thick natural cowhide leather with a hard steel buckle. "You'll need something to hang that frog sticker on."

Floyd looked it over. It was beautifully hand tooled and was a perfect fit. Owen was a master of leather.

He looked across the table at his brothers. "This is like Christmas. I don't know what to say."

Matt, the oldest, said, "Thank you will do, brother, and a promise to come back to see us with all your hair."

Floyd nodded. "Thank you, all of you. I'll be back with all my hair and looking way handsomer."

Everyone laughed, and Owen said, "That wouldn't be hard, the way you look right now."

More laughter erupted.

Owen continued, "I made you these. Once those heathens stole your pistols, I wasn't going to give these to you, but . . ." He tossed Floyd a pair of holsters he had made that would fit across a saddle. They were perfect for the Harpers Ferry pistols, but he no longer had them.

When he recognized what the holsters were, Floyd raised his eyebrows at his brother.

"I guess this is where I come in," the store owner said. He placed a bag on the table and removed an almost exact copy of the stolen pistols. "After your pa came to me last night and told me what happened, I remembered this one other pistol that I had for sale. I'd like to give it to you—"

Floyd started shaking his head. "Mr. Webley, I can't accept this pistol, but I'll pay you for it." He reached for his poke.

"No you won't, boy," Webley said. "You can consider this a loan. You'll have another reason to return home, to pay me back."

"Thank you, sir, I will."

"There's one more thing, Floyd," Ma said. "Martha, go get it from the bedroom."

He watched his sister run into his folks' bedroom and come out carrying something big, folded in her hands.

"Well, go ahead," Ma said. "Put it on him."

His sister came over and shook out a long coat. He looked at it. It was all heavy wool with a sewn-in lining.

"We split it in back so it could fit over a horse," Martha said, holding up the coat for him to put in an arm. He thrust first his right arm and then his left in the sleeves. The coat was heavy and warm. It was loose on him. He still had room for more clothes under it.

"How does it fit?" Ma asked.

"Perfect." He was already getting hot. "This will keep me warm in those mountains."

Ma nodded. "Good. Both your sisters had a hand in making it for you. We hoped it would be another year before you needed it, but at least it's ready."

Martha spoke up. "Ma worked on it most of the night, when she and Pa weren't getting your things together."

"That's enough, Martha," Ma said.

With the coat on, Floyd walked across the room to his ma. He put both his arms around her, hugging her tight, and whispered, "Thank you, Ma. Thank you for everything."

She looked up into her son's eyes and placed a hand against his right cheek. "You're welcome, my son. Come back home to me."

"I will."

Pa cleared his throat. "All right, now. We can't be holding Mr. Brennan up from his trip. Let's move this outside so they can take their leave."

Floyd, sweat breaking out on his forehead, slipped out of the heavy coat and started back to his room.

"Where you going, son?" Pa asked.

"I've still got to pack my stuff, Pa."

"No, you don't. All your clothes, along with extra lead and gunpowder, are already in the wagon. All you've got to do now is climb aboard."

Everyone followed Floyd and Brennan outside to the wagon. Tied to the back were two horses. A roan and a big black.

"Put your things in the back, Floyd," Hugh Brennan said. "You can drop the mister now and just call me Hugh." He winked at Floyd. "Like I told you to do yesterday."

"Yes, sir. Hugh."

He told everyone goodbye, giving Martha an enormous hug. She was trying to smile through her tears, with little success. He hugged his ma one last time. All that was left was Pa. He stood looking at the man who meant so much to him.

"Bye, Pa," he said, thrusting out his hand.

His pa took the hand and said, "I'm proud of you, Floyd. I want you to remember, always be honest with your fellow man, protect women, kids, and the mistreated, and step aside for no man. This Porter has shown you what he's made of. You don't have to be fair with him. Kill him the first chance you get."

"Yes, sir. I expect I will."

He turned from his pa and climbed into the wagon. Brennan clucked to the team, and they started out. Floyd looked back, waving until they made the first turn and were out of sight. He was going west. Why was he so empty? He looked up the road, his head turned so that Hugh couldn't see his watery eyes. *I'm supposed to be a man, not some sniffling little crybaby,* he thought.

"Don't let it bother you, Floyd," Hugh said. "Every time I leave my family, I get a little teary-eyed."

"I'll be fine."

Now he was looking to moving west. He was on his way.

"Yes, you will, boy," Hugh said. "You up to driving this team?"

"Yes, sir, anytime."

Hugh handed the reins over to Floyd. "Then take these ribbons and show me what you can do."

4

After a month at the reins, Floyd learned more about mules than he thought possible. He'd never had much to do with Blacky, Pa's mule, unless plowing. Pa or Matt usually worked her. However, Pa insisted on never forcing her to do anything.

Hugh agreed. In fact, he explained to Floyd the greater intelligence of mules over horses. Some riders figured they were just stubborn. Far from stubborn, they wanted to know their task would do them no harm. Once they developed trust in the action and the man, the task clearly explained, they completed it.

With his recent knowledge, he drove the six mules like a longtime hand. Driven through sunny days and wet, dry roads and muddy, the animals had become good friends.

Thanks to Hugh, who worked at fulfilling his promise to Pa, each new day moving west brought fresh experiences and sights to see.

Floyd admitted the first week he was homesick. Pa had taught him to be a hard worker. To combat the initial loneliness, he threw himself into his work, driving, taking care of the mules, digging out a stuck wheel, and, his favorite part, hunting. The hunting also provided Floyd the chance to learn his new firearms. The rifle Matt gave him could have been the sister of his. At a hundred yards, it threw the .54-caliber round ball as close to center as his stolen one did.

Each reflection on his rifle and pistols brought the old anger near the surface. *I'll find you one day, Porter. We'll settle our account. You can bet on it,* he thought.

Hugh spoke from the back of his horse, drawing Floyd from his dark thoughts. "There it is, Floyd. That's Independence, Missouri, the eastern end of the Santa Fe trail."

Excited, and rid, for now, of the somber musing, he said, "I've read about it, Hugh. But I never considered I'd be looking at it, at least not for a few more years."

"Well, you're seein' it now. Let's get on down to our barn." Hugh rode ahead.

Floyd popped the reins and made a clucking noise with his tongue. The wagon jerked as the six big animals stepped forward in unison. He smiled, enjoying the sight between the six mules' ears. He was living his dream. Many a night, since they left, Floyd felt like he might wake up any moment and be back home, sleeping in his bed. But he hadn't, and here he was, headed to those mountains to be a mountain man.

He had been learning more caution from Hugh. Though he grew up in the woods, Hugh explained the differences in the west. Alone, necessity required you to be constantly vigilant. If your horse threw you, or you slipped and broke a leg, or even got a rattlesnake bite, in most cases, there was no doctor around. Something as simple as a broken limb could keep a man from hunting or defending himself. It could mean death.

I already knew a lot, he thought, *but I'm learning more from Hugh.* The older man had even taught him a unique way of fighting. Pa had taught all the boys how to fight, but there was always another way to kick or a punch to learn.

As he pulled into town, Floyd saw several covered wagons much like Hugh's. *Wonder if they're going west like us.*

Hugh waved from a tall barn up ahead. He had dismounted and was allowing his horse to drink while he spoke with an old man at the barn. The man looked ancient. He was thin. His shirt hung from wide, bony shoulders. Thick gray hair hung past his neck, bulging from under his big hat. Behind his waistband, he wore a pistol. Floyd pulled the team up in front of the barn.

The man yelled at him, "Git off yore rear, boy, and git down here and take care of those mules. Ain't no time to be relaxin' up there. And don't forget the horse you got tied in back."

Floyd gave the old man a hard look, wrapped the reins around the brake handle, and jumped to the ground.

"Come over here first, Floyd," Hugh called. "I want you to meet Salty Dickens."

Floyd walked up, still eyeing the old man.

"Salty, this here is Floyd Logan. He's goin' west with me."

Salty eyed Floyd, then turned his head to the side, looking at him sideways. "You givin' me the snake-eye, boy?"

"I work for Mr. Brennan. I don't work for you. Save your orders for somebody else."

Salty eyed him for another moment or two, threw his head back and laughed, sounding like a chicken cackling after laying an egg. His face broke into a wide grin, exposing missing front teeth. "Boy, you *sound* like you're a little salty yoreself. Shake."

Floyd frowned for a moment, then grinned back, taking the bony hand. "Pleased to meet you, Mr. Dickens, I think."

That sent Salty into another spasm of cackling. "You are, boy, you are. You just ain't realized it yet."

"I find myself seldom surprised at anything Salty does or says," Hugh said. "He runs the stables for me on this end of the trail, now and then making a trip with me. Now let's get these animals taken care of."

"Yes siree," Salty said. "Drive that wagon into the barn, boy.

We'll unhitch in there and allow these fellers to get a drink and put on the feed bag. I bet they'd like that."

∼

Hugh watched Floyd trot back to the wagon and climb onto the seat. It was at least six feet from ground to wagon seat, but the boy grasped the top, took one step on a spoke of the front wheel, and vaulted up.

He popped the reins, spoke to the animals, and turned them into the street, making a loop so he could head the wagon straight into the long barn. The roan resisted only for a moment, trying to angle over to the outside water trough.

It was a wonder how Floyd had taken to the mules and the big wagon. Hugh could feel the excitement and determination from the lad, and it brought memories to him of his first venture west. A smile creased his dirty face. Hugh had always been an impulsive man. It had gotten him into trouble on occasion, but he always managed to either think or fight his way out of the problem.

Something had nudged him in Limerick as he watched the young man shoot. The calm with which the boy went about winning impressed him. He wasn't intimidated, shooting against the older men. Even when Porter spoke to him on the firing line, obviously threatening him, he remained calm. The young man exuded confidence. Maybe some of the attitude was just the brashness of youth, but there was something else, and that something else impressed Hugh. After meeting Floyd's pa, he could see whom he got it from. Ethan Logan was a man to be reckoned with.

Hugh had been thinking of hiring another man to return to Independence with him and on to Santa Fe. He was feeling his years. His old bones ached after a long day on the trail. He had been fortunate in his life.

He'd always had a knack for trading, and that talent had paid off in his first venture. It hadn't hurt that he was educated, fluent in Spanish, and could read men. These talents allowed him to make friends, not only with many of the merchants, but several of the Spanish aristocrats.

And now he had hired a young man, not yet seventeen, and taken him away from his family. But he felt no guilt, for he could tell Floyd would have left soon enough. That boy, whether he knew it or not, had vision and the potential to grow into just what the western country needed.

He also had a temper. Hugh had watched as Floyd swept Pike from his horse with the butt of his rifle. Hugh had also observed how quickly Floyd snapped back at Salty's orders when he felt the man had no right to be ordering him around. He'd need some guidance. The boy needed to learn to put a harness on that temper. Flying off the handle to the wrong man would get him killed. This country and the men in it were anything but forgiving.

~

FLOYD PULLED the team to a halt inside the barn. He looked up at the tall ceiling extending over the extended parking area. To his left there were individual stalls, and well above the stalls ran a hayloft that was only half filled for the season. On the peak of the roof, light filtered through the cupola that sat on top to help ventilate the barn.

There was an additional door at the opposite end, allowing a wagon to drive straight through. To his right, between wagons already parked in the large barn, doors opened into a corral. The corral was big enough to allow the thirty or more mules and horses occupying the space to move around and accept the mules he was driving.

Floyd jumped down as Hugh came from the stall where he had led his horse.

"Salty," Hugh said, "I don't see but two wagons. Where are the rest?"

"Those impatient hardheads already headed west."

Floyd watched Hugh take a deep breath, keeping a rein on his temper. "When did they leave?"

Salty shook his head and let fly a stream of tobacco. "August, about two weeks ago. Flagan said they wasn't about to wait for you. They had to beat the snow."

"What did Edward Flagan have to do with it? Isn't he the new banker in town?"

"Yep, he is, he and his son. This here Flagan don't know nothin' about trailing, though he convinced the rest of those inexperienced traders waiting on you that he had more sense than you ever had. Them boys even elected him wagon master."

"How many wagons?"

"Well, let me figger." Salty reached up and scratched the side of his head with his thumb. "Flagan had two wagons, and Wilson one. Smith had him two brand-new wagons he bought from us, mules too, Norris two more, and Jenson had three."

"Albert Jensen went with them?"

"Yes siree. He's the onliest one what's supposed to have any sense. I tried to talk him out of it, but he told me he couldn't wait, not knowing if you got waylaid or was even coming back."

"Albert knows I have a family in Santa Fe."

"Yep, he do, but he still joined 'em."

Floyd watched Hugh walk around in a circle, slapping his hat against his leg. It was the first time he'd seen his employer upset. Hugh slammed his hat back on his head and turned to Salty.

"Well, it can't be helped. How many men total went?"

"Now there's the rub. They've got five extra men to help with the mules, but Wilson and Smith took their families. Said something about starting their own place."

"What?" Hugh shook his head again. "The w during the day. The Indians will be chasing bu plains, trying to stock up with wintering meat. almighty big chance with their families and so few wag

"Flagan and his scouts told 'em everything would be fine. He talked up the importance of gettin' in before you, to get the best prices for their goods."

"Flagan's a fool. You said scouts, more than one?"

"Yore gonna love this. Flagan hired Trace Porter and his cronies. Porter came in a few weeks ago, deposited a little money in Flagan's bank, and got in tight with him."

Hugh shoved his hat back and rubbed his forehead. "Good night alive. Didn't anybody tell him about Porter and his bunch?"

"Boss, all them folks are new, 'ceptin' Jensen, and Flagan ain't listening to no one but Porter. You gotta admit, Porter's been in those mountains for quite a few years."

"I wish we had arrived earlier, but they were on horseback, and there's no way this wagon could keep up with them. Porter's a thief and a murderer. If he doesn't figure out a way to kill those folks and steal all their goods, it'll surprise me. Not to mention what that bunch will do to the women and girls."

"Porter pushed gettin' out ahead of you. He had Flagan and all the other new ones believin' if they beat you to Santa Fe, they'd git plumb rich."

"Don't they know the market's big enough for all of us? They should have waited. The additional men and guns would've provided greater protection for them and us." Hugh stopped, considered his last statement, then jabbed his finger at Salty. "That's what Porter didn't want! If the Indians don't get them, Porter will."

Hugh was silent for a few moments. Then, after an enormous sigh, he said, "Water under the bridge. They're well gone. We just need to be on our way. The reduced number of wagons and men put us in more danger, but there's nothing we can do about it. How soon can we be ready?"

"Everything's ready 'ceptin' for the wagon you brought in. I need to unload it and make sure the tarring is fresh over them joints. If it ain't, first river you try to cross, water'll come in faster'n I can spit. Axles and hubs will need greasin', too. You've also got two tires what need replacing. Noticed the iron was loose when you come in." Salty waved his hand toward the wagon. "Ain't no telling what else I'm liable to find."

Salty glanced at Floyd and winked. "If I can have the boy to help, we'll get it done today and you can pull out in the morning."

"Sounds good to me. What about the drivers?"

"I've hired drivers and helpers, just waitin' on you at Emma's Boardinghouse. Still need a scout, but I think that young feller Jeb Campbell is partakin' at the Trailhead Saloon. He's been to the mountains and Santa Fe. Jeb don't talk much, but he's smart and experienced. You'll have a fine scout if you can drag him away from Nora. They've become a pair."

Floyd dusted his hands off. "Mules are unhitched and lined up at the trough. Soon as they and the roan finish, I'll get them rubbed down. After that, I'll be ready to help Salty."

"Floyd," Hugh said, reaching into his coat pocket and pulling out a jingling leather bag, "here's your first month's pay." Hugh counted out five coins: two eagles, gold ten-dollar coins; one half eagle, a gold five-dollar coin; and two quarter eagles, each worth two and a half dollars.

Floyd was used to receiving pay for his trapping in currency and occasionally silver coins. He had only seen gold coins in Pa and Ma's savings jar. He held the five gold coins in his left hand, felt them with his right thumb, and looked at Hugh.

"Mr. Brennan, you're the first person ever paid me in gold. I swear, they are mighty pretty."

Salty spoke up. "They spend well too, boy. Most people I know like gold. Especially the crooked ones. They'll be happy to relieve you of that ballast mighty quick. So don't go 'round flashing those things until you need 'em."

Hugh nodded. "Salty's right. There're all kinds in town. Mostly honest citizens and traders, but there's also the element that prefers to make a living on other people's efforts. Watch yourself. You can eat and sleep at Emma's Boardinghouse. Just tell her you work for me.

"Now I'm going to find Jeb Campbell." He looked at the waiting wagon. "Looks like you two have a lot of work to do. Salty, when you're done, show Floyd to Emma's."

Hugh spun around and marched out of the barn.

~

JEB CAMPBELL, at a table in the Trailhead Saloon, had a slim, long-haired blonde at his side, clutching his left hand and talking earnestly. Jeb's skin, burned brown by the years in the mountains and plains, was in sharp contrast to that of his companion's. Her smooth skin rivaled the whitest ivory.

They both had celebrated their twenty-first birthday, though Jeb looked ten years older than the beauty who had his hand in a death grip. The hardness around his eyes and mouth that elicited caution from other men was gone, replaced with a smile that widened his mouth and crinkled around his eyes. On his right side, a chair was pulled close to brace his rifle. A pistol lay on the table.

Though it was only afternoon, the saloon was almost half full of thirsty men eager to win their next stake, or the company of a pretty girl. Smoke rested thick as a prairie fire in the enclosed room. Only the door presented an outlet for the smoke, but no one seemed to notice.

Jeb, distant, his mind back in the mountains, listened, not so much to the words, but to the musical lilt of Nora's voice. She extolled the virtue of his remaining in Independence and settling down.

He liked Nora. He liked her a lot. But he hadn't yet met a woman who could keep him from the mountains. He had been here nigh on to a month and was getting restless. He nodded a couple of times to her voice and motioned the barkeep over to give her another drink.

Nora was paid based on how many drinks she sold. Though he knew the house only served the girls a weak tea, for the price of whiskey, so they could continue to work until closing, he didn't mind. Everybody needed to make a living, and he enjoyed hearing Nora's voice. That was *one* of the reasons he came out of the mountains occasionally, to hear a woman's voice.

The barkeep walked up with Nora's drink just as a big bearded teamster staggered from an adjoining table. His feet tangled in the chair rungs, he stumbled back, jarring the bartender and causing him to stumble toward Nora, almost spilling the drink he was carrying.

Jeb enjoyed the action. In fact, grinning, he watched it all play out. Watched it right up to the point the teamster turned to the bartender, who had steadied and was placing Nora's drink on the table.

The big man shoved the bartender, this time causing the drink to splash onto Nora's neck and chest and the bartender to fall into her lap. The teamster wasn't finished. Swaying, he yelled at the bartender, "Stay out of my way when you're serving that slut!"

Jeb exploded from his chair. His right hand slid back to his tomahawk, resting in the belt loop on his right hip, as his powerful legs drove him up. While drawing the weapon, he stepped around Nora's chair and slammed the flat slide against the man's temple. The teamster dropped like a sack of feed, while his companions at the table slid back chairs, their obvious intent to seek revenge for their friend.

5

Jeb turned to the men, pulling his pistol from his waistband and waving the tomahawk back and forth in front of him. "Now you boys done seen what happened here. If you're hankerin' to help yore drunk friend, keep on a-coming."

Hugh had stepped into the saloon in time to see everything. With a drawn pistol in each hand, he said, "You men would be wise to drag your rude companion out of here. The people of Independence frown on his type of action."

The three men looked at the pistols and the deadly-looking tomahawk weaving back and forth like the head of a snake. They moved as one to the side of their companion still out on the floor. One of them looked at Jeb. "He'll be looking for you, mister. Butch here can hold a grudge."

Jeb lowered the hammer and slid the pistol behind his waistband, keeping the tomahawk ready. "Friend, you tell Butch here my name's Jeb Campbell. I'll be around town for a few more days, and I'm a real accommodating feller should he have a craving for me."

At the mention of his name, the three teamsters looked at

each other and wasted no time carrying their unconscious friend from the saloon.

Jeb looked over at Hugh, a big grin spreading across his face. "Been a while." He motioned to a chair at the table with the tomahawk, then slid it back into its loop.

Hugh pulled up a chair, removed his hat, and nodded to Nora.

"This here is Nora. Nora, this is my good friend Hugh Brennan, a trader out of Santa Fe."

Nora extended her hand to Hugh. He took it while dropping into the chair.

"Pleased to meet you, ma'am."

She gave him a cautious smile. "I sense you two have business." She stood, her hand lingering on Jeb's wide shoulder, and said, "I'll see you later?"

He grinned up at her and nodded. The two men watched her walk to the back, the exaggerated sway of her hips missed by no one. Then they shook hands.

The bartender started over to the table. "All I want is a coffee," Hugh called.

The man shrugged, turned and yelled back into the kitchen, "Send me a black coffee!" Moments later an older woman emerged with the steaming cup. The bartender pointed toward Hugh. She brought it over and set it in front of the trader.

"Anything else, sir?"

He shook his head, dropped a nickel on the table, and smiled up at the woman. "No, ma'am, I'm fine." Turning back to Jeb, he said, "What brings you east this time of year? Shouldn't you be getting ready for the season?"

"I stayed in those mountains the whole winter, had a good spring season, and decided to hear me a woman's voice. I miss that in them canyons."

"Get married."

At that, Jeb threw back his head and roared, "Cain't you see me settled down behind a plow. I'd be stark ravin' mad in less than a month. It's a whole lot easier to come back here." At this point he broke out into a wide grin. "Or go to Santa Fe. I know some mighty pretty girls there."

Hugh gave a mock frown. "Don't you be coming down to be a wicked influence on my daughters. Their mother is dangerous when some mountain man starts making eyes at her girls."

Again Jeb laughed. "You're sure right there. Lucia can be a fiery lady. Anyway, I came out to replace some old traps and add a few more. I almost went south to Santa Fe, but came out here."

Jeb could tell his last statement spurred Hugh's interest.

"You're buying more traps? Isn't seven or eight about all you can handle, considering hauling the weight in those mountains?"

"Well, yes and no. Normally you'd be right. But I've found a place in the San Juan Mountains that's easy to get to, with lots of beaver. I figured I'd set up a couple of extra lines, even take on a partner." He shook his head. "Although I can't think of a soul I'd trust, at least anyone who ain't already committed to another outfit."

Hugh nodded. "I think I might have a deal for you."

"I'm listening, but it can't take me out of the mountains. I'm about to head back."

Hugh nodded. "Good. This is something that might work for both of us. When are you planning on leaving?"

"Anytime. I'm itchin' to git back to them mountains. I already may have stayed too long, so I need to be leaving mighty quick."

"All right," Hugh said, "here's the deal. I'm leaving in the morning, and I need a scout. You're lookin' to head back. From here in Independence, we could make it in as little as seven weeks. That would put you in Santa Fe by the end of October. If you hustled, you could be in the San Juans by the middle of November."

"Hugh, that leaves me no time to trap. Streams'll be frozen up by November. As it is, if I ride straight through, I'll only get a little over a month, six weeks at the most, to trap before I'm iced out. I don't see how I can help you."

"Have you bought your traps?"

Jeb shook his head.

"Do you have a packhorse?"

"Not yet. I sold mine when I sold the plews."

Hugh nodded. "All right. Here's what I'll do. If you'll hire on as a scout and take us all the way to Santa Fe, I'll give you ten new traps, that's at least a hundred dollars. On top of that—"

Jeb held up his hand. "Hugh, stop. I really need to head straight to the mountains. I'll make a lot better time than I would with you and your wagons."

"Now wait," Hugh said, shaking his head. "Let me finish. I'll give you a packhorse and pay you three hundred dollars, plus a two-hundred-dollar bonus when we get to Santa Fe. Now that's more than fair, and you know yourself that a man traveling alone through that Indian country stands an excellent chance of losing his hair."

Jeb leaned back and looked hard at Hugh. "You sure want to get to Santa Fe almighty bad."

"Yes, I do. By the time we get there, it'll be over nine months since I left. I know my wife and children are worried about me. I'm sure you know about the train that left two weeks ago."

Jeb nodded, a frown crossing his face. "Yeah, I told Flagan he needed a better scout than Porter, but he wouldn't listen to me. Porter's a thief and so's his crew. And some of those men are takin' their families. That's plumb crazy in a train that small."

"It is crazy. I hope they make it through, but I've an awful feeling about that outfit. Since they're two weeks ahead of us, I doubt we can help them. But I'd like to be on our way on the off chance we might catch up with them before Porter's bunch makes their move. I'm taking extra horses, and with you as a scout, we can push hard, and maybe . . ."

Jeb stared through the doorway, watching the thick smoke

from inside the saloon mix with the fine dust from the wagon-cut streets. He gave a sharp nod. "I'll do it. When do we leave?"

"Good," Hugh said, relief in his voice. "We'll be pulling out at first light in the morning. Can you be ready?"

Jeb flashed his grin at Hugh. "Ole son, all I've got to do is grab my possibles bag, throw a saddle on Buster, and I'm ready to hit the trail. I'll see you west of town in the morning."

Hugh's chair scraped across the rough-hewn floor as he slid it back and stood. He thrust his hand across to Jeb. "It's a deal. Pick up whatever you need at the Western Supplies General Store and tell them to put it on my bill. Now, I've got to round out my teamsters."

Nora, a frown on her face, slowly made her way back to Jeb's table.

∽

FLOYD STOOD at the side of the big wagon, the wool coat Ma and the girls had made him pulled tight around his shoulders. He watched the low, broken clouds race by overhead, spitting out intermittent drops of rain. The wide brim of his slouch hat kept most of it from his face.

The scattered rain dampened his clothes but not his spirits. Floyd's face carried a wide grin. He was headed west to the tall mountains, glass-clear, snow-fed streams full of trout, and enough adventure to satisfy any man. He could feel the pressure of his pistol against his waist and thought, *I'll find you, Porter. You'll regret your thieving ways.* His thoughts darkened only momentarily, as gazing west, his young mind flipped back to his mountains.

He hadn't met the new scout yet, but Salty said he was a good one. Though he was young, he was whip-leather tough and knew the country and the Indians. Salty had laughed, saying, "Why, Floyd, that feller's even saltier than me."

Floyd turned his gaze along the row of wagons. By adding those traders who had waited for Hugh, they had twelve wagons. From the rear of the wagon train, Hugh was making his way to the front, stopping at each wagon to speak to the driver.

He reached the third wagon from the end and stopped, as he had done with the others. After talking for a few moments, one of the three men climbed down and followed Brennan forward.

The big black Hugh was riding stomped his front feet in impatience when Hugh pulled him up again.

"Floyd, my boy, are you ready to head west?"

"Mr. Brennan, I'm about to bust open I'm so ready."

"Good, we'll be on our way shortly. Floyd, this young man is Albert Riley. Everyone calls him Muley because he's so good with the mules."

"Howdy," Muley said, and shoved his hand forward.

Floyd took the boy's hand and shook it while giving him a close once-over.

Muley wasn't as tall as Floyd, though he looked to be about two years older. He didn't appear as if he had an ounce of meat on his bones. To call him lanky would have been generous. His thin face emphasized the enormous grin that seemed to stretch from ear to ear.

Floyd grinned back. "Howdy."

Brennan continued. "He's helped Salty around the barn, both driving short hauls east and working on the wagons. I was thinking you might need some help, and Muley was dying to go west, like you. Thought you men might enjoy the like company."

"Thank you, Mr. Brennan," they both said in unison and grinned.

"Well, toss your things in, Muley, and you two mount up. Let's lead this wagon train to Santa Fe."

"Yes, sir," they again shouted in unison. Floyd double-checked the mules' harness, jogged to the opposite side of the wagon, and followed Muley's example, who had turned and almost catapulted himself up to the wagon seat.

Hugh Brennan laughed and turned to the man trotting up to him from the remuda.

"I thought Salty was through ridin' the trail," Jeb said as he pulled up to Hugh.

"I told him I wouldn't have any wagons coming back until next summer, but he still insisted he would make one more trip west. You can't argue with him when he gets like that, so I put him in charge of the remuda."

"Reckon you've got some mighty fine horseflesh, though they won't be so fat when we reach Santa Fe."

Hugh nodded. "None of us will."

"You still want to push hard?"

"Yes, especially early in the trip. I know we'll run into difficulties along the way that will cost us time. But I'm thinking we should be able to make fifty miles today if the trail doesn't get muddy." He looked across the prairie at the tall grass glistening in the light rain.

"All right, I'll find us a stopping place a ways down the road." Jeb looked over at the lead wagon. "I recognize Muley, but who's the feller with the ribbons? Haven't seen him around. He looks mighty young."

Floyd, only ten feet from the two men, heard their conversation above the west wind. He winced at the reference to his age. He felt sure the big man talking to Hugh was Jeb Campbell, the scout, but no matter who he was, what he said rubbed him the wrong way.

Before Hugh could speak up, Floyd called over from the wagon, "The name, Mr. Campbell, is Floyd Logan, and I'm old enough to outshoot any man on this train."

Muley, sitting to Floyd's right, between him and the horsemen, jerked his head around and gave Floyd a wide-eyed stare. "You know Jeb Campbell is the best shot in the country?"

Floyd ignored him and kept his gaze on Jeb.

Jeb, a twinkle in his eye, looked at Hugh and back at Floyd. "Boy, you sure talk a good game. Can you back it up with that old rifle?"

"Anytime, any place."

Hugh nodded. "He can shoot, Jeb."

Jeb chuckled and gave a curt nod. "Lookin' forward to it." He grew serious as he spoke to Hugh. "We'll need to check everyone's skills. I'll stop us early enough to have a little shoot off. First, though, I'll ride ahead. I ain't expectin' no Injun worries until we get farther west, but Buster needs to stretch his legs." He touched a finger to his hat and galloped off over the hills.

Hugh turned the big black to face the rest of the train, raised his right arm, and as he swung it forward, called, "Forward, ho!"

The pop of reins and calls could be heard from the teamsters down the line, and, with Floyd leading off, the wagon train started west. Muley was still looking at Floyd like he was a crazy man.

∼

THE DAY HAD GONE SMOOTHLY. Around noon they had stopped, changed teams, and kept moving. The wind had blown the clouds and rain away while blowing itself out. The afternoon warmed to where Floyd tossed his coat into the wagon, the sun feeling good against his chilled body.

They were coming upon a creek with a bend in it forming a wide U with the open portion facing west. Jeb was signaling for the teamsters to cross on the rocky flats south of the proposed camp and circle up in the U. Crossing, Floyd could see Salty and two other riders holding the horses in the shallow creek, allowing them to water. Hugh rode alongside Floyd's wagon.

"Follow Jeb's signals. We'll get a little practice circling up.

After we're circled, take care of your stock and we'll have some fun."

Floyd waved as he guided the horses up the west bank. The bank had been cut into a wide road climbing out of the creek. Western travelers before them had cut down and sloped the walls of the bank, leaving a shallow gradient for an easy exit from the riverbed back to the prairie.

Leading the remaining wagons, Floyd followed the previous tracks. They turned from the crossing, paralleled the timbered creek, and led into the camp formed by the meandering flow of the creek. Cottonwood, black willow, ash and box elder, along with a few elm trees, stood out along the water course, providing a perfect windbreak for the wagons.

Floyd guided his horses in behind the last wagon in line, forming a loose circle of wagons within the protected space. The grass here was much shorter than across the prairie. It had been tromped and cropped by many other pilgrims who had also chosen this spot to pause their wagons for the night.

From a thick low limb on the north side of the clearing hung the skinned carcasses of two whitetail deer. Jeb had done more than riding. Tasty venison would be included in their supper tonight.

As Floyd eyed the deer, he was envious but not ungrateful. Thrilled and beholden to Hugh Brennan to be going west, he was anxious for the time he would be on horseback. To gallop out across the prairie held much more appeal than following the east end of the westbound mules.

He looped the reins around the brake handle and vaulted to the ground, glancing around at the other teamsters. They were all busy unhitching their teams. Salty had left the remuda with the other riders and was riding toward Floyd.

"Howdy, boys, got some mules for me?"

"Sure, Salty," Muley replied before Floyd could speak. "Floyd and me will unhitch 'em and they'll be all yours."

Salty swung down and looped his reins over the left front wheel. He walked forward and took the bridle of the lead mule, holding the team in place while Floyd and Muley raced to finish first.

Beating Muley by a hair, Floyd said to Salty, "Thanks, that made it a lot easier."

Muley glared at Floyd and said, "Yeah, thanks."

"Don't mention it," Salty said, walking back to his horse. He untied him, swung aboard, and said to Floyd, "Hear you challenged Jeb to a little shooting exhibition."

Floyd turned to Muley and said, "Gimme a second, Muley, and we'll get the harness stowed in the back of the wagon." He looked up at Salty. "Yeah, I guess I did. Sometimes I fly off the handle."

The mules had gone to cropping the short grass where they stood. Salty leaned forward, his right arm across his saddle, slid his hat back, and stared at Floyd. "Word to the wise, boy. I see you as a good lad, but you're out in a man's world, and you ain't yet full grown. You don't learn to keep a tight rein on that temper, it's gonna get you or someone else kilt, and that's for danged sure."

Salty turned his head and let loose a long stream of brown tobacco juice, some of it dribbling down into his beard. He straightened, took a long swipe across his mouth with his forearm, and said, "Challenging Jeb to a shoot off, now that's gonna be something to see."

He nodded, turned his horse and pushed the mules ahead, talking to them and the teamsters he passed. Salty moved around the circle of wagons until he had them all gathered, and headed the animals to the creek.

Floyd stood for a few moments longer, contemplating what Salty had said. That was almost word for word what Pa had told him before he left. He'd always had a quick temper, but it disappeared as quick. It was time he started growing up. There was no desire in his heart to kill anyone, and he could see how his temper could drag him down that road.

Muley and Floyd had finished laying the harness in the back of the wagon when Jeb rode up. He swung down, tied his horse to the back wheel, and said to Floyd, "Grab your rifle."

Floyd moved up to the front of the wagon, reached up and over the side, where his rifle stood, grabbed it and turned around.

"One thing you never forget," Jeb said, "is your rifle. No matter what you're doing, always have your rifle with you."

"But you said no Indians were close around here."

"I've been wrong before. Don't let any man's words cost you yore life. There will come a time when having or not having your rifle will mean life or death. Don't forget that. Now come on."

6

Floyd felt his temper rising. Only Pa talked to him like that. He remembered what Salty had said, and thought, *I've got to learn*, and tamped down his anger.

Jeb had dragged a big log out to the edge of the tall grass. Next to the log, he had stacked a pile of stones, each stone about the size of a man's fist. He stacked three from one end of the log with about a foot between each stone. When Floyd saw what he was doing, he pitched in and started from the other end. Quickly they lined the rocks across the log.

Jeb turned back toward the wagons and stepped off fifty paces. Floyd watched Hugh gather all the men, who were now trooping out from the wagons with their rifles and shooting gear.

"How's that for you?" Jeb asked.

"Mr. Campbell, I was mouthy this morning, but to tell the truth, I could dang near hit those with a slingshot."

A slight grin tugged at the corners of Jeb's mouth. "You're right."

Floyd stood wondering which part of his statement the mountain man was agreeing with.

The rest of the men arrived. Jeb looked over to Hugh, and

Hugh stepped out of the group, clearing his throat. "Men, many of you know Jeb Campbell here. For those of you who don't, you're looking at a real high-country mountain man. He knows the plains we'll be crossing and the Indians we'll be dealing with. So I'm trusting him with the success of our endeavor."

The men who knew Jeb nodded in agreement, some saying, "Howdy, Jeb."

Hugh continued. "We'll soon be moving into Indian and renegade country. Our scout mentioned it would be a good idea for everyone to get a chance to test their rifles and their shooting skills. So we will have a brief shooting match."

A murmur passed through the men. They'd been up early, which most were used to, and pushed hard to make the fifty miles their wagon master had asked for. All were tired and hungry. They'd seen the venison hanging in the trees and were eager to flop their lips over some of it. For sure they all liked a shooting match, but most, their stomachs growling, wanted to eat.

Hugh heard the murmuring and held up his hands. "Now, I realize you're tired and hungry, but I've set up some prizes for the shooters."

Now the men perked up. Winning something made it a lot more acceptable to delay supper.

"First prize," Hugh said, "is a ten-dollar gold piece."

At the mention of gold, the men let out a whoop. Their excitement banished their hunger and fatigue.

"Second prize is a five-dollar gold piece, and third prize is a two-dollar-and-fifty-cent gold piece. Now is that worth waiting a while for your supper?"

The men cheered in assent, and Hugh nodded to Jeb.

Before Jeb could speak, Salty spoke up. "The boys back with the horses will be a mite upset if they're left out."

"I'm way ahead of you, Salty. The first two men eliminated will go back and relieve your men."

Salty gave a sharp nod in agreement.

Jeb began. "Now, here's what's gonna happen. Each of you shoot until you miss. One miss and you're out. We'll start here at fifty paces. Those who miss will set up the next batch of rocks, and we'll move back another fifty paces." He turned to Floyd. "You and I will shoot in the last round of each if you're agreeable."

Floyd nodded, and ten shooters stepped up.

Jeb said, "When you're ready, fire away."

Shots rattled out. Rocks split and others remained stationary. After the smoke had cleared, there were four still standing.

Hugh pointed to two of the men who'd missed. "Why don't you boys go relieve the others, and so you all know, I'll not be competing against you. It wouldn't be fair for me to take back my money."

The remaining shooters laughed and cheered while the two selected men nodded and started toward the horses and mules, where, in the distance, the two riders could be seen watching. The remaining two stepped forward to set up the rocks.

The wranglers made it up in time to shoot in the last round at fifty yards. It was also time for Floyd and Jeb to shoot.

Floyd glanced over at Jeb as he walked up, threw his rifle to his shoulder, and squeezed the trigger, all in one effortless motion. The two men fired at almost the same time, and their two rocks exploded as one. Five of the remaining shooters missed. That meant that out of thirty men, twelve of them had missed at fifty paces. It was all Floyd could do to keep from shaking his head.

Jeb marched off another fifty paces, bringing them to a hundred. This time there would only be two groups shooting, the first of ten and the second of eight.

Immediately after shooting, Floyd had started his reloading, noticing Jeb had also begun. Finishing quickly, he was surprised to see Jeb already pacing off the next distance. Face flushed, he turned and walked back to the new line.

At a hundred paces, six out of the first ten missed. Floyd, Jeb, and Salty, with the two wranglers, were firing in the second group. Again, Floyd fired as soon as the rifle reached his shoulder, as did Jeb, their rocks exploding, along with Salty's and the two wranglers'. The other three missed.

While two of the men who missed jogged forward to reset the stones, Jeb paced another fifty paces off to make it one hundred and fifty paces. The nine rocks looked tiny sitting on top of the log. The setting sun was in the shooters' eyes, making it even more difficult.

This time, when the men were back from setting up the stones, Floyd brought up his rifle above his target and let it settle onto his rock, and squeezed the trigger. The rock shattered at the sound of the blast.

Jeb had waited until he fired, as he had done at fifty yards. He threw his rifle to his shoulder and fired. His rock exploded, along with Salty's and one wrangler's. Two of the teamsters were also successful.

Six men remained as Jeb stepped off another fifty paces. Floyd had been impressed when at one hundred and fifty paces Jeb just stepped up to the line and, in one motion, fired. He was also surprised that Salty was still in the competition. He hadn't expected that. From talking with his pa, he knew that when a man grew older, his eyes weren't able to focus on those distant objects like they did when he was young. But Salty didn't seem to have any problem with his eyes.

While they waited for the men setting the rocks up to get back, Salty caught Floyd looking at him—and winked. Floyd grinned at the older man and scanned the others. They were now at two hundred paces, the sun had only moments before dropped behind the far hill, and shadows were reaching for the rocks, making them even harder to see. That didn't matter. He had made farther shots than this one.

He stepped up to the line and aimed down his barrel. The

front sight nestled evenly and level between the blades of his rear sight and settled onto the rock. He raised it up the width of two rocks, for elevation, and squeezed the trigger. His rifle fired at the same time as Jeb's. Both rocks exploded, along with one other.

The men were shouting in excitement at the amazing marksmanship they were observing. Floyd could hear them making side bets on what the winning lineup would be.

Jeb stopped the teamster as he started out to set up more rocks. "If you can find three about half the size of those we've been shooting, that should do it." He turned to the crowd. "Since we're almost against the wagons, we ain't gonna be able to move back no more. So we'll use smaller rocks."

The men cheered again.

Floyd stared into the growing darkness. This was the most challenging shooting he had ever done. He watched the man pick out three rocks and set them on top of the log. They were almost impossible to see. Salty cleared his throat.

"Boys," he said, "I hate to quit, but there ain't a pinch of sense in me trying to make that shot." He shook his head and said, "I ain't even seeing those blamed rocks."

At Salty's statement, the men roared and flocked around him, slapping him on the back and congratulating him. Many agreed with him, they couldn't see the rocks either.

Floyd thought, *If I hit it, I'll be riding with lady luck.*

Once the man returned from positioning the rocks, Floyd brought the rifle to his shoulder, steadied on the barely visible rock, raised the muzzle a smidgin, and squeezed the trigger. With the blast, smoke hung around for only a moment and cleared, bringing his target back into view. The rock was still there. He shook his head and moved away.

"Hold on a second, Floyd." Jeb had waited for Floyd to fire. He now brought his own rifle up, waited a fraction of a second, fired, and the rock exploded. The men let out another roar, gathering around Jeb and pounding him on the back.

Floyd turned to him and smiled. "You beat me fair and square. You may not believe it, but I haven't been beat in a long time."

Jeb stuck out his hand, and while the two men shook, Jeb said, "Let's take a look at your rock."

In the dim light, the two shooters, followed by the crowd of men, walked the two hundred paces to the log with the rock still sitting on it. Hugh had joined them.

Jeb picked up the rock, looked at it, held it up and pointed to the chip knocked out of it showing the gray lead transfer. "After Floyd shot, I saw a faint cloud of dust fly off this rock. He didn't miss."

Floyd nodded. "Thank you, Mr. Campbell. I surely appreciate you showing me this. I may not have missed, but I didn't hit it dead center like you did. It's a pleasure shooting with you."

Another cheer burst out of the men. Hugh stepped in front of the crowd, holding his hands up. "I think everyone will agree with me. This has been some amazing shooting. I'm announcing Salty as third, Floyd number two, and Jeb Campbell wins the first prize!" He flipped a coin to Salty, then to Floyd, and to Jeb.

"Well," Salty said, after catching the coin, "I thankee, boss, and this here has been fun." He looked around at the rest of the men. "I don't know about you fellers, but I'm gettin' almighty hungry. Let's eat!"

With his last statement a shout of agreement went up. The men turned and, everyone talking among themselves, made their way back to the wagons and the waiting supper.

Floyd, Jeb, and Salty moved off to the side and started cleaning their rifles. Hugh joined them.

Jeb nodded his head to a group of the teamsters who were also cleaning their weapons. "Glad to see they're taking care of them rifles. Those other fellers need to learn to take care of their firearms before they feed their bellies."

Hugh stood, turning toward the men around the cookfire.

"You men get those rifles cleaned before you eat. You can never tell when Indians may show up."

Two burly teamsters said something among themselves. A big man who appeared to be the ringleader spoke up. "Reckon we oughta eat first. Your scout said there ain't no Injuns this far east. Don't make no sense to wait on eatin' only to run a swab down a barrel."

Hugh stood and moved toward the group. "Your name's Watson, right?"

The burly man nodded.

"Watson, you've never made this Santa Fe trip with me. How many times have you traveled this road?"

The big man's face scrunched in a confused frown. "Well, I ain't never made this here trip, but I've plenty of experience drivin' mules and horses. Why, I've made the trip from Independence all the way to Chicago several times."

"How many Indian attacks did you have?"

Now the man looked around and gave his group a sardonic grin. He turned back to Hugh. "Course I ain't had no attacks. But if I had—"

"If you had, you would have been lucky to get off your first shot with a dirty rifle. Since we have only started, I'll allow you this one chance. Clean your rifle before you eat, like everyone else is doing, and I'll forget this."

"If I don't?"

"If you don't, you're fired, and you can walk back to civilization. It's only about thirty miles."

Hugh stood facing the teamster.

Jeb, Salty, Floyd, and several other men, including Muley, stood relaxed at his side, their hands resting on the pistol butts extending from their waistbands.

Finally Watson spoke up. "What if I just come over there and kick yore old butt?"

Hugh gave the man a slow smile, but there was no warmth in

his icy calm voice. "Mr. Watson, I am too old to roll around in the dirt with you. If you so much as start toward me, I will pull my pistol and blow a sizeable hole in your belly.

"You have three choices. Clean your weapon and then eat, take your gear and head back for Independence, or start my way to, as you so politely put it, 'kick my butt,' at which time I shall kill you. Make up your mind!"

"I can still make the trip?" the teamster asked in surprise.

"And get paid in Santa Fe," Hugh said.

The big man looked at the ground, then up at Hugh. "Sorry, Mr. Brennan. I'd be much obliged to stay on. I'll clean this here rifle right now."

All the men laughed and cheered.

Hugh turned back to the smaller fire Salty had built, and motioned to Jeb, Floyd, and Muley. The smell of broiling venison spread through the camp. The men cleaned and loaded their weapons. Each grabbed a plate of beans and venison. While the food disappeared, there was not a word spoken. They cleaned their utensils and returned to the fire.

Jeb looked across the fire toward Hugh. "I guess you know what I'd like for you to do."

"I've got an idea," Hugh said, looking at Floyd, who sat next to Jeb.

Shorty barked out a short laugh and sent a shot of tobacco juice into the edge of the fire. They all listened to it sizzle for a moment.

Hugh, his eyes still on Floyd, said, "Would you like to join Jeb as a scout?"

Floyd stared back in shock. This was his dream. Scout and hunter for a wagon train headed west. "Yes, sir! I sure would."

Hugh continued, "Floyd, you're an excellent shot, but it takes more than a good shot to be a scout. Jeb will report back to me. You have much to learn, and your life and ours depends on you learning. Though Jeb isn't more than six or seven years older than you, he's spent those years learning in the mountains and on this prairie. He knows the country and the Indians. You will listen to him. Do I make myself clear?"

"Yes, sir. I'll listen to Jeb. I'll do what he says. I'll learn to control my temper."

"No." Jeb stepped in. "I don't want you to *learn* to control your temper, I want you to control it. It's your choice. Make it right now. This is the one thing I can't teach you. You have to do it, starting this very moment."

Every eye in the small group was on Floyd. He gazed into the darkness. Jeb was right. It was a decision. "Jeb, it's done. No more flying off the handle." Floyd grinned. "The next time I challenge you to a shoot off, I'll win."

The laughter from around their fire had all the men in camp turning, looking, then shrugging their shoulders and going back to their conversations.

"Floyd," Hugh said, "you'll ride with Jeb when he needs you, and when he doesn't, you'll drive the wagon.

"Muley, that means you'll be the regular driver most of the time, and I'll pay you as a driver and not a helper. Can you handle switching back and forth, depending on where Floyd is needed?"

"Mr. Brennan, wherever you need me. I'm happy to be going west."

"Thank you, Muley. You're a good man."

"So, Floyd, I'll pay you as assistant scout, but you will still fill in as driver when needed. Is all of this agreeable to you?"

"Mr. Brennan, I don't think I can say it better than Muley. I'm just happy to be going west."

7

Floyd, on the roan he had named Rusty, galloped beside Jeb. They were a week out of Independence, and for all that time Floyd had driven the wagon only one day. Muley was doing so well, that after the first day with Muley, he had not been asked again to drive. Before topping a wooded hill, Jeb pulled up, Floyd stopping next to him. The two men dropped from their horses and tied the reins to a tree, leaving enough slack to allow the horses to graze on the tall grass.

"Over this hill is the Neosho River," Jeb said. "Normally this is an easy crossing, but we'll check it to make sure. Once we're across, I want to stop by the post office."

"There's no post office out here, is there?"

"You'll see. Now take it easy up here. This is Pawnee and Osage country. Back in twenty-five, the army signed a treaty with them, so it should be safe. But they can be notional."

Hardly visible in the tall grass, they moved from tree to tree. Near the top they removed their hats, then eased far enough up, in the five-foot grass, to see just over the wide ridge.

At the bottom of a long sloping draw was the river, running low and slow.

"Water's low. That's good," Jeb said. "We'll circle the wagons in that open area west of the river."

"Yeah, looks beaten down."

Jeb nodded. "It's popular with travelers. There's water and still plenty of grass. Also, a week out from Independence it gives folks a chance to settle for a day before they head out for the long stretch. Plus, folks want to check in at the post office."

"Now that's the second time you mentioned a post office. Jeb, there's not a building down there."

Jeb nodded again and grinned at Floyd. "Come on, I'll show you."

The two men moved back and mounted their horses.

Rifles ready across the pommel of their saddles, they rode down the slope to the river.

"This is about the best place for crossing," Jeb said. "Notice the sloping banks. Right now it's running low, but in the spring, it can be a handful, deep and fast. When high running, you've got to be careful of it."

Floyd logged Jeb's information in his memory. He had been learning much during the past week, for his companion, though not talkative, seemed to have no hesitation in sharing his knowledge. Sometimes Floyd wondered if he was back in school, but he was grateful for Jeb's generosity. A lesser man would keep some things to himself to show he was smarter.

Once in the river, they stopped the horses when nearing the other side and let them drink. Floyd followed Jeb's direction, eyes roaming across the surroundings.

Not only looking at the trees and grass in the grove and along the river, but studying each bush, alert for something out of place. Skin was smooth, a limb or bush wasn't. Often, when someone had their eyes on you, it was possible to sense their presence. This wasn't something taught by Jeb, but by Pa, to all of his sons.

In fact, Pa had talked to him when he made the comment

about wanting to go to the shining mountains to become a mountain man. Pa told him he already was a mountain man, traveling the mountains of Tennessee and some of Georgia. Taught many skills by Pa and his brothers, it wasn't necessary to go to the tall mountains to learn them. Often, those reminders rattled around in his head. *You all taught me,* he thought. *Maybe one day I can come back and teach you, or at least share some of the things I've done and seen and learned.*

The two scouts rode out of the river, up the bank, and into the grove. Gigantic oak trees dominated the area, with a few scattered elm and ash. A particularly large oak stood off by itself. Thick spreading limbs with dark green leaves, several of which hung low enough to the ground a person might sit on them, covered a wide radius.

Jeb headed straight for it. Reaching the tree, he swung down and walked up to a big hole in the tree that had escaped Floyd's scan until they were close. Jeb thrust his hand into the hole and pulled out several papers, turned around, and held them up to Floyd. "The post office."

Floyd swung down, his rifle in hand, and, leading Rusty, walked to Jeb. "Post office?"

"Yep. Folks post news about the trail, the condition, rivers, Indian activity, and washouts, just to name a few. They stick 'em in this here tree so travelers headed where they've been will have some idea of what's happening."

Jeb looked hard at Floyd. "You're a readin' man, aren't you? Now if you ain't, no sense in bein' embarrassed. Many's the man who cain't."

"Yep," Floyd said, "Ma made sure we were able to read, write, and do our figures. She was a stickler for that. She always said that a man who wasn't versed in reading had the deck stacked against him. It didn't mean he would never succeed, it just meant it would be harder for him."

"Sounds like you've got yourself a smart ma. Folks set a heap of importance on learnin'. Course, there's all sorts of learning. There's school learnin' and people learnin' and country learnin'. To be safe where we're headin', a man needs the last two a lot more'n the first, but the first is important." He handed the notes in the tree to Floyd.

While Jeb watched, he found the one about the Pawnee and looked up.

"Seen that, did you?"

"Yes," Floyd said. "It seems the Pawnee attacked them not far west of here."

"True, but we haven't met any wagons or mule trains, so I'm not sure how old this is. Most times they date it, but I ain't seein' nary a date."

As the two men continued to look at the notes in the tree, they maintained their vigilance. Jeb had a saying about Indians. "When you ain't ready for 'em, that's when they hit you."

Floyd's head jerked up.

Jeb rammed the notes back in the hole and leaped into the saddle.

Floyd was right behind him, moving his horse close and whispering while his eyes roamed down the river. "It sounded like metal bumping something."

Jeb's only answer was to ease his rifle's hammer back to check his powder in the pan. Floyd didn't need anyone to tell him to check. It was the first thing he did when his rear hit the saddle. Jeb, with Floyd following, moved his horse toward the sound, using the large oaks for concealment. They worked their way through the glade, no sound from the horses except a soft whish as they moved through the tall grass.

For a short distance, the river made a bend to the west, and where it turned back east there was a break in the trees.

The first movement Floyd caught was not quite fifty yards in front of them.

"Dang," Jeb said, "it's a woman."

They could see her coming back from the creek, carrying a bucket of water.

The bucket must have hit a stump or limb. That's what we heard. Floyd thought.

Jeb burst out, "What the blue blazes is a woman doin' here? Come on."

The two men rode into the clearing, surprising her. Though surprised, she hurried to the large log that functioned as several seats for the campsite. From it, she picked up a rifle, and holding it with the casual manner of someone who was experienced in how to use it, she turned to face them.

At the end of the log was a walled tent. The tent looked to be at least nine feet wide and almost twelve feet long. The woman, calm, called to the tent, "Dorie, we have company. Please come out with your pa's rifle."

A much younger woman, Floyd's age or younger, stepped out swinging the long barrel of the rifle toward them.

Jeb held up his hands. "Hold on, ladies. We ain't meanin' you no harm. We just heard your bucket and rode down to see what the noise was."

The woman turned her head toward her daughter. "Dorie, it isn't necessary to point the rifle at these men."

As the daughter lowered the barrel and leaned over to prop the rifle against the log, the older woman said, "I didn't say put it down. Keep it handy. It's just not polite to point it at visitors."

It was obvious to Floyd, the long-barreled smoke pole was too heavy for the girl. "Ma'am, we're not meaning you any harm. In fact, we'd like to help. You ladies shouldn't be here by yourself."

The woman, after watching them closely, decided they meant no harm. She again turned to the girl and smiled at her. "I think we can put our rifles down. These men seem trustworthy."

She looked towards Jeb, whose hands were still up. "You can put your hands down, sir. You'll need them to get off your horse. Won't you gentlemen join us for some coffee?"

"Thank you, ma'am," Jeb said. "It'd be a pleasure. Ma'am, if you don't mind my askin', what's a pair of nice ladies like you doing so far from Independence by yourself?"

"Oh, my heavens no, we are not by ourselves, Mister...?"

"Sorry, ma'am, my name is Jeb Campbell, and this young feller is Floyd Logan."

The woman stepped forward and extended her hand first to Jeb and then Floyd. "It's nice to meet you. In fact, you cannot begin to understand how nice it is. My name is Eleanor Ryland, this is my daughter, Dorothy, and my husband, Oliver, is in the tent, injured. I am so glad you are here."

Jeb said, "Thank you, ma'am. If you'll go ahead with that coffee, Floyd and me will step into the tent and check on your husband."

"Oh, thank you so much." Eleanor dumped out the stale coffee and started making fresh.

Floyd followed Jeb into the tent and stood over Ryland. The man was in terrible shape. His face was red and sweaty. In fact, it appeared sweat covered all his body.

Jeb leaned forward and touched the man's forehead. "Why, he's hot as fire."

The man's left arm was under the sheet. Jeb pulled the sheet back and the smell hit them both. Ryland was a large man, and his hand had swollen almost twice its normal size.

Floyd stepped nearer Jeb, bringing the man's hand into view. From the wrist forward it was as red as a strawberry and huge. There were red streaks starting up his arm. None had reached his elbow, but they were close. Floyd wished he were home, because Ma had fixed up many a cut and scrape, even after he had filled them with dirt and debris.

"Looks like he stabbed something in his thumb," Jeb said.

"Sure does. Wish Ma were here. If she were here, he'd be fixed up lickety-split, but now, he's heading down a dangerous road."

Jeb turned to him. "Do you remember what she used?"

"Sure, garlic, onion, and honey. Crush the garlic and onion, mix it with the honey, and smear it on the wound. She said that all three of them work to suck out the poison. It doesn't take long, either."

The two men walked back outside.

"Mrs. Ryland?"

The lady looked up from the coffee she was preparing. "Yes, Mr. Campbell?"

"My partner here, Floyd, he knows a little about doctoring. Do you have any garlic, onion, and honey?"

Puzzled, she stood, dusting her hands off on her dress. Dorie seemed to be unable to take her eyes from Floyd, though Floyd had no idea.

"I have both garlic and onion, but no honey."

"Jeb," Floyd said, "there were bees near the big oak." He turned to Eleanor Ryland. "Ma'am, please bring me an onion and a garlic pod. I'll get started mashing them. Jeb, you think you can find that hive?"

Jeb grinned. "That'll be my pleasure. I think everbody would enjoy some fresh honey." He leaped on his horse, rifle in hand, and rode back to the post office tree.

Before he was out of sight, Dorie was handing Floyd the garlic and onion, her eyes glued to him hopefully. It was dried garlic, but not too dry. Floyd turned to Eleanor again. "Do you have a bowl I can mash this up in?"

She wheeled to a large wooden box, opened the lid, and pulled out a bowl. She held it up for Floyd to see. "Will this do?"

"Yes, ma'am."

He took the bowl, pulled out his long knife, and sliced the onion into small pieces. When finished with the onion, he started on the garlic pod.

Eleanor and Dorie watched.

"How long's it been since he hurt his thumb?" Floyd asked as he worked.

"Three days," Dorie said. We had stopped here, built a fire, and set up the tent. Then Pa asked me if I wanted to go with him to get some water. We were walking and talking about our adventure when Pa stepped over a log. He must have caught his foot on a limb and he started falling. He grabbed at a small oak right by us to keep him steady, and suddenly said, 'Damn.'"

"Dorie!" Eleanor exclaimed. "That's no way for a lady to talk. I don't care how old you are, I'll get you some lye soap if I hear that again."

"Mama, that's what Papa said. I don't talk like that."

But even in her protest, Floyd saw that there was a sassy glint in her sharp blue eyes.

"Well, go on," her mother said, "tell Mr. Logan what happened."

"When Pa stumbled and grabbed for that limb, it had a short little stob on it that had a tiny splinter sticking out. That splinter went deep under Pa's thumbnail."

"That's right," Eleanor said, "and we had a terrible time getting it out. I heated a needle over a match, and I had to dig and dig to get it out. Poor Oliver, I had to shove that needle over an inch under his thumbnail to reach the last piece. It had to hurt so bad, but he never uttered a sound."

Floyd had just completed smashing the garlic and onion. He added a few drops of water and began mixing it. The onion had been strong smelling, which was good, but the fumes were hard on his eyes. They burned and tears flowed down his dirty cheeks.

Jeb rode up with a sizeable piece of honeycomb, honey dripping from his hand. Floyd looked up as Jeb swung down from the saddle. "Oh my," Jeb said. "I was gone too long. Floyd missed me so much he's started cryin'."

Dorie giggled.

Floyd huffed and said, "You get over here and smash this onion. We'll see how long you last."

Jeb held the honeycomb over the bowl and squeezed it.

Eleanor had run for another bowl, and as soon as Floyd said, "That's enough," she slipped it under Jeb's hand.

Floyd kept mixing until he had a thick concoction of honey, garlic, and onion. He stood and looked at Eleanor. "Do you have anything we can use to make a bandage?"

Dorie said, "I know where it is," and raced over to another of the large boxes, opened it, and pulled out a large batt of linen.

Without asking, she tore a bandage about six inches wide and two feet long.

Floyd nodded. "Good, that'll do. Mrs. Ryland, can you help me?"

"Certainly," she said, seeing the disappointment on her daughter's face. She was sure Floyd missed it.

"Are you sure you removed all of the splinter?"

"Yes," Eleanor said. "It was difficult and extremely painful for Oliver, but I dug all of it out."

"All right then. Sit down and hold his hand where I can get to the end of the thumb."

Eleanor grasped her husband's forearm, turned the hand up where the thumb pointed at Floyd, and held it stationary.

"Perfect," he said, and using a portion of the linen as a swab, he dipped it into the mixture, then spread the mixture over the injured thumb. Before it started dripping, he picked up the bandage and made two wraps around the thumb, followed by wrapping the remaining portion around Oliver's hand. Completed, he tucked the end of the bandage between the back of the hand and the bandage.

He rose from the injured man. "That's it." He handed the bowl with the mix to the woman. "Best get that covered up. Keep the flies out of it. Now all we can do is wait. We'll wait two hours, apply some more, and put on a fresh bandage."

"When will you know?"

"Understand, Mrs. Ryland, I'm not sure this will work, but my ma always said the first thing that would happen is the fever would break. Now I don't know that, I just remember her telling us. I'm sorry, but we'll just have to wait and pray."

The two walked out of the tent. Jeb was sitting on the log, drinking coffee. "Tell me, Floyd. What's the verdict?"

He shook his head. "Jeb, like I told Mrs. Ryland, we'll just have to wait and see."

"Please, both of you, call me Eleanor. You've been so much help, I feel like I know you. I can't thank you enough for all you've done."

"We haven't done much, Eleanor," Jeb said. "Wish it were possible to say your husband will be fine, but we'll just have to wait. What's got me puzzled is what the blue blazes you folks are doing out here in Indian country by yourself?"

Eleanor turned to Floyd. "Would you like some coffee, Floyd?"

"Yes, ma'am, I'd appreciate some. Let me get my cup from my saddlebags."

"No need, we have cups right here." From one of the wooden boxes placed near the fire, she pulled out a china cup and filled it with coffee, then handed it to Floyd.

After pouring herself one, she closed the box lid and sat on the box. She took a small sip, sighed, looked up at the blue sky for a moment, and gazed at Jeb.

"Oliver is a marvelous man, with few faults. I am blessed to be his wife."

"Sounds like there's a but coming, ma'am," Jeb said.

"Oliver is one of the best gunsmiths in this country. Any of the major firearms companies would hire him, but Oliver has itchy feet. We were living in St. Louis, doing quite well, and he decided he wanted to go west. So here we are."

"Where are you planning on going?" Floyd asked.

"For now, I think Santa Fe, but I believe his ultimate destination is somewhere in California."

Jeb shook his head. "Santa Fe is a long way off. You're traveling alone?"

"We got into Independence a short time after Mr. Flagan's train left, and we had hopes of catching them. So we bought fresh mules, additional supplies, and left the day after we got there, but we never caught them." She looked around and shrugged. "Here we are. I'm just glad you came along. Are you traveling west?"

"We sure are," Jeb replied. "This might be your lucky day if you can talk Mr. Brennan into letting you join up. Though I'll tell you he don't cater to women on his trains. He's a businessman and aims to travel fast.

"We're scouts for his train and headed for Santa Fe. In fact, they should arrive here in a couple of hours."

"Oh, my goodness," she said. Her shoulders relaxed and Floyd saw it was all she could do to keep from crying. "I am so relieved. With Oliver sick, there was only me and Dorie. I've been scared to death Indians might come upon us."

Jeb shook his head. "Ain't just Indians, ma'am. There's a high number of no-good critters that walk on two legs. It wouldn't do for them to find you and your daughter. They wouldn't be gentle."

She shuddered. "I'm so thankful we're saved."

Floyd looked over her at Jeb. During his brief time with Hugh, he had figured out that his boss was never pleased having women on the wagon trains he ran. Those trains moved fast with few delays. But even with his penchant for traveling woman-free, Floyd was sure he wouldn't leave this family here to fend for themselves. Or would he?

8

Two hours had passed. It was time for a new dressing. Floyd walked into the tent with Mrs. Ryland. He examined her husband. He didn't know if his imagination was playing tricks on him or not, but the man seemed to be resting better. They cleaned his hand, applied a fresh honey poultice, and wrapped it with a clean bandage.

Jeb had ridden back to guide Hugh and the wagons. Before leaving, he warned Floyd to keep his eyes peeled. They would be an opportune target for any marauding Indians or thieves.

The woman stayed with her husband as Floyd exited the tent. He checked the pistol behind his waistband and his rifle. Then he walked over and checked the two rifles belonging to the family. He picked the one up that Eleanor had used. The thought of using her first name bothered him. He was used to calling older women ma'am. *Oh well,* he thought, *get used to it. Times are changing.*

The rifle had no flint, no pan. He pulled the hammer to half cock. A cap had replaced the pan. He inspected it and found a shorter barrel and smaller caliber, .50. Swinging the rifle to his shoulder, it seemed to leap up and settle snugly into place. He'd never had a rifle fit so well, not even the one that Porter had stolen. He lowered it and snapped it to his shoulder again.

Floyd marveled at the fit. When it hit his shoulder, the rear and front sight aligned perfectly. He didn't have to move the rifle at all. He repeated his action, and again.

"It points quite well, doesn't it?" He turned. Eleanor was watching him.

Laughing, Floyd said, "That doesn't even begin to explain it. This rifle fits like a glove, though I suspect that with this shorter barrel it doesn't hit as hard or travel as far as my fifty-four."

She brushed back her brown hair, sprinkled with a few strands of gray, and smiled. Floyd saw the smile wrinkles form at the edge of her tired dark eyes. Worry clouded those eyes, but she still smiled.

"Don't make the mistake of betting on your suspicion, or you'll lose your money. I don't know how he's done it, but Oliver has shortened the barrel while still producing a rifle that shoots as far, if not farther, than those long rifles."

Floyd said, "I reckon you love your husband, but that's saying an awful lot."

She just continued to smile. "It is, isn't it?"

Floyd was still holding her rifle when he saw movement in the brush. The rifle was up and against his shoulder faster than before. Over the sights, as he fired, he saw the Indian loose his arrow moments before the round ball struck him. Floyd immediately dropped the rifle and grabbed his, bringing it to his shoulder. From the corner of his eye, he saw Eleanor reaching for the rifle her daughter had held.

He had no time to worry about her, for they were coming. Six of them. Tall, wide shoulders, wearing only breechcloth and moccasins, now less than twenty yards away. He fired again as a weapon fired to his right. He handed his rifle back, and she took it.

With one smooth motion, his hand came to his waist and

pulled his pistol. Hammer back, he fired point-blank into a hideous face painted red from the nose up, with a black and white feather hanging from the topknot. The man's face exploded, and he collapsed toward Floyd, falling at his feet.

The remaining two Indians raced forward, almost on top of him. He flipped his pistol into the air, grabbing it by the muzzle as it came down.

The lead Indian was a big man and mature. He had a smile on his face, recognizing how young Floyd was. The man was carrying a nasty-looking tomahawk that was drawn back to split Floyd's head like a cantaloupe. It fell, following an accelerating arc, with all the power in those wide shoulders. Floyd blocked it with his pistol, but it was a glancing blow that slid past his face, opening his shirt and leaving a red line across his chest. With his free left hand he hammered a left cross into the Indian's nose, smashing it.

Indians, great wrestlers, rarely fought with their fists, and the blow came as a surprise to the man. He staggered back. Floyd reached to his waist and yanked out the long blade his brother Nathan had given him. About that time another rifle roared behind him, but he was too busy to turn. He pictured a knife slashing between his shoulder blades at any moment, but he had to take care of the threat in front of him first.

The big Indian shook his head, recovering quickly. After losing his tomahawk, the man had pulled out his knife, not as long as Floyd's, but proficient hands made it more deadly.

The man wiped his nose with his left hand and spread the blood over his face and chest. A bloodthirsty grin flashed at Floyd, exposing even white teeth, which made him look more sinister. He held his knife low. The knife had a double edge. He knew this Indian had survived other knife fights from the confidence he showed. They slowly circled each other. Out of the corner of his eye he saw Eleanor loading her rifle, and spoke to her quickly while keeping his eyes on his opponent. "Keep loading. Get everything loaded you can and be ready. There may be more. Don't shoot this one."

The Indian feinted with a low jab. Floyd stepped back and twisted to his right, slashing down across the man's wrist. That move should have sliced the man's hand off, except the Indian's hand wasn't there. Quick as a snake he retracted the jab and came up, aiming for Floyd's throat. With the speed of youth, Floyd turned and twisted away, bringing his head down, essentially blocking the blade from his throat.

Though his throat was now protected, his jaw was open and took the power of the thrust. The blade point grated on his jawbone below the left corner of his mouth. Driving in deep, the Indian ripped up and out. The blade traveled the length of Floyd's jaw, exiting in front of his ear. He felt the blood gushing from his jaw and his chest. *I don't have much time,* he thought. *With this bleeding, I'll start weakening soon.*

The two separated and started circling again. The Indian nodded his head and smiled. A quick thought ran through Floyd's mind. *He's confident. I bet he's already weighing my scalp on his belt. Maybe...*

Floyd was moving backward with the Indian pursuing. He had to get this right, or he was a dead man. Glancing at the edge of the log that had been dragged to the fire, he backed faster, as if trying to get away from the Indian.

The experienced knife fighter was grinning now, his knife flicking out like the tongue of a snake, reaching toward the boy.

Now, Floyd thought. Acting as if rushing to get away from the knife that had already tasted his blood, he dragged his foot along the edge of the log, seeming to stumble backward.

Already extended, the Indian pushed off, out of balance, to take advantage of his enemy's fear and confusion. Immediately Floyd wheeled farther to his right, turning into the Indian's exposed left side. He drove his knife deep, pointed upward to reach the man's heart. From confidence, the man's expression changed to shock and pain. He tried to bring his knife around to stab Floyd, but his fingers no longer obeyed his commands and loosened, allowing the knife to fall to the earth.

Floyd held the brave for what to him seemed like an eternity. When he no longer felt the man breathing, he pushed him from his blade. The Indian collapsed to the ground.

Floyd was limp and weak. For the first time he looked around. Five other Indians, plus the one behind the bush, lay dead in the grass. Eleanor was moving toward him. He glanced at Dorie, who was staring at him in horror. In the tent's door stood Oliver, holding on to the tent with his left hand, a smoking pistol hanging in his right.

Floyd took a step, staggered, and caught himself. Pa had said that would happen in a knife fight. Too many or deep cuts will bleed you out, but he won. He was still alive. He smiled at the three people watching him and collapsed in the grass.

∽

WHEN HE AWOKE, he was stretched out on his bedding under the post office tree. There was a breeze blowing, keeping most of the mosquitoes away. The coolness beneath the shade of the old oak was relaxing. He realized he should be up and helping with the team and the horses. As he tried to get up, a firm hand pushed him back down.

"Looks like you did this on purpose, boy." Jeb was leaning over him. "You didn't tell me about those Injuns. I guess you wanted all the fun. Yes, sir, I'll have to remember that."

Floyd looked around in confusion. "I swear, Jeb, I didn't know they were there. They surprised us."

Hugh Brennan walked up. "Don't pay Jeb any mind, that's his way of funning you. Floyd, I'm sure glad you didn't let them Indians kill you. If that had happened, I'm afraid your entire family would have been after me."

Floyd grinned at Hugh. That was the wrong thing to do. Pain shot up the left side of his face, and he reached for his cheek.

Jeb grabbed his hand. "Now don't go feelin' of that for a while. You got you a right nice cut there. You'll have a scar that'll last till they put you in the ground. That nice Mrs. Ryland sewed it up mighty fine, and the one on your chest. But I'll tell you, boy, you'd better stay out of bear country for a while. They smell all that honey on you, they'll be coming over to lick you to death, if the onions and the garlic don't run 'em off. Whew, you stink."

"Jeb, dang it! Don't make me grin."

Hugh squatted down next to Floyd. "You did real good, son. That one you had the knife fight with had a load of scalps on his lance, some fresh. He was one salty old Indian. Mrs. Ryland told us about it, and how though he had cut you bad, you kept your head and suckered him in. I'm right proud of you."

Floyd looked up at the trader. "Thanks, Hugh. How is Mr. Ryland doing? I seem to remember him standing at the tent, holding a pistol."

"Looks like he'll live, and keep his hand, thanks to you."

"Don't forget Jeb. He found the honey. Ma always says that's the prime ingredient."

Hugh chuckled. "You're right about him finding the honey. I think every man on this train thanks him for that. There'll be plenty of biscuits and honey for several days."

"What about the Rylands?" Floyd said to Brennan. "Will they be joining us?"

"Sure, Floyd. I plan on taking them all the way to Santa Fe. We can always use a good gunsmith in town. I'm not particularly pleased about having the ladies along. This will be a hard, fast trip, but after your Indian attack, I think the Rylands can stand up to just about anything. Now you get some rest. We'll be leaving bright and early."

Hugh strode off to make sure the guards were placed and ready.

Jeb hung around. "Mrs. Ryland told me what happened. You shore enough had your hands full. Reckon you've got the sand I'm lookin' for in a pard. When we get to Santa Fe, I'm hoping there's still time fer some trappin' this year before the heavy snows set in.

"Either way, I'm plannin' on headin' up to my place in the Rockies. Got me a mighty fine cabin with plenty of room for two. What I'm saying is, I'd be particular pleased if you'd throw in with me.

"Don't you worry, it'll be on the halves. Whatever we make trappin', we'll split right down the middle. That is if you've got a mind to go."

Floyd pushed himself up on his elbows, excitement coursing through his entire body. He shoved his hand out to Jeb. "Yes, sir. I can't believe it, but for sure you've got a partner, and thanks. I'll do my best for you."

Jeb grinned at the boy's excitement. "I'm sure you will." He glanced toward the Rylands' camping spot. "Looks like you've got yourself some more company." His eyes crinkled at the edges, devilment playing in them. "Why, it's Mrs. Ryland, with that cute little daughter of hers. I think she's got her eye on you, boy."

Floyd twisted his head to see. Pain throbbed in his jaw, and though he tried to hide it, there was an initial involuntary wince. "No such thing. Why, she's just a baby."

Jeb, still grinning, said, "She ain't so much a baby, I'm thinkin'." He stood to greet the women, touching his hat brim. "Ma'am, Dorie."

Eleanor smiled at Jeb. "Hello, Jeb, how's our heroic defender doing?"

"Oh, I think he's gonna live."

She kneeled down beside Floyd, whose face was red at her words. "How are your cuts, Floyd?"

"Fine, ma'am. I'm fit to ride, but Mr. Brennan is making me

rest up tonight. I'll be riding out tomorrow with Jeb. How's Mr. Ryland, his hand?"

Standing at her mother's side, Dorie, her blue eyes wide, spoke up. "Oh, Floyd, he's doing so much better. When the Indians came, he heard the shooting and got out of his sickbed, with his pistol, to kill one of them." Her animated voice dropped. "But he was so tired, we had to help him back to bed."

Eleanor looked up at her daughter. "Yes, but remember, he had the strength to get out of bed." She turned back to Floyd. "He is much better, thanks to you." Remembering Jeb standing by them, she looked up at Jeb. "And you also, Jeb. If you hadn't been able to find that honey . . ." Her voice caught, and she cleared her throat. "I'm am so glad you did."

"Me too, ma'am, and all the men in the camp. We all like honey. If you folks will excuse me, I've got to go make a round out there, to make sure everything is set for the night." He nodded to the ladies and winked at Floyd.

Floyd tossed Jeb's departing back an annoyed look and turned back to Eleanor. "I'm glad we could help, ma'am. It was good timing we were there."

"Providence, Floyd," Eleanor said. "That's what it was. If you hadn't been there, we would be dead or worse, captured by the Indians . . ." Unconsciously, she placed a protective arm around Dorie's waist.

"Oh, Floyd," Dorie said, "you saved Pa, and you saved us from those horrible Indians. Why, you are our knight. You are a true modern-day Ivanhoe."

Now this was more than Floyd was able to take. He grinned at Dorie and said, "Child, I'm no one's knight. I was there. If it had been Jeb, he would have dispatched those Indians much quicker than I did."

It was obvious Dorie had heard nothing past *child*. After taking a deep breath, she said, "I am no child, Mr. Logan. I would venture to say you are not much older than I." With that, she spun around and stomped off to their tent.

Eleanor shook her head, smiling at Floyd's baffled gaze. "Don't mind her, Floyd. She sees you as her hero, and I'm afraid she might have feelings for you."

"No," Floyd said. "I've never even showed . . . Why, she's so young." Puzzled, he turned his gaze from the stiff, retreating back of Dorie to Eleanor's face. "I'm sorry, Mrs. Ryland."

"No, no, Floyd. Don't apologize. This is something she must overcome for herself, and she will. Now, back to you. How are you? It looks like Jeb got the honey mixture on your chest and jaw. That is a deep cut in your face. Will you be all right?"

"I'll be fine, ma'am. I'll be up and around tomorrow. It bears watching for a few days, but other than a long scar, I'll be fit as rain."

"I'm so sorry. It can be hard to suffer such a severe wound at your age. Is there anything we can do?"

"No. Seriously, I'm fine. Why, I never was what you'd call handsome, so this little scratch won't make any difference. I'm headed to the mountains, and I wouldn't imagine those bear and beaver and elk that I've heard about will care a whit."

She stood and looked down at the boy. "Well, understand, Floyd, we owe you a great deal. We would consider it a favor if you and Jeb would take your supper with us each night when we stop."

"Why, that ain't necessary."

"I insist, and so does Oliver. Please. We will expect you. Now, I must get back and check on my husband. Get some rest. And, Floyd? Thank you again."

With her last statement, she spun around and headed back for their tent. Floyd wasn't sure, but it looked like she had tears in her eyes. He shook his head. *Goodness,* he thought, *will I ever understand women?*

He leaned back and started dozing off.

"Howdy, Floyd. I brung you some stew."

Floyd opened his heavy eyes. There was Muley standing next to him with a plate of stew and two big biscuits with butter and honey.

"Cookie wanted you to get some food in you before you went to sleep. I volunteered to bring it." He squatted down. Floyd first pushed himself up on his elbows and then slid to the rear, bringing himself close enough to the tree to lean against it.

"Thanks, Muley." He smelled the stew as he took the plate and realized he was hungry. He made short work of the stew, without a word, while Muley watched. Finished, he looked up and said, "How are the mules doing?"

"Oh, they're fine. Wagon's doing good, too."

"Muley, I sure appreciate you driving that wagon so I can scout with Jeb. I hope that ain't much of a burden on you."

"Burden? Pshaw. A burden was getting whipped by my pa almost every day for not workin' hard enough. Why, this ain't nothin' more than a vacation that I ain't payin' for. In fact, I'm gettin' paid. On top of everything, I've got a friend what's a hero. Now, I'm tellin' you, there ain't no way you can beat that with a crooked stick."

Floyd's face hurt when he grinned. "Muley, I ain't no hero."

"Why, of course you ain't. All you did was kill a few Injuns who was trying to take that pretty hair off those lady folk's heads. I was talkin' about Jeb. He done found that scrumptious honey!"

9

Floyd pulled Rusty to a stop and gazed across the short-grass plains. Two weeks had passed since the Pawnee attack, and his face pained him only occasionally.

Jeb said they were making good time, now about halfway to Santa Fe. His eyes had adjusted to the interminable distances. Now, the third week of September, the summer sun had parched the plains to a soft buckskin color. Occasionally the brown sea was broken with the dark green of elm and cottonwood along a river or creek. He felt at home. This was what he had dreamed of back in Tennessee.

He was alone in the west's vastness. His eyes were the first to spot those antelope slowly grazing in the distance, or a point of rock jutting from the plains. Sure, others had been here before him, but not today—unless they were Indians. He pulled himself from his musing, hearing in his head, Jeb telling him to stay alert.

From the arroyo behind him, his friend topped out and cantered over to him.

"Pretty, ain't it," Jeb said, stopping his horse alongside Floyd, and unlimbering his spyglass.

"Mighty," Floyd replied, still searching near them for

anything or anyone that didn't belong in the wilds surrounding them.

Jeb handed Floyd the glass and pointed toward the dusty blue hill that rose out of the plains. "'Bout ten mile. That's Pawnee Rock. Reckon that puts us near halfway." He grinned at Floyd. "We keep this up and we'll get to the mountains in time to trap beaver fore hard winter sets in."

Floyd looked through the glass, amazed each time he used it at how it reduced the distance, making objects appear near close enough to touch. "Pawnees camp there? Is that how it got the name?"

Jeb laughed out loud. "Naw, it's kinda funny. Kit Carson, a few years ago, when he was just startin' out, was on guard duty. He reckons a Pawnee was on top of him and shot him dead. Only he didn't shoot a Pawnee, he shot one of their own mules. When we meet him, and we will, I don't recommend askin' him about Pawnee Rock."

Floyd grinned. "Thanks, I'll remember that." Without thinking, he reached up and scratched his chest. The sting reminded him and he stopped scratching.

Jeb caught the movement. "Itching?"

"Yep, sometimes they both drive me crazy with the itching."

"Leave 'em alone. That means both them cuts are healin' fine. Before long, you'll forget all about 'em. Anyway, the girls like 'em. They'll want to know how it happened, and you can tell 'em yore hero story. You'll have all of them swooning all over you."

Floyd fingered the long red gash along his jawline. "Yeah, I'm sure." He was slowly sweeping the glass along the horizon when he stopped. He thought his eyes picked up movement.

When Jeb observed him stop the glass of a sudden like, he said, "What is it?"

"Not sure. I thought there was something at the edge of the horizon, but it isn't there now. Wait, there it is again."

He handed the glass back to Jeb. "There's something out

there. Way out there. Looks like on the horizon. I can't make it out, but—"

Jeb rammed the glass closed, turned, pulled the saddlebags open and dropped it in. "Come on. We've got to get back to the wagons."

With his last words he spun his horse around and disappeared into the arroyo he had just come from, Floyd right on his tail. They rode full-out for the wagons, their dust plume rising and catching up with them in the constant wind.

Floyd felt Rusty's exuberance. The horse loved to run. His muscles rippled under his red skin as he drove after Jeb. Racing back to the wagons, Floyd's mind was awash with questions. What had Jeb seen that set him off like this? He had never seen his friend anxious. First tense when Jeb spun around, Floyd relaxed, enjoying the dash and watching ahead to keep Rusty from stepping in a gopher hole.

Hugh came riding out to meet them.

Without slowing, Jeb yelled, "Fire," and they raced past Hugh to the wagons. Jeb slowed his horse to a lope, turned to Floyd and shouted, "Ride down the train and tell them prairie fire. I'm headin' to the river with Hugh." With that, Jeb pulled his horse up.

Floyd continued down the wagons, telling them about the prairie fire. He pulled up at the Ryland wagon. "Oliver, there's a prairie fire out west coming our way. Jeb says to follow the wagon ahead, like you've been doing, but be prepared to swing toward the river."

He saw the fear in the eyes of each person he told. He'd heard about these big fires that stretched for miles and had the potential to destroy an entire wagon train. Floyd was learning about himself. He was finding out that there wasn't much that scared him, but he knew he was scared now. Hopefully Jeb knew what to do. If not, they'd be fried like a brittle piece of bacon.

Lucky this fire caught us alongside the Arkansas River, Floyd thought. *If Jeb found a crossing, maybe we'll be able to outrun the fire.* He returned to the lead wagon, where Jeb and Hugh were guiding it through the soft sand toward the river.

Jeb leaned over to him as they rode. "I've found a spot where the river's pretty shallow. Banks aren't shallow enough though, so we'll have to cut them down so the wagons can get in. Ride back and let the helpers know we'll need them with their shovels when we get there."

Floyd did as he was told. Reaching the river, men piled out of the wagons, shovels in hand, to race toward the bank, where they started cutting down the bank. Only now that he'd stopped did he turn to watch for the fire. What had been first barely discernible was now taking up most of the northwestern horizon. It wasn't yet close enough to see flames, but the smoke billowed to the sky.

He flung himself off his horse and grabbed a shovel from Muley's wagon, racing to pitch in.

The boy had continued to grow during the few months since he'd left home. He wasn't a stranger to work, nor did he shrink from it. A boy on a farm spent many hours of hoeing, digging, stump pulling, and plowing. From those many hours of work at home, his shoulders were wide and sinewy, but now they were filling out with man-muscle. His upper arms were thickening along with his shoulders. A long neck jutted out of matted muscle that helped throw the big shovelfuls of dirt clear.

It took only a brief time for the men to slope the cutbank enough for the wagons to start down.

"Clear the trail," Jeb shouted to the hardworking men while motioning Muley forward.

Muley, concentrating on the steep bank, guided the six-mule team down and into the water.

Floyd saw the mules holding back, and he leaped forward, grabbing the lead while talking softly to the mules, which knew and trusted him. With a slight tug, he guided them into the water.

Jeb was riding alongside the wagon.

Muley turned to him and said, "That far bank looks mighty steep."

"You're not going up it," Jeb shouted over the din of wagons and men. "You pull into the middle. It's hard, I've already checked it. Once in the middle, turn your team upstream and drive till I tell you to stop."

Confused, Muley shouted back to Jeb, "You want me to stop in the river?"

"Yes, the bottom's hard and the water's shallow. Brennan is out there already. Follow him." As an afterthought while Muley rolled past, he said, "This will be the safest place with this fire. Now keep it moving!" Jeb raced to the next wagon.

Floyd, tossing the shovel into Muley's wagon, overheard the brief conversation. He ran back to Rusty, leaped for the saddle, his left foot slipping into the stirrup, and spun the horse back up the length of the wagons. He passed three of them before he pulled up and passed on the message. When finished with those three, Jeb did the same thing, racing past Floyd.

The wind had been out of the west. Now it was calm. The sweltering afternoon sun beat down on them, wringing every drop of sweat possible out of the travelers.

Floyd felt the wetness of his shirt as he rode through the artificial breeze Rusty's dash created. He pulled up at the last wagon. It belonged to the Rylands. Oliver's thumb had healed, and he could use it sufficiently to drive the team. Mrs. Ryland was sitting next to her husband.

When Floyd swung around beside them, she asked, "Are we crossing the river?" At that moment a small herd of whitetail deer dashed between the wagons. A big doe was in the lead, her neck stretched and long legs extending as far as they would go in each fear-ridden leap. Two half-grown fawns, their tongues hanging out from the heat and exertion, followed the doe. A majestic buck ran behind them. He halted for a moment, staring at the wagons, his eyes wild with fear, then bounded between the Rylands' mules and the freight wagon in front of them. His wide antlers were so close the mules jerked their heads back.

Floyd watched the deer for only a second. "Follow the wagon in front of you," he said to Oliver. "They'll be turning upstream. We're staying in the water."

Eleanor started to ask him a question, but he cut her off. "As soon as you're stopped, jump out and wet down your canvas. Also, get a few pieces of clothing and wet them. You'll need one for each of you, and several to keep the mule's nostrils clean from soot or cinders."

Dorie, who was looking at him, wide-eyed, said, "Will we be safe, Floyd?"

He had already wheeled Rusty to head back to Jeb. He pulled up and grinned at the girl. "You bet we will. It won't be fun, with all that smoke, but we'll be fine as frog's hair."

He waved and said to Rusty, "Let's go, boy."

The horse leaped forward, while his rider hoped what he had said was true. He didn't have any idea, but was relying on Jeb.

Pawnee Rock had disappeared in the flames and smoke. The flames were easily visible now. He had seen forest fires back home, and it amazed him at the damage they did, but this was his first prairie fire. Jeb and Hugh had talked about the danger, and how other travelers had died, burned to death. There wasn't much worse way to die. He pulled up to Jeb, who sat his horse on the ledge, watching.

The calm wind had disappeared. Now out of the east, it ruffled his hair at the back of his head, moving toward the fire. He rubbed the back of his neck. Jeb caught his movement.

"Fire draws wind into it from all around. It's still moving east, but sucking the wind toward it from the east."

Floyd gazed at the flames, chasing the rising smoke. The smoke seemed to go almost straight up and then lean over and dash east. He smelled the first acrid hint of it. Thick clouds of smoke and cinders were high above him.

"Get on down into that river," Jeb shouted. He watched the leaping flames, only three or four miles away and well above the height of the wagons and many of the trees along the Arkansas. "Help Salty with the remuda. Last thing we need is those durned animals stampeding. I'm just hoping this don't jump the Arkansas."

Floyd let Rusty make his way down the slope into the river, then turned him toward the remuda. The smoke was getting thicker, and the heat from the approaching flames was intense. He yanked off the bandana he'd been wearing, leaned down, and soaked it in the cool Arkansas River, rose back up and tied it around his face. The burning, cracking, and popping of the grass and brush, combined with the roar of the oncoming fire was almost deafening.

Salty pointed to the herd and yelled, "Keep 'em in the water! Don't let 'em run. That fire's gonna jump this danged river for sure."

Floyd circled the animals on the downwind side, trying to keep them from charging up the opposite bank. He knew the river would stop the fire. It was so wide. There was no way those flames could jump it. Then he saw the live embers carried in the smoke.

He tried to keep the horses and mules calm. People were in the river, standing against the fast current, throwing buckets full of water on the canvas tops and wood wagons. He saw all three of the Rylands, the water above Dorie's knees, trying to wet down their wagon.

Up the river, flames reached the north bank, then raced down the tree line toward them, towering above the little people like evil flaming monsters. An ember landed on his hand. He slapped at it with his opposite hand and saw it fall into the river, but couldn't hear it sizzling for the roar of the fire.

It turned and leaped, hit the trees and raced up, tops bursting in flames.

The horses and mules were rolling their eyes at the fire, dancing in fear at the burning death. Just when he thought it impossible to get worse, someone yelled, "We're all gonna die!"

He watched as a wagon pulled out of the line and charged for the opposite bank. Jeb, Hugh, Floyd—they were all too busy to stop the man. He charged his mules up the steep bank. The animals strained to pull the heavy wagon up the south side of the river. It appeared they might not make it, but their fear of the fire, the burning embers scorching their hides, gave them the power to yank the wagon over the crest. The team dashed across the plains to the south of the river. After almost five hundred yards, the man pulled the team up, motioning for everyone to follow him. He waved and shouted, but his voice was lost in the fire's roar.

Floyd recognized the man as the one who argued with Hugh about cleaning his rifle at the first stop. Watching the man, he thought, *It might not be such a bad idea*, as another ember, driven by the upper wind, sailed above him. His eyes followed it floating in the wind and settling into a stand of bunch grass. A moment later the grass burst into flame. Up and down the south side of the river the ember's action was repeated. The flames roared overhead, from the north bank and treetops. The heat was overpowering.

Floyd knew they wouldn't be able to hold the animals much longer. *Now I know what hell must be like,* he thought. Animals leaped from the bank, more deer, rabbits, wolves, coyotes, rats, mice, everything trying to escape the flaming death. A flock of turkeys launched from around the burning trees to the opposite bank, several with their tails on fire, only to bring more fire to the prairie upon landing.

The heat, smoke, and stench from the burning grass, trees, and animals filled his nostrils. *Will it never end?* his mind screamed. And then it did. The fire passed, heavy smoke receding. Floyd turned to watch the wagon in the distance. The man had stopped beckoning and now stood on the wagon seat, watching the expanding fire. As it grew, flames dashed toward him. He turned and raced futilely away, the fire chasing him until the smoke and flames blocked him from view.

Floyd coughed and looked around at the animals. Eyes were rolling, and several attempted to buck from their harness, but with fire also on the south side, they no longer tried to race in that direction. He examined the wagons. One had a part of its canvas burnt away, but a bucket of river water quickly quenched the flames. Other than a lot of coughing and sneezing from the people and animals, except for the one wagon, now lost for sure, they had survived. Jeb's fast thinking had saved them.

Salty rode up next to Floyd. "Outstanding work, son. Reckon if it hadn't been for you and Jeb gettin' back here so quick and gettin' us into the river, we woulda been goners. Them prairie fires are scary."

"All Jeb, Salty. He's the one who spotted it. All I saw was something I couldn't identify. He did it, not me."

"Boy, don't you be so cantankerous. You spotted it. He knowed what it was and what to do. It needed you both. 'Cause we just barely got everyone into the water before it got here. Those things move almighty fast."

"That one sure did," Floyd said, riding off to the Ryland wagon.

Mr. Ryland was up front with the mules, cleaning out their noses. "Everybody all right?" Floyd asked.

"I would say so." He looked around at Floyd. There was black soot under and to each side of his nostrils. Floyd figured that everyone looked like him. Splashing behind him caused him to look around. It was Dorie, and he was right. There was black under her nose.

She pointed at him and laughed. "You're funny, Floyd. Looks like you're trying to grow a black mustache."

He grinned back at her. "Reckon you might want to find yourself a mirror, yourself."

Her laughter died, and she leaned over to check her reflection in the moving water. She gasped, pulled the end of her dress from the water and wiped her lip and nose, smearing the sticky soot all over her upper lip and one cheek. Her chin snapped up and her soot-blackened lips pursed. "It isn't nice to laugh at a lady."

In the water, her dress in her hand and black soot smeared across her face, she might have been a chimney sweep's assistant. Grinning, he said, "Yes, ma'am," turned Rusty, and rode toward the lead wagon. He could hear Oliver chuckling, and Eleanor saying, "Now, now, Dorie, you shouldn't get upset. We are all funny with this soot on our faces."

10

They drove the animals out of the water and onto the blackened prairie. To the west, as far as the eye could see, the scorched earth shone in the sun. Not a sprig of fresh or dried grass remained for the animals to graze. Every step taken kicked up a cloud of burnt grass and brush. Trees along the Arkansas stood like black and white skeletons.

"What do we do now?" Floyd asked Jeb and Hugh. The three of them sat astride their horses at the front of the wagons.

Jeb looked at Hugh. "I recommend we keep moving. We've got to get to fresh grass, or these animals will starve. The longer we keep 'em movin', the closer we'll be when we have to stop. We were lucky the fire pushed no buffalo our way. A big herd woulda run us over."

Hugh nodded. "I agree. We'll keep pushing. This fire had to start somewhere. There's fresh grass waiting for us up ahead. We just have to find it. We'll hang close to the Arkansas till we cross it. At least the stock will have water."

"Let's move," Jeb said.

Jeb and Floyd moved out at a lope ahead of the wagons. The two men had switched horses before starting out again. Floyd rode a little buckskin mustang. It didn't look like much, but Hugh said it was quick and a stayer. They rode steadily for several miles in and out of scattered arroyos. Reaching a slight knoll, Jeb pulled up, took off his hat, and pulled his glass from the saddlebags.

He nudged the black forward until just Jeb's eyes and forehead extended above the rise. There he sat, scanning the open country. He motioned Floyd up. Upon topping the rise, Floyd saw a black plume rising in the distance.

"Buffalo?" he asked.

"No. Injuns. Not many, ten, fifteen. Looks like several of the women are pulling travois. I can't make out any braves or horses. I'm surprised they're alive. They must have found a cave or something to hide in, but still appears some are hurt." He dropped the glass into its carrier. "Come on, but keep yore eyes open. No tellin' what we might be ridin' into."

Floyd checked the powder in his rifle and pistol, pulled his knife around where it rested near at hand, and bumped the buckskin in the flanks.

The two men loped toward the Indians.

Closing on the group of Indians, they slowed to a walk. Jeb whispered, "Cheyenne. Women and kids and a couple of old men. Long way south for them. Might have been split up by the fire."

The Cheyenne had stopped. The women pulling the travois lowered them to the ground, and an older man came toward them. Floyd saw one travois carried a young woman, and another an old man.

The Cheyenne man approached and began speaking in sign language. Floyd, thanks to the Cherokees he had known in Tennessee, had learned quite a bit of Indian sign language. As Jeb conversed with the elder, Floyd understood much of their lingo.

The man first asked for tobacco. Jeb reached into his possibles bag and pulled out a square of tobacco. He cut off half of it and tossed it to the Indian, who caught it deftly, held it to his nose and inhaled, then grunted with satisfaction. He turned and said something to one of the women behind him. She pulled a blanket from a skin sack she carried on her back and spread it on the blackened ground. She also produced a pipe, handing it to the man. He took it, sat on the blanket, motioned for Jeb and Floyd to join him, and pulled out his knife.

While he prepared the ceremonial pipe, he shared his name, Long Arm. With his knife, he shaved enough tobacco from the square to fill the bowl of the pipe and packed it down. He then produced a flint and striker, lighting the tobacco. Once lit, he took several deep breaths, holding the pipe with one hand and using the other to direct the smoke over his chest and head. Then he passed it to Jeb.

Jeb followed the same actions, inhaling several deep breaths while moving his free hand as if to push the smoke over his body.

Now the pipe came to Floyd. He did not smoke, nor had he even tried it, but realizing the importance of the ritual, he took the pipe and inhaled. An explosive fit of coughing immediately followed. Fortunately, throughout the coughing attack he clung to the long pipe.

He looked across at the Cheyenne. No smile crossed the old face, but the corners of his eyes wrinkled more, giving the sense of a twinkle in the dark brown orbs. After the fit of coughing passed, Floyd calmed himself down and took another deep breath, followed by only two short hacks. He remembered to use his free hand to encourage the smoke toward himself. At last, he passed the pipe back to Long Arm, who gravely took it in two hands, turned it and again placed the mouthpiece in his mouth, once more inhaling.

Floyd sat still, with a calm demeanor, while he battled to keep from bursting out in uncontrollable coughing. He watched and listened while Jeb conversed with the Cheyenne. The man told Jeb how they had moved south with the buffalo, preparing for the long starvation time. There had been a great storm in the west, and it had no sooner passed than the fire approached.

The men were off searching for buffalo, leaving only the women, young and elderly. Most had escaped around the southern edge of the fire, but some were not as fast. In a canyon, to the northeast, they found a shallow but protected cave, where they hid. The cave would not hold them all, and two, he pointed to the ones on the travois, accepted burns by the fire gods. Now the group searched for their families, but they had little food and no horses.

Jeb turned to Floyd. "Did you get that?"

"I did. What's your plan?"

"Well, we can't leave 'em to die. Reckon Hugh can spare some food and a pair of horses. That should make it easier on 'em. I'll let the old feller know, then ride back to the wagons, load up some supplies, and bring the horses back. You can stay here and get to know the Cheyenne. Looks like this bunch is pretty peaceable. If the others show up before I get back—" a faint grin broke through his serious expression "—I'd recommend being friendly."

"Thanks," Floyd said.

Jeb turned back to Long Arm and told him his plan.

The Indian became animated, turned, and started speaking to the women and children. Excitement ran through the group.

Jeb mounted and turned east, leaving a black-brown cloud of dust and cinders behind him. Floyd walked to his horse, opened his saddlebags and pulled out his packet of jerky. His hand also hit the bag of hard candy he had purchased in Independence. He grabbed it and turned to the old man.

He extended the jerky to the man and watched as he gave it to an older woman, who started passing it around to the children. Floyd then pulled a piece of hard candy from his bag and gave it to the Cheyenne. The man examined it, turning it over between his fingers, then holding it up to the sun, trying to look through it.

In sign language, Floyd told him to "Watch me." Then, taking a small piece from the bag, he put it in his mouth, made sucking sounds, and smiled, rubbing his stomach.

The old man stuck out his tongue and laid the piece of candy on it. All eyes watched him. The candy disappeared into his mouth, replaced by a smile. He tried to bite on it and winced.

Floyd shook his head, and holding the piece he had placed in his mouth earlier between his teeth, he sucked. This time the man got it. He maneuvered his candy between his teeth, and with his lips around it, sucked.

"Mmm," erupted from him and he rubbed his stomach. Floyd saw the children watching, eyes wide. He motioned to a little girl. She looked up at her mother, got a nod, and walked to Floyd hesitantly. He pulled a bright yellow lemon drop from the bag and gave it to her. She put the drop on her tongue, and like the old Indian had done, drew it back to her teeth, gripped it tight and sucked. A smile broke out on her face. She turned and ran to her mother, jabbering.

Now all the kids dashed to Floyd. He handed each a piece and, after laughing at their antics, walked to each adult and gave them one. They were all laughing and talking when they heard horses pounding toward them.

The children flocked back to the adults.

Floyd knew the horses didn't belong to Jeb. It came from beyond the rise to the west. Jeb would arrive from the east, and he wouldn't have the number of horses now racing toward them.

The Indian riders burst over the rise at a hard gallop, over a hundred of them, all in war paint, but little else. They had painted their bodies, faces, and their horses. Some wore leggings, but bare chests and shoulders stood out in the red, black, and white paint. In their paint they looked magnificent, and deadly.

Upon spotting Floyd and the lost Cheyennes, they split and galloped into a circle, surrounding him and leaving the women, children, and old people behind them, protected. He stood his ground, making eye contact with the leader.

Floyd's mind was working overtime. *I hope Jeb can see this before he exposes himself, so he can warn the wagon train. Don't know if I can make it out of this situation. I sure can't fight them all.*

The leader rode forward. He lifted his lance and, with the point, traced the livid scar along Floyd's left jaw. Then he said, "Did a Cheyenne give you this?"

Floyd hid his surprise that this Indian spoke English so well. He shook his head and said, "No, Pawnee."

A murmur went around the riders as the chief asked, "What has happened to the Pawnee?"

"He is dead."

The chief said, "Ah, and who killed him?"

"I did."

"How?"

Floyd reached behind him and drew his long knife, holding it up. "With this."

The chief spoke briefly with the other warriors, and there were many nods and exclamations.

"So, white man, what is your name, and why are you here?"

"Name's Floyd Logan, and I'm headed to Santa Fe."

"Flo-yd. A strange name."

"Where I come from, it means flood."

"You are a white man, no?"

"Yes, but my ancestors come from Scotland. It is across the big water yonder." Floyd pointed east.

"Ah," the man said. He thought on it for a second, then made a fist with his right hand, and with it, bumped his chest. "I am Standing Wolf of the Cheyenne."

Long Arm interrupted the interrogation. He started speaking rapidly in Cheyenne. Several times he pointed east. He also pointed to Floyd, his saddlebags, and the children, who, eyes wide, watched the proceedings.

He finished speaking but did not leave. He stood next to Standing Wolf, his hand resting on the horse's shoulder.

"He says you have a friend."

"I do."

"Where is he?"

"He went back to gather food and horses for them." Floyd pointed toward the women and children.

"So he will return?"

"I'm planning on it."

"Is he a good tracker?"

Floyd didn't like where this might be heading. "The best."

"Good, come with us."

Floyd knew that no Indian respected fear. Hopefully, he would survive this encounter, but if he showed any fear or hesitation, his life might be very short. He stepped forward, toward the chief, before saying, "Good, I would learn of the Cheyenne."

He turned his back on the man and strode to his horse. The chief had said nothing about taking his weapons, which he thought was an excellent sign. Two men rode over to the travois and, after checking the supine individuals, tied the travois to their horses. Long Arm mounted behind the chief, while they lifted the rest to ride behind other riders. Once mounted, they moved west, no faster than the speed of the travois.

The chief motioned for Floyd to ride at his side, others making room for him. He rode silently, waiting. Sure enough, the chief spoke. "This man"—pointing with his thumb at the man behind him "—is my father. We were hunting many miles to the west and knew nothing about the fire until arriving near our camp. There we found an old tree on a dry creek, hit by lightning, starting the fire. It is good these members of our tribe escaped the fire."

"Did everyone escape?" Floyd asked.

"Yes, Flo-yd, they did."

They rode on in silence.

The sun lowered as they left the scarred land behind, entering the unburned prairie. Spears of orange shot through the golden clouds that floated lazily overhead. Slowly the brilliant orb disappeared beneath the horizon.

In the distance, Floyd made out points of light, fires. It must be the Cheyenne village.

The cloak of darkness wrapped around them long before they arrived at the camp.

Fires burned in front of each teepee. One fire, larger than the others, blazed in the middle of the camp. The people in the camp rushed to see those who had survived. Much talking and gesticulating took place around the new arrivals. The children, who had tasted Floyd's candy, chattered about it and pointed toward Floyd.

The riders split off to separate teepees, the chief motioning for Floyd to stay with him.

Three women, plus a young boy and girl, stood in front of a teepee outside the ring of light from the fire, their features not yet discernible. Standing Wolf pulled up there. Floyd followed suit. The women hurried to the aid of Long Arm. After Standing Wolf jumped to the ground, Long Arm, worn out, slid down from the horse.

All three women had stepped forward into the flickering light of the fire. Floyd felt like he lost his breath. His eyes locked on the youthful woman who had stepped out to assist the other two. *She must be the most beautiful girl I've ever seen,* Floyd thought. He sat his horse like a statue, nothing moving but his eyes.

She looked to be near his age. Her dark eyes reflected the dancing light of the fire as she turned her head toward him. She had the prettiest eyes he had ever seen. Black hair fell in two long braids that hung to her waist. A fringed buckskin dress draped from her shoulders to near the ground. Running down the sides of the buckskin were blue and white beads painstakingly sewn, accentuating her figure. She wore a belt of the same buckskin and beads pulled tight around her tiny waist. The long fringe almost hid her dainty moccasined feet.

"Flo-yd!"

Floyd had forgotten about everyone and everything else. With the gruff bark of his name, he snapped his head toward Standing Wolf.

"Get down, Flo-yd."

Floyd cleared his throat. "Thank you." He tossed a long leg over the horse and, like Standing Wolf, jumped to the ground, his face burning red, and just hoped no one else noticed in the firelight.

He didn't know whether the shadows and flickering firelight were playing tricks, but it looked like Long Arm's eyes were twinkling. He glanced at Standing Wolf, his eyes involuntarily slowing as they passed over the solemn face of the girl.

Using the bow in his hands, the chief pointed at the women. "This is my family. My mother, Little Dove, my wife, Quick Rabbit, and my daughter, Dawn Light."

Floyd wasn't sure, but it sounded like Standing Wolf emphasized daughter. *Oh boy*, he thought. *I sure hope I haven't messed things up.* "Nice to meet you," he said to each, nervously reaching out to shake hands. It wasn't until much later he wondered if the shaking of hands was their custom.

Each, in turn, took his hand, and while giving it one firm shake, they spoke his name, "Flo-yd." When Dawn Light grasped his hand, he felt the warmth and strength flowing through her. The musical tone of her voice gave him a thrill he had never felt before. He held her hand a second too long, and she jerked it away, looking at her father, who was frowning.

"Come," Standing Wolf said.

"I must take care of my horse," Floyd said.

Standing Wolf said something in Cheyenne, and two older boys came running to take the horses. Floyd walked back to his horse, untied the saddlebags and stripped them off, turned, and followed everyone except Standing Wolf toward the teepee. The chief motioned for Floyd to go inside. He nodded, crouched to pass through the opening, and stepped in, followed by Standing Wolf.

Beds were lined along the walls. A small fire burned in the center, with buffalo robes on the ground. Though the air was cooling outside, it was warm inside the teepee. The chief laid his bow and arrows on a small stand and sat so he faced the entrance from the far side. He motioned for Floyd to put his weapons with the chief's and join him on his left. Floyd considered keeping the pistol, but only for a moment. He realized, if they planned on killing him, there was no way he could get out alive, so he pulled his pistol from his waistband and laid it with his rifle. Before laying the saddlebags with the weapons, he pulled out the hard candy.

11

Turning, he joined the family, sitting to the left of Standing Wolf. Long Arm saw the sack he was carrying and spoke swiftly to the youngsters. All eyes swung to Floyd. With grand ceremony, he arose and bowed. First to Standing Wolf, again to Long Arm, and finally to the three women. He peered at the children, tilted his head, and winked.

He passed the candy around, starting with the chief, while Long Arm held a running commentary. No one tried to gnaw the candy. Each repeated the process used by Long Arm and began sucking. At the initial taste, and in their own way, each showed their wonder and pleasure, Even Dawn Light's face lit with delight.

"What is this that tastes much like hard honey, but different?" Standing Wolf asked.

Floyd grinned and said, "We call it candy. Is it not good?"

"It is good, Flo-yd," the chief said. "But let us not have more now. We must eat."

With his remarks, the women started dishing from a large cooking pot into individual bowls. Floyd noticed they had spoons carved from some type of horn. Dawn Light handed him a bowl.

Their hands touched briefly. To him, it was like lightning had passed between them. Looking into her face, he saw no acknowledgment of what he was feeling.

Floyd waited until the women had their food and had started eating, and he began. He had no idea of what type of meat was in the stew, but it was delicious. He finished his bowl and set it down in front of him. Quick Rabbit motioned toward the large pot, showing he should have more. He looked around. Others were getting seconds, so he nodded, and Dawn Light extended her hand for his bowl. This time the corners of her mouth crinkled slightly. His heart leaped.

After the second helping, Standing Wolf said something to his wife. She handed him his pipe, and he turned to Floyd. "Come, we go sit by the medicine fire."

Floyd looked at the pipe, hoping the distaste he experienced did not make it to his face, and followed Standing Wolf out of the tent toward the enormous fire. Other men were now exiting their teepees. Floyd tried to count teepees, and he lost count. *There must be three or four hundred men here,* he thought.

He again sat to the chief's left and waited. After talking to several of the warriors, he turned to Floyd. "Your friend comes."

Floyd worked to remain as stoic as his companions. "That is good. He will be tired and hungry."

Standing Wolf said something to his wife. She left, soon returning with a bowl of the stew, just as Jeb came riding into the village.

He led two horses, each saddled and packed with supplies. He spotted Floyd and rode straight to Standing Wolf and his friend. Jeb jumped from his saddle and strode toward Standing Wolf, his arm extended. The chief stepped forward, and the two shook by grasping the other's forearm.

"Good to see you, Standing Wolf. I'm surprised you are this far south."

"Jeb Campbell, my friend. I did not know it was you we waited on."

Jeb glanced at Floyd, who only shrugged.

"Did you have any of your tribe die from the fire?"

"No. Some burned, but not bad. You?"

Jeb shook his head. "No, but it was touch and go. By the time it got to us, it was roaring. We pulled the wagons into the Arkansas, that's all that saved us."

"Come, sit. Sit down by your young friend."

Floyd shook Jeb's hand as he stepped over. "Glad to see you."

Jeb grinned. "I bet."

Jeb sat to the left of Standing Wolf, and Floyd to the left of Jeb. While Jeb spoke with the chief about the buffalo, Floyd's eyes kept straying to Dawn Light, standing with the other women. Once, she glanced his way and gave him an almost imperceptible smile. His heart flew.

He broke his gaze at Dawn Light and looked at the men forming the circle around the medicine fire. Most were lithe, athletic-looking warriors. They were relaxed, laughing, and gesturing. Everyone was jubilant since no one had died in the prairie fire. As he was scanning the circle of men, almost straight across from him, there was one man, five or six years older. He was glaring at him with a cold and hate-filled stare.

Floyd turned around to look for the person the man was staring at. There was no one. He was definitely staring at him. *Now what is that all about?*

While he was contemplating the thought, Jeb leaned nearer. Floyd had been riding with Jeb for almost a month now and had learned quite a bit of his partner's expressions. He picked up on the barely evident worry line, low across his forehead, and leaned closer to Jeb.

His partner said, "Floyd, you keep your *moon-eyes* off that Dawn Light. She's a mighty purty girl, I agree, but she's the chief's daughter. She's off the menu. You keep lookin' at her, and you'll have us burning on a stake. I'll tell you if that starts, they won't finish until they do in the wagon train and every living soul there." Jeb motioned across the fire with his eyes. "Look across the fire. See that feller watching you? He's an up-and-coming warrior, and he's romancin' her."

Standing Wolf, as if on cue, said something in Cheyenne. The man Jeb was talking about rose and, circling the fire, walked to his chief. He stood in front of Standing Wolf, and while the chief continued to speak, the Indian remained solemn, except for once, when he gave a short, high-pitched yell, drew his tomahawk and thrust it skyward. Everyone around, not just in the circle, joined in the yell. Once the yelling had quieted, Standing Wolf continued while the brave returned his tomahawk to his belt and turned a bitter gaze at Floyd.

Once the chief finished, the warrior, shoulders back and thick bare chest thrust forward, strode back to his place and sat. The chief turned to Jeb and said something low. Jeb nodded.

Standing Wolf had other braves stand and spoke of them. While this was going on, Jeb leaned back to Floyd. "Well, if you was gonna pick a girl to make moon-eyes at, it is impossible for you to have picked a worse one. That feller what's been glaring at you ain't only romancin' her. He's about to be hitched to her, and the chief likes him. Seems he's one of the big braves about to make war chief."

Standing Wolf continued to speak.

"Now he's talkin' about buffalo. They found 'em west of here. One more thing. That black hand painted on the bridegroom's chest don't mean he likes to play patty-cake. It means that he's killed a man close in with his hands. It means he's a fighter."

Floyd had allowed Jeb to talk to him like he was a kid and had said nothing, but he'd had enough. "I ain't afraid of him."

Jeb looked at Floyd like he was crazy. "Well, I am. I'm afraid for losing my hair. I'm afraid for every white man and woman comin' west losing their hair. Get some sense in your head. Fear can be a smart thing."

Standing Wolf had stopped talking to the others, and Jeb took the opportunity to speak to him. "Those two horses, plus the supplies I brought, are for Long Arm to do with as he sees fit. I told him I would bring these things, and I keep my word."

The chief eyed Jeb, then nodded. "It is a good thing you and Flo-yd have done. Long Arm will be pleased. You and Flo-yd are good friends of the Cheyenne."

"Thanks, Chief," Jeb said. "I was wondering if you might have seen another wagon train pass? It would have been seven to fourteen suns ago."

With no hesitation, Standing Wolf said, "Yes. Nine suns ago. They were traveling fast. Thirsty Knife"—he pointed at the man across the fire whom Jeb had been talking to Floyd about—"wanted to attack them, but I said no. We do not need trouble with the white man."

Floyd had been listening to the conversation. *So that's his name, Thirsty Knife.* He looked across the fire at the man, who was still glaring at him. Floyd stared right back, thinking, *I'll remember you, mister. I've a feeling our paths will cross again.* With Jeb, he stood. His friend was busy telling Standing Wolf they would leave before daylight. For this reason, they would sleep outside the chief's teepee so they wouldn't disturb the old ones' sleep when they rose to leave.

Standing Wolf nodded. Floyd thought a knowing look passed between the two men. "You must be careful, my friend," the Indian leader said after a moment. "The Comanche is out in force. They are hunting the great buffalo, as we, but the Comanche is always ready for a fight. Though they are an ally for us, we keep a lookout when they are around."

"Thanks," Jeb said. "Would you mind askin' Quick Rabbit to bring our things out here?"

"Yes," Standing Wolf responded, then turned to his wife and

fired out what sounded very much like a request, not a command. She smiled at him and disappeared into the teepee. Moments later, she and Little Dove emerged with Floyd's things.

"Thank you, ma'am," Floyd said as each handed over what they were carrying. They nodded. Quick Rabbit, Dawn Light's mother, smiled at him and said, "You are welcome, Flo-yd." Then she turned and disappeared into the teepee, as the others of the tribe were doing, except for the first shift of the night guard.

Jeb shook hands with the Cheyenne chief, followed by Floyd. Floyd nodded his head and said, "Thank you, Chief Standing Wolf, for your hospitality."

The chief, with a bit of mischief in his eyes, asked, "Did you learn much of the Cheyenne, Flo-yd?"

"Yes, sir, I sure did. I look forward to seeing you again sometime."

"Yes, hopefully on friendly terms."

"That too is my wish."

With that, Standing Wolf entered the teepee, dropping the flap. Jeb's eyebrows moved up only a little, but Floyd caught it. With their gear, they moved over near the horses, where Jeb had left his things, and where Floyd's tack and bedroll had been left.

He started to speak only to stop at Jeb's quick headshake. Then Jeb whispered, "Get some rest. We'll be out of here early."

∼

Daylight found them at least an hour from the Cheyenne camp. They were just beginning to stir when Floyd and Jeb had ridden out. They were still north of the Arkansas and, according to Jeb, quite a distance from the wagons.

Jeb pointed to a single small tree in the distance. "That's our next stop. We'll find water there. Mark the place in your mind. It might save your life. In fact, every water hole you find, pick landmarks that will guide you to it. Out here, about the best you can do is line up two, better three hills. You can't depend on that tree being there when you need it. You also want to mark your point from going and coming. Places always look different when you look at 'em from a different direction." He bumped his horse, starting toward the tree.

"Jeb?" Floyd said.

"Yep?"

"What did the closed flap on Standing Wolf's tent mean?"

"What do you think it meant?"

"Well," Floyd said, keeping his head swiveling for danger, "the way he closed it, looked like he didn't want us to follow him in."

"You got it. A person's always welcome into a teepee when the flap's turned back, but you can get into a mighty ruckus by walkin' in when that flap's closed. That's about the only way the Cheyenne has of having any privacy in camp. So most folks honor it. Now last night, he was making a loud point when he closed that flap right in front of us. Though we're friends, he was sendin' us a message, loud and clear, that we were not welcome inside."

The two men rode slowly to the edge of a dry wash. It was at least fifteen feet deep with steep sides. The wash was too steep for them to cross here. They would have to ride either north or south to find a crossing.

Jeb turned to Floyd. "Which way?"

Floyd felt the breeze on his left cheek, meaning the wind was out of the northwest. Without hesitating, he said, "North."

Jeb nodded. "Good. We want to head into the wind every chance we get. No sense letting some Pawnee or Comanche smell us. You know they can smell us, don't you, Floyd?"

"Yep, I sure do. Learned that from Pa. Not only that, we can pick up their scent."

"You got yourself a right smart pa. Darned tootin' you can smell 'em. Most tribes have a different scent, depending on what they eat and what kind of rancid grease they spread on their hair."

They continued up the side of the wash until reaching a point where the sides tapered and it shallowed out. The two men turned their horses, crossed, and started for the little tree.

"Jeb?" Floyd asked again.

"Yep?"

"I like that girl. I ain't"—he thought of his ma—"I haven't ever seen anyone or anything that beautiful."

"She's mighty easy on the eyes, for sure, but you've got to understand. She's not for you. You go after her, and the entire Cheyenne nation will come down on you. You don't want those folks after your hide, 'cause they won't stop. Don't matter how long it takes. They'll keep coming. Remember that. Now's the time to put any thought of her out of your mind. Be thankful you're sucking in this mighty fine air and not smellin' your own flesh burning."

They rode in silence after Jeb's last statement. Reaching the tree, Floyd took in the view of the crystal-clear water bubbling from the arroyo bottom. It flowed for no more than two hundred yards, then disappeared in the sandy earth.

"Go ahead," Jeb said, tossing Floyd his canteen. "I'll keep watch."

Floyd rode to the bottom and took his horse a ways downstream to let him drink. When the horse finished, he rode back, filled the two canteens, and bent over, cupping the water in his hand while drinking. This was what Jeb had shown him. Lying down and drinking from a stream left a man vulnerable to an attack. It was possible for an enemy to be on top of him before he could even get to his knees to respond. This way kept his eyes and head in play, always watchful.

He finished, mounted, and rode to the top on the opposite side. Without a word spoken, Jeb rode down and, using the same method, watered his horse and got a drink. Soon they were again on their way.

Around nine that morning the wagons rolled into sight. The two scouts bumped their horses and took off into a lope. As they approached, Hugh, riding his big black, rode out to join them. Upon meeting him, they swung their horses alongside, and the three walked their horses west.

"Glad you boys are back. I was wondering if the prairie had swallowed you up." He looked pointedly at Jeb. "Looks like it swallowed up my horses and supplies."

"Consider it an investment in keepin' yore hair," Jeb replied. "When I got to where I left Floyd and that little bunch of Cheyenne, they were gone. All that was left was the tracks of well over a hundred mounted and unshod ponies. So I lit out after 'em."

Hugh looked toward Floyd. "Looks like you found him pretty much intact."

"Yep," Jeb said, "I did. In a Cheyenne camp of so many teepees I couldn't count them all. And guess who's leading 'em?" Without waiting for a reply, the scout said, "Standing Wolf."

"Well, I'll be danged. He's still alive and kicking. It's been at least five or six years since I last saw him. We parted friendly."

"Good thing you did," Jeb said. "He wasn't real happy about me bringing more white men to this country, and he let me know it. But when I told him it was you taking supplies back to Santa Fe, he calmed right down."

"Excellent. Any sign of Flagan's bunch?"

"Other than a few tracks up ahead, nothing. Standing Wolf said they seen 'em about nine days ago. Said they took the cutoff. He also told me the Comanches are out and about, chasing buffalo."

Hugh shook his head. "I hate to hear that. Didn't expect much different, but those Indians never seen the day they were friendly with whites. Any suggestions?"

Floyd turned and looked down the wagons. Muley raised a hand and waved. He stood in his saddle, gave Muley a wave, and turned back.

Jeb replied, "No suggestions until you decide whether you plan on taking the cutoff."

Hugh didn't dodge the question this time. "Yes. I want to get these folks to Santa Fe safely. If we take the cutoff, we might meet the Comanches. If we take the mountain route, we could get delayed or even trapped by early snow. So, Jeb, I've made up my mind. We'll chance the Indians and take the cutoff."

Jeb nodded. "The cutoff it is, but you'd best be ready to fight. The buffalo have moved south. Standing Wolf said they are ranging from just before the cutoff to way north and west. So we'll see the Comanche, I guarantee it, and he'll be huntin' hair. I just hope we eyeball him first."

12

"By the by," Jeb said, "couple more miles, and you'll be out of the burn. You're not moving as fast as you were. Figured on picking you up farther west."

"The Rylands had an axle break. They had an extra one, but it's sure a good thing we had Salty along. He had her changed quick, but it slowed us down."

"We'll say hi to Salty. Need to change horses. Anything else?"

"One thing. The animals have gone without good grass for almost two days. Find us a suitable spot with water and grass and we'll stop early. Give the animals and the people plenty of time to eat and rest."

Jeb waved acknowledgment, motioned to Floyd, and headed back along the wagons. Several of the drivers wanted to talk, but the scouts had to change mounts and get back out front.

Salty must have seen them coming, because he and another wrangler had Rusty and a horse for Jeb roped and waiting for them when they pulled up.

Floyd slid off the little mustang and patted him on the neck before stripping his tack.

"How'd he do, boy?" Salty asked.

"He's an excellent horse, Salty. I never had to push him, but he rides like he's got plenty of bottom. I'd be happy to ride him anytime."

"Good. I'll keep that in mind."

Floyd pulled the cinch tight on Rusty, checked the bit, grasped the reins, and, with his rifle, swung into the saddle. Jeb was swinging up at the same time. Both of their horses pranced as they mounted.

Jeb grinned over at Floyd. "Looks like they want to run."

"Let her rip," Floyd called, and the two men raced the horses by the wagons and past Brennan, who was shaking his head as they passed.

After less than half a mile, Jeb pulled up with Floyd alongside.

"All right," Jeb said. "I'm crossing the river to see if I can find any tracks. If you see anything, don't be brave. Figure out what it is and hightail it back to the wagons. If not, find a spot near the river with good grass where you figure the wagons should be around midafternoon, and shoot some game. Elk, deer, buffalo, don't matter, but those folks have gone without fresh meet for almost two days. We owe it to 'em."

Floyd nodded and Jeb was off for the river. After watching him cross, Floyd held Rusty to a walk and examined every bush and the trees along the river. He was learning each day. His eyes moved constantly. After weeks of experience, he knew the prairie, which appeared flat, wasn't really. Arroyos and canyons cut across the land, where any number of Indians could be hiding. He kept his eyes moving.

The hours clicked by. He figured the wagons were about an hour behind. *I'd best find a good campsite,* he thought. After ruling out two he passed, he found one he considered perfect. Grass was thick, and it was near the river, but not too close, so the mosquitoes wouldn't be bad. Those little devils could be rough around sunset.

Floyd marked the camp for Hugh and continued riding west, hunting, hopefully, only for game. After a scant distance, he spotted mule deer moving toward the river. The velvet antlers of a nice buck peeked above the bank of a wash, which ran down to the river. Turning Rusty back, he rode a short distance, dismounted, and tied the horse to a wad of bunchgrass. He bent low, took an angle on the deer's movement, and went off in an easy run.

A good position presented itself, where he would have a good field of fire. He checked his rifle, thinking, *Wish I had two rifles,* and squatted down behind a young cottonwood. He had chosen well. An unhampered view of the arroyo greeted his eyes. He didn't have long to wait. The big mule deer whose antlers he had seen came into view. Another buck followed, then another, and another, until he counted seven. The deer were on their way to water, using the arroyo for concealment.

By this time, the first buck was at a perfect angle for a heart shot. He slowly eased the rifle to his shoulder so the sharp-eyed deer would not spot him. Since the deer were quartering toward him, he leveled the sight in front of the left shoulder and pulled the trigger. Almost as one shot, another rifle fired from behind him, the bullet striking the second deer.

Floyd spun around, and there was Jeb, not twenty-five feet away, reloading. Floyd immediately reloaded and swung his rifle up. Before he could fire, Jeb fired again at one of the escaping bucks that made the mistake of coming out of the wash in their direction. Watching the buck stumble and fall, he thought, *Three are enough for tonight.*

He stood and waved to Jeb, then headed to the arroyo, where two nice bucks lay sprawled in the sand. *Beautiful animals,* he thought. *If we didn't have to eat, I'd never shoot one again.* A smile crossed his lips as the next thought crossed his mind. *But they do taste good.*

Floyd glanced around and saw Jeb move to the animal he had

killed on the prairie. He watched him check it, turn, and come walking toward him.

"Good shooting, ole son," Jeb said, "though you seemed a little surprised when I shot."

Floyd, feeling stupid for allowing Jeb to get so close without seeing or hearing him, said, "Guess I was a little too fixed on those deer."

"Reckon so. I could've easily been one of them Pawnee or even Comanche. That's about the quickest way I'm knowin' to lose yore hair." Jeb laughed. "But seeing those bucks just moseying down that there arroyo like they ain't had a care in the world could get any man's blood up. It might even make him do something he'd never do on calmer occasions."

While Jeb talked, his head moved constantly, looking out for Indians. "We'd best get these boys gutted and hauled back to your camp spot. We can finish dressing them out there."

The two men made quick work of the three animals. Jeb loaded two of them on his horse. Floyd took the big one he'd killed. Once loaded, they headed back to the campsite.

They arrived in plenty of time to get the deer hung and skinned before the wagons arrived. After scraping the hides clean of meat, they stretched the three of them.

"We don't have time to soften or remove the hair," Jeb said, "so we'll dry 'em and toss 'em in Muley's wagon."

∼

THE TWO SCOUTS had helped with the mules when the wagon train arrived. Now they were sitting around the Rylands' campfire, along with Hugh, Salty, and Muley. Mrs. Ryland had turned out to be an excellent cook. She had agreed to feed Hugh, Muley, the scouts, and the wranglers. Floyd wondered if the other men of the train were jealous of the arrangement.

Dorie and Eleanor were filling the plates of the men from the pot of venison stew. When Floyd extended his metal plate, Dorie gave him not only a brilliant smile, but an extra helping of stew.

Floyd glanced around, well aware there was not an eye that missed her action, but he said, "Thank you, Miss Dorie. I'm almighty hungry."

Jeb had already started on his stew. After two big bites, he said, "I swear, this is the best stew I think I ever et."

"Why, I can second that, ma'am. We got to be careful around here, because all those mule-whackers what drive them wagons?" Salty said, pointing his thumb to the other men sitting around their fires. "I'm bettin' they'd likely cut our throats for the chance to be over here." His enthusiasm and full mouth caused some stew to dribble onto his beard.

"Mr. Salty," Eleanor said, "thank you for the compliment, but I doubt seriously that any of those fine men would kill you to eat here."

From a fire across the inner circle of the wagons, a voice called, "Gospel truth, ma'am. Say you'll feed us, and we'll take care of those gents."

At the last statement, laughter rippled around the camp.

Eleanor waved and said, "Thank you all, but I wouldn't want anyone hurt."

"Ma'am," Hugh leaned forward and in a low voice said, "I'm planning on taking a day's rest after we cross the Arkansas. If I bring you the sugar and dried apples, would you be willing to fix enough pies to feed this bunch? I think they'd like that."

Dorie was nodding her head and clapping soundlessly.

"It seems my daughter agrees with me. We'd love to, Mr. Brennan. Just tell us when."

"Thank you, ma'am. I sure will."

The men finished their stew in silence. When they set their plates down, Dorie turned to her father. Her blue eyes danced in the flames. "Papa, isn't it time?"

A puzzled expression crossed his face. "Time for what?"

Now those blue eyes flashed. "Don't tease me, Papa. I'm not a little girl."

Oliver Ryland stood, placed his arm around his now embarrassed daughter, and said, "You'll be my little girl when I'm old and gray."

She turned to Eleanor. "Mama!"

Eleanor smiled and said, "Oliver, get on with it, and stop teasing your daughter."

Smiling back at his wife, he said, *"Yes, dear."*

The exchange had baffled the men around the fire. But western men did not question family conversations of others, not unless they were good friends or a lady was being insulted.

Oliver stepped to the back of the wagon, stopped, turned, and faced the group. "First, Mr. Brennan, thank you for allowing us to join your wagon train. I have since learned that you frown on having women on this trip."

Hugh started to speak up, but Oliver held his hand up, palm toward him. "If you'll wait a moment. I have also learned what a gentleman you are, and the only reason for your desire to have no women along is the danger of the passage."

Hugh nodded. "That's correct, and I mean no offense to you, Mrs. Brennan, or to you, Dorie, but this is a dangerous road. In a few years it will not be so bad, but now, with so few wagons and men, it's very dangerous."

Oliver made a slight head nod toward Hugh and looked to Jeb. "And you, Jeb, you have been such a help, raiding the beehive, helping us along the way. We thank you."

By now everyone at all the other fires had stopped their conversations and were watching the proceedings.

Oliver opened his arms, encompassing all the men. "Thank you, Salty, and all of you. On behalf of Eleanor, Dorie, and myself, we extend our thanks and gratitude to you for taking us in. Thank you all."

When he stopped speaking, the men from around the fires broke into applause.

He held his hands up to quiet them. "But if it hadn't been for a young man sitting here, I would not have survived my sickness, and none of my family would have survived the Pawnee attack."

Floyd's face reddened with embarrassment. He glanced at Dorie, and she was beaming. Mrs. Ryland's eyes were moist. He looked down at his worn boots, hoping that Oliver would stop. But he didn't.

"He shared a remedy that worked." Now he held up his hand and wiggled his thumb. "I'm a gunsmith, and without the use of my thumb, it would be very difficult, if not impossible, for me to continue my work." He gazed at Floyd. "I believe you saved my life. Thank you."

There was a roar from the camp, and the applause built again. Floyd wanted to find a hole and crawl in. He thought, *I have never been this embarrassed in my whole life. Please, Mr. Ryland, sit down and shut up.*

But he didn't. "Now you gents know," Oliver Ryland continued, "that this young man was not through. Pawnees attacked us, and he ended up killing four of them. The last one in a knife fight. Something I have never witnessed. Floyd stood toe to toe with a bigger, more experienced man and suffered a most grievous wound, the scar of which he will carry for the rest of his life. Yet he won the day. For that, I, we"—he indicated his wife and daughter—"would like to present him with this."

Finished talking, Oliver reached into the back of the wagon and from the darkness withdrew a new and shiny Ryland Rifle. The firelight danced along the shiny brown barrel, caressing the smooth lines and soft reflection from the forearm. It slipped past the grip, into the curving beavertail butt of the stock, brass shining.

Astonished, Floyd stood to meet Oliver. The man was thrusting the beautiful rifle toward him. "Mr. Ryland, I can't accept this," he said, even as his eyes took in the graceful lines of the weapon.

"My boy," Oliver said, "you cannot refuse it. I have spent hours on this trail making this rifle specifically for you. It is yours. Please take it." He continued to hold the weapon out toward Floyd.

Floyd waited and slowly reached out to grasp the grip with his right hand. His left hand found the forearm and rubbed along the checkered surface. He looked for the flint and frizzen. His eyebrows rose in confusion. This rifle had none. Instead, there was a hammer, and after looking at the mechanism in the firelight, he realized it was a hollow post. *How does that create fire?* he thought.

Oliver must have read his mind. "May I see your rifle for a moment?"

Puzzled, Floyd handed it back to Oliver. The gunsmith produced a tiny object that looked like a tin hat and slid it over the hollow post. He pulled the hammer back to full cock and fired. The hammer fell, striking the hat, which exploded. Oliver pulled the hammer back and, with a fingernail, flipped the spent cap off the nipple and pulled out another one.

He held it up to Floyd, who took it from his hand and, following his example, slipped it over the nipple and looked up at Oliver. Oliver nodded. Floyd threw the rifle to his shoulder to squeeze the trigger, with the same result. He lowered the rifle and grinned at Oliver.

"What is this?" Floyd asked.

Oliver took a moment to explain to Floyd, and those standing around watching, how this new muzzleloader operated. He finished the explanation by saying, "I first saw this back east and knew it would be perfect for rifle and pistol alike."

Jeb and Salty had stepped up, with the drivers and helpers crowding around.

Salty said, "What happens if that newfangled hat thing gets wet?"

"If it gets wet, it won't fire," Oliver said. "Tell me, Salty, what happens if the powder in your pan gets wet, or the wind blows it out, or your flint breaks?"

Salty stood, smacking his lips and rubbing his beard. "Humph! Well, I ain't impressed. Not one little bit." He turned to Floyd. "You be careful with that thing, boy. It'll get you killed." He turned to Eleanor. "Thankee for a fine meal, ma'am." He stomped into the dark toward the remuda.

Hugh grinned. "He'll come around. Salty doesn't take to unfamiliar things easily."

Floyd continued to caress the stock and forearm, careful to keep his fingers from the lightly oiled barrel. In the firelight, he picked up what looked like writing on the barrel near the forearm. He turned the barrel so it caught the firelight, and he could make out, above the wooden forearm, the engraving. On the lock side of the rifle, it read: *Made by O.R. Ryland.* On the opposite side the engraving read: *In Remembrance of Council Grove, September 1830.*

He stared at it, speechless. Dorie had moved next to him while he read the inscription.

"Do you like it, Floyd?"

Floyd looked down at the girl. "Dorie, it's about the finest gift I've ever had. Why, look at it. I know it must be a foot shorter than my flintlock, and it must weigh at least a pound, maybe more, less. And watch." He threw it to his shoulder, and it fit like it was built for him. As the butt neared his shoulder, he could see the sights starting to align, and when it rested in that shoulder notch, the sights aligned perfectly. He dropped it down and looked at Dorie again. "I love it, and this engraved part." He stopped to peer at both Eleanor and Oliver. "Why, this is the prettiest thing I've ever seen."

Eleanor and Oliver smiled back at him, and Oliver dipped his head in acknowledgment. Dorie beamed.

Hugh broke the spell. "Men, we've got an early start in the morning."

The crowd dispersed, men heading for their bedrolls.

Muley hung around for a moment. "Floyd, that's a mighty pretty gift, but I reckon you earned it."

"Muley, there ain't a chance I earned it. I'd have to do what I did over and over to earn something like this. But I'm sure glad to have it."

Dorie had moved over to her mother's side.

"Yep, it's really nice. Speaking of nice, that Dorie's right nice, too."

Floyd grinned. "Yes, she is, Muley." Floyd looked over at her, and she smiled back. "You like her?"

"Well, I could, if'n you weren't interested."

"I like her, Muley, but not like that." His voice stiffened. "Just be sure and treat her right."

Muley leaned back and frowned. "That's the only way I'd treat a fine lady like her."

"No offense, Muley. You should know where I stand."

Muley nodded, smiled at Dorie and headed back for his wagon.

Oliver walked up to Floyd. He had a leather sack in his hand. When he reached him, he opened it so Floyd could look in. It was a pile of those caps. On each side of the bag were smaller pockets. One pocket held three of the nipples the caps slipped over, while the other pocket held a small wrench that fit the nipple.

"Take these, and you're ready to go. Shoot it and get used to it. It's lighter, so it will kick a little more, but you will be surprised at what you can do with this rifle."

"Thank you again, Mr. Ryland. I don't have the words to describe how I appreciate this." He patted the forearm. "It's the first new rifle I've ever had, and the only custom-made rifle or pistol."

"You take it, Floyd, and use it to keep yourself safe. From what I've heard about the Comanches, I've a feeling you might need it in the coming days."

13

The wagons pushed west, following the Arkansas River. Their travel had slowed because of the expanse of buffalo. The enormous wooly animals were thick across the high plains. So thick at times, the wagon train had to pull up and wait for the massive beasts to move past. Though forced to slow, an abundance of meat was readily available.

Floyd had found he liked it so much, he could eat the dark red meat every day. Which was good, for that had been their only meat since finding the buffalo.

But with the abundance of game came more Indians. So far, none had approached. Usually they sat their horses at a distance and watched the wagons slowly pass.

Floyd recognized one of those who rode closer. It was the Cheyenne Thirsty Knife. He recognized Floyd and glared at him as they passed.

"Don't stop yore horse, ole son," Jeb had said. "There's way too many of them to try and fight 'em off, them being such fighters too. Keep riding, and dang it, Floyd, stop yore staring!"

Floyd had slowly broken his gaze with the Cheyenne, but he was seething. He didn't like to turn tail from anyone, especially that particular Indian. Plus, he didn't appreciate the way Jeb had spoken to him. *Why,* he thought, *I'm almost seventeen, will be in January, and I'm bigger than a lot of those full-grown Indians.*

He cooled down rapidly as he continued to think about what Jeb had said. *Why am I getting so riled up? Jeb is right. The last thing I want to do is start a fight that would bring harm to the other folks. I've got to get this demon under control. If I don't, someday someone will get hurt because of me. Anyway, Dawn Light doesn't want to have anything to do with a scarred-up white man.*

After riding more than an hour or two, Jeb spoke up. "We want no trouble with any of these Injuns. Most of them are good people. Like the white man, you've got the good and the bad. Like that bunch watching us." He nodded to the knoll to the north. Ten warriors sat their horses, lances in hand, watching the two of them proceed.

"Those are Arapaho, been mostly friendly with the whites. Course, they don't like their hunt being interrupted. Sometimes, you can get some big fights between different tribes out here. You toss in some Pawnee, or Sioux, them Arapaho get mighty unfriendly, and they fight. So will the Cheyenne. None like fighting during this big hunt. They're trying to stock up their larder for winter. Winter's a hard time out here, a dying time.

"Now, reckon there's one tribe what would rather fight than eat. That be the Comanche. I'm mighty surprised, and thankful, we ain't seen hide nor hair of that bunch, but in a couple more days we'll be turning south, right into their country."

Floyd waited, but Jeb had stopped talking, and they continued west. *That's the way Jeb is,* Floyd thought. *Occasionally he starts talking and talks a blue streak, but most of the time, he's tight as a miser with his words.*

∽

Sixteen days had passed since Pawnee Rock. It had been easy travel, even if it was slow. The buffalo showed no signs of thinning, nor did the Indians. Everyone was on edge. Though, so far, all had been peaceful.

The wagon train was only an hour behind them when Jeb pulled up at the river's edge. "Here we be. This'll be the crossing. Headin' south, we'll be leaving the easy water."

Floyd sat watching the fast-moving water. "How deep, you reckon?"

"Up to you to find out. This here is a rocky area, so we ain't got much chance of the wagons bogging, but the current's a mite swift. Hugh's been worried about this crossing. There's been many a wagon or its goods lost here." He paused, staring at the whirling, jumping water, and added, "A few lives too.

"You go on and ride across. Shouldn't be much of a problem on a horse since it ain't too deep, no more'n three feet or so at the deepest. But with its speed, it'll pile up against them flat wagon sides and could push 'em right over, or downstream."

Floyd made a clucking noise with his mouth, and Rusty stepped down the sloping bank and into the swift water. Once in, he dipped his head for a drink. Floyd let him have a drink and bumped him lightly with his heels. Rusty obediently raised his head and started across the river.

The water rushed around the horse's legs, gradually rising to his belly. It stayed there for three or four yards and slowly began to shallow. Once on the other side, Floyd cautiously rode up the slope until his eyes broke the plane, and he scanned past the top. He scoured the prairie to the south, then brought his eyes around to each edge of the river, nothing threatening visible. Turning Rusty, he rode back across.

Once back with Jeb, he pulled up and said, "Not as deep as first thought."

"Nope, sure ain't. Reckon that's mighty good. I'm figuring those wagons ought to be along any minute."

The two men rode back up the bank and gazed east. Sure enough, the white, dingy now, wagon tops were slowly advancing.

"When they get here," Jeb said, "we'll take 'em right across. Once over, we can talk to Hugh. Were it me, I'd take a rest. The stretch ahead is long, with sparse water. To make camp here might take a little more time, but the mules can get plenty of water and rest fore we head 'em out there." He pointed to the plains to the south. "Plus, we oughta be rested so we can keep a sharp eye out for the Comanche."

Floyd rode to meet the wagons. As usual, Hugh was in the lead. The trip was telling on the older man, but he wasn't shirking his duties.

"Got a spot to cross," Floyd said as he rode up and turned Rusty in next to Hugh. "Water's swift, but the bottom's hard. The water is only a couple of feet deep."

"Good," Hugh said. "How far?"

"Next rise, you'll be looking at Jeb."

"Glad to hear it. We're all purely bone-weary. I don't know how Jeb feels, but once we've crossed, I'm ready to hold up for two days to give the animals and folks a bit of a rest."

Floyd grinned. "That'll make Jeb happy."

Hugh nodded, took a deep breath. "So, what are you planning when we get to Santa Fe?"

Floyd looked at Hugh, surprised he had asked. "I guess I was planning on heading to the mountains with Jeb. He wants to get a little trapping in before the streams freeze, and then hole up. You know, get ready for the spring trapping."

"Is that what you want to do?"

Floyd contemplated the question. "Yes, sir, I believe so. I came west for the mountains, and I sure enough need to learn to trap beaver."

"I can teach you that, Floyd. Besides, mark my word, the day of the beaver is coming to a close. Oh, a smart man can still make money, but the beaver will disappear in another ten years. You need to learn more than trapping. I can teach you that. There's business to get the hang of, how to tell which people to trust, and those to give a wide berth. Land to buy. I'll tell you, you can't go wrong with land."

Hugh made a wide sweep of his arm. "All this wide-open country you're looking at right now needs is water. When men calculate how to get water here, the buffalo and the Indian will follow the beaver, and you'll be looking at ranches and farms."

Floyd shook his head. "Hugh, I am not a farmer, and I'll never be." He pointed west. "I belong in those mountains out there, and that's where I want to be. I appreciate your offer, but I'd like to go with Jeb. It may sound crazy, but I feel like those mountains are calling me."

Hugh was quiet as they came over a rise, and less than a half mile away, Jeb was waving. "All right, we'll talk more later. Tell Muley what's going on, and I'll inform the rest."

Floyd pulled up, waiting for Muley's wagon to come up to him. Muley was back up front. They had been rotating the lead wagon so the ones in back didn't get stuck eating dust all the way to Santa Fe. As he pulled by, Floyd swung Rusty around and, riding next to the wagon, said, "Crossing's up ahead, Muley. You see Jeb?"

Muley, looking almost as tired as Hugh, a good thirty years older than him, said, "Yep, I sure do."

"Follow his signals. You'll be the first across. The crossing has a hard bottom. River is wide there, though the water is fast it's only about two feet deep. Suitable surface is plenty wide. Don't stop. Keep those mules moving. I'll be riding on the upriver side of the mules. Any questions?"

"Yeah. When you gonna let me shoot that fancy rifle?"

Floyd laughed. "Today or tomorrow. Depends on what Hugh and Jeb have planned."

The short distance fell away quickly, and Muley was at the water's edge. He walked the mules into the water, and though they tried to stop to drink, he kept them moving. Halfway across, the water started piling on the side of the wagon, pushing relentlessly. It bounced along over the rocks, and with each bounce it moved a little farther downstream.

"Speed 'em up, Muley!" Floyd yelled.

Muley popped the reins, and the tired mules threw their weight against the harness. Floyd dropped back, throwing a loop over the rear corner of the wagon and whipping two turns around his saddle horn. At Floyd's urging, Rusty threw himself against the rope. Immediately the wagon stopped drifting. The mules continued to pull, finally reaching the bank.

Floyd yelled to Muley, "Take 'em on up. Give the other wagons plenty of room and pull up. Jeb'll be up there shortly."

Muley waved a hand full of reins at him, guiding his mules up the side of the riverbank.

Floyd turned to look back. There were two wagons in the river, with another starting to enter. He saw that Hugh and Jeb had roped the back end of each of the wagons, and with their help, the wagons crossed with ease. He rode back across to help another wagon entering the fast water.

Alternating, the three men braced the wagons through the fast-moving water, preventing any losses. When the last wagon rolled up the far side of the river, Salty and the other wranglers brought the mules and horses across. Near the far side, they let them stop and drink the sweet water coming out of the mountains.

Finished with the last wagon, Floyd rode to help Salty with the animals. He joined up with them in the river and, after letting them stop for a drink, pushed them across and up the bank.

The drivers circled the wagons and lit their fires. They had tied a rope corral at one end for the animals. Drivers and helpers worked to release their mules so they could be taken back to the river for a more satisfying drink. After helping herd the animals into the makeshift corral, Floyd relieved one of the wranglers and helped Salty take the remaining mules to the river.

"How you holdin' up, boy?" Salty asked.

Floyd looked at him askance. "I'm holding up real good, Salty. How are you doing?"

The old man took one loop around his saddle horn with the reins, placed both hands on his lower back, and leaned back. Once straightened, he said, "I've seen better days. I'd give anything to have a younger body, like yours. You ain't got an idea how lucky you are, no aches or pains."

He unlooped the reins and watched the animals drink. "Why, I disremember being a youngster, no older'n you." He grinned at Floyd.

Floyd was well aware the old man knew he was sensitive about his age and was probably needling him.

"Salty, I suspect you can't remember back that far."

"Don't insult yore elders, boy. That ain't nice."

Floyd looked to the west, and Salty watched him.

"What you thinkin', boy?"

"Salty, does the Arkansas River come out of the Far West mountains?"

"You can bet yore saddle it does."

"Have you seen it?"

Salty gave a long and misty look to the west. "Why, boy, I've been all over those mountains. I trapped those mountains when all you had to do was lay yore traps out on the bank, circle around, and herd them plew towards 'em. They'd just naturally like line up and step right in.

"I knowed John Colter and trapped with Bridger and Beckworth. That Beckworth could spin a yarn better'n any ole soul I ever met. Knowed them Britishers of the Hudson Bay and North West."

Salty blinked and gradually pulled himself back to the present. "You was askin' about this river. It heads up in them tall mountains, nigh on to two hundred miles west of here. Those mountains just righteously reach up so far they tickle the sky's belly, and even the trees can't hang on. It's all bare rock at the top exceptin' for the snow that stays around into the summer. Don't let it git in yore blood, boy. 'Cause once it's there, you ain't never gettin' rid of it."

He looked around at Floyd and shot him a sheepish grin beneath his almost solid white beard. "Sometimes an old man talks too much. We let these here animals drink any more, they're liable to founder. Help me get 'em back to camp."

The two men drove the herd back to the wagons. Someone spotted them coming, moved a wagon far enough out of the circle so they could ride in, and closed the circle behind them. One of the wranglers opened the corral rope gate and let them ride in. Floyd had been silent. He remained that way while he unsaddled Rusty and, with some dry grass, rubbed him down. He stepped back so the horse could roll in the dust, and with his tack slipped under the rope.

"Thanks, Salty," he said, "but I think those mountains, even though I haven't seen them yet, are already in my blood."

The old man put his tack down. Within arm's reach, he laid one hand on Floyd's shoulder. "I reckon you may be right, son. You already carry the mark of the west on your face, and I ain't meanin' the scar. I saw it when I first met you in Independence. Mountain men are like a good horse, they're stayers. They don't quit, and quitting the mountains is the last thing they want to do. I'm thinkin' you're liable to be out here for a long time, but let me give you a word to the wise.

"Sometime, five, maybe ten year from now, go home. Visit yore folks before they're gone. I waited too long. And you don't want to do that. It'll cost you a season or two of trappin', but don't worry about that. You can always make up a trappin' season, even though the plew aren't like they used to be. Promise me you'll go back, 'cause yore sweet mama will be hankerin' to lay eyes on you."

Floyd nodded. "I will, Salty. I'll make that trip."

"Good, now let's get some grub."

Salty split off to stow his gear, and Floyd headed to Muley's wagon. He'd never heard Salty or anyone else talk about the mountains like that. It sounded like they were almost like a drug a man had to have. *Well, it might be so,* he thought. *Look at me. I've pulled up stakes, left home, not even seventeen yet. I've got a pretty girl mooning over me, and all I can think about are the mountains and Dawn Light. Will I ever get over either?*

"Floyd."

He looked up, and there was Muley at the wagon, calling.

"Come on, Floyd, I want to shoot that rifle."

"Let me check with Jeb. We're in Comanche country now and probably want to keep the noise down. Have you seen him?"

"He and Hugh are over at the Rylands' wagon."

The two boys turned and headed toward the gunsmith's wagon.

Sure enough, both Hugh and Jeb were there drinking coffee with Oliver and Eleanor Ryland. Dorie looked up, and when she saw Floyd, her face broke into a wide smile.

"Hi, Floyd," she said.

"Hi, Dorie," Floyd said, and turned to Jeb. "Muley wants to shoot my rifle. Is it all right to fire it here since we're in Comanche country?"

"Sure," Jeb said. "They probably already know we're here. Hugh says we're staying for two days, so we need a buffalo. Why don't you walk out to the edge of the wagons and let Muley use it to kill us some fresh meat?" He turned to Muley. "Think you can do that, Muley."

The boy was almost bouncing with excitement. "I sure can, if Floyd don't mind."

"Come on," Floyd said. "Let's get you a buffalo."

"Bye, Floyd," Dorie called.

Floyd waved his hand in a short wave.

Muley turned and smiled. "Bye, Dorie. I'm fixin' to get you a buffalo."

Floyd had looked over his shoulder at Muley, in irritation for him slowing down, and saw Dorie watching him.

Almost as a second thought, she glanced at Muley and said, "Bye, Muley."

14

The two young men strode west from the encampment. After moving only fifty yards, Floyd pointed out a cow hardly thirty yards away. "Right behind the front shoulder, Muley. Same place as a big deer."

Muley brought the lighter rifle to his shoulder, settled on the cow's shoulder, and applied pressure on the trigger. It was a good thing he had gotten his sight on his target quickly, because the rifle fired long before he expected it.

"Holy smokes, Floyd. You don't have to do anything other than touch that trigger and it fires. You gotta be careful with that thing."

Floyd was pointing to the cow. "You got her."

It was down on its forelegs now, blood running from its mouth. Floyd reloaded the rifle, scanning the surrounding territory. The wagons were less than a hundred yards away and he saw Dorie clapping. He looked back at the cow. It had dropped to its side. Buffalo standing around it smelled and then shied off a few feet from the blood scent, but didn't run.

"I did, didn't I. That's the first buffalo I've ever shot."

The two walked toward the dead animal. "Congratulations, Muley. That's a young cow. It'll cook up mighty good tonight."

"Look at the wagons. You've got an audience."

Muley turned around, his face split with a toothy grin as he saw Dorie and waved to her. She waved back. Men had already started from the wagons to help butcher the animal.

Floyd and Muley reached the buffalo, and each grabbed a leg on the same side and rolled it onto its back. Floyd straightened out the head and neck and pulled out his knife. Men from the wagon train walked up.

The leader, knife in hand, said, "Good shot, Muley. She never took a step. Guess she'll weigh in at near five hundred pounds. Be some mighty good eating." He looked at Floyd and Muley. "If you fellers don't mind, I've been a butcher a better part of my life. Me and these boys with me will take care of her and then divvy the meat."

Floyd tossed a questioning glance at Muley.

"Fine with me," he said.

"Yep, that'd be just fine, if you'd take the tongue to Salty. He sure likes buffalo tongue."

"I'll do 'er," he said.

The boys stood back for a few minutes watching the men make short work of the buffalo.

"My first buffalo," Muley said as the two headed back toward the wagon.

"That was a fine shot. How do you like my rifle?"

Muley grinned and rubbed his shoulder. "It's nice and light, but it shore rares back." After a short pause, he said, "But it gets the job done."

Floyd nodded. "It tends to kick more than those heavier rifles, but did you see how fast I reloaded? I didn't have to mess with a pan or worry about the wind scattering my powder. I just slipped that little cap on. Slicker than hog lard."

"I'd best get to work," Muley said, turning toward his wagon.

"Got some harness repairs and wagon cleanin' that need to get done, since we're stopping for a while."

Floyd stepped off with him and Muley stopped. "Where you goin'? Ain't you got some scoutin' work to get done?"

"If I do, Jeb will come get me. Until then, we can double up and we'll finish twice as fast. Then you can go help *Dorie* clean those pans."

Muley's face turned the color of a red evening sunset. He grinned at Floyd. "I sure like her, but she's sweet on you."

"You just be nice to her and spend time with her. She'll see the error of her ways."

The two boys stretched the harness out and went to work.

∼

THE NEXT MORNING, after Jeb and Floyd had returned from their first scouting of the day, Floyd rode over to continue working with Muley. Hugh Brennan, seeing the two return, mounted his big black and rode over to Jeb. "Let's ride."

Jeb nodded, and the two of them loped to the south, riding in silence for over a mile. Then Hugh slowed the black to a walk, and Jeb stayed with him.

"I have another request for you," Hugh said.

Jeb looked off to the west, across the backs of thousands of buffalo. He turned back, and heaving a hefty sigh, he said, "*Mr. Brennan,* you talked me into scouting for you all the way to Santa Fe." He pointed to the west. "Less than two hunert miles thataway be the mountains I'm goin' to. I'll take you to Santa Fe, but I double-danged-sure ain't staying a minute longer than I have to."

Hugh laughed, which brought a deeper frown from Jeb.

Hugh held up his hand. "I am not about to ask you to stay a minute longer than necessity requires for you to get your new traps and supplies and be on your way."

"Fine," Jeb said, "then state yore business."

Hugh examined the young scout. Jeb had to be no more than six years older than Floyd, yet it seemed he had been in these mountains forever. The man looked and sounded like he was much older than his twenty-two years. Like most mountain men, a thick beard covered most of his face. The flop hat he wore hung down over his ears and covered his light blue eyes, making him appear either intriguing or ominous, depending on the person viewing.

"Well?" Jeb asked.

Hugh realized he had been staring, cleared his throat, and continued. "I want Floyd to spend this winter with me. He still needs to learn much, and I believe having him with me will help make that happen."

Now it was Jeb's turn to stare. After a moment he said, "You figure he won't learn anything from me?"

"Sure he will, Jeb. You've a great deal to teach him, but if he goes with you first, he'll never return to me. He'll never have the chance to learn what I can teach him. We both know that boy is destined for the mountains."

"Yep, you're danged right. What makes you think he'd stay with you for the winter?"

The two men continued to walk their horses south, over the rocky ground, allowing their animals to stop and pull at the sparse grass.

"I'm sure he wouldn't without your help. He trusts you, and he'll come closer to following your suggestions than mine. Here's what's on my mind. He's a smart lad, but he needs to learn about trading, more about people, fighting, and knife fighting. He can shoot remarkably well, but he is still a boy in a man's body."

"Reckon that dead Pawnee back at Council Grove might disagree with you."

"Well, yes, perhaps. However, Floyd was almighty lucky, though I won't take away what he did. We all need luck. I just don't believe he is ready to handle himself hand-to-hand."

Jeb thought on it for a moment while he guided his horse around a large loose rock. "I'll admit to feelin' much like you about it. The youngster was mighty lucky to have survived that Pawnee. He needs more training. I was thinkin' on teachin' him some myself when we get to the mountains."

"You can still do that in the spring. But for now, help him realize how important it is that he stay with me over the winter. I'll take care of him and get him trained. Why, he will reside with my family. I'll treat him like my own son."

Jeb threw a knowing glance at Hugh. "I reckon those daughters of yours'll be mighty glad he ain't yore son."

Now it was Hugh's turn to frown. "Jeb, what do you mean by that?"

"Well now, boys bein' boys, and girls bein' girls, and you with a houseful of mighty-pleasin'-on-the-eyes daughters, what do you think I mean?"

"Jeb, nothing will happen. But at least we might get the boy's mind off that Cheyenne girl. Why, he might go with you, get to pining over her, and head out to look for her tribe. In the winter! If he didn't die from exposure, he'd die from Thirsty Knife's blade."

Jeb considered what Hugh had just said. Hugh watched him turn it over in his mind, as if he was examining it from every direction. "I reckon you're speaking the gospel truth on that one. You should have seen him when I got there. He was like a lovesick calf. He couldn't take his eyes off her. I'll admit, she's mighty pretty, but he don't know the dangers involved with his actions."

Hugh nodded. "Exactly what I'm saying, and he has to learn to control his temper. I've watched him. He's better than he was when we first left Tennessee. He tries very hard, but he still hasn't gotten control over it. I've got a plan, a man who, if he's willing, can cure him of flying off the handle."

"That's a real problem," Jeb agreed. "I'm with you, he just ain't able to hang onto that temper. That one fault will get him killed.

"All right, Hugh. I'll try to help get him to stay in Santa Fe with you. Understand, I may not be successful. He's got his heart set on them mountains."

Hugh turned his horse back toward camp and rode for a ways before either man spoke. Hugh broke the silence. "Good. Thank you. I know he has his mind made up, but the two of us may persuade him to delay the mountains for just a few months. I know it will be in his best interest."

Silence returned, both men deep in their own thoughts about a boy neither had known before a couple of months ago.

Hugh's mind was racing. *Now,* he thought, *I have at least the winter. I think the world of Floyd. If I had any sons, I would want them to be like him, but that is not going to happen. But possibly my daughters can be better persuaders than I. One of them might capture his heart, and I can have the son I've always wanted.* He continued to ride on with Jeb, a faint smile on his face.

∼

THE TWO DAYS had passed with no disturbances. New shoes were on the mules and horses that needed them, harnesses were patched, and wagons repaired.

Floyd swung up onto Rusty. It had been two days well spent. Everyone looked happy to be on the trail again. They were all rested, and he would see mountains before too many more miles. Jeb had wanted to get an early start, so the two of them rode out of camp long before the others, besides the guards, were up.

The wind was still, and silence was on the land. *It's like the earth is enjoying a quiet morning,* Floyd thought. His mind drifted to the days spent in camp. *Muley sure didn't waste any time. Why, he was at the Ryland wagon every chance he had, which was quite a few since I helped him with the wagon and harness.*

He continued thinking about his friend. *But I'm glad, because it looks like it may pay off with Dorie. I'm sure Dorie likes him.*

"What are you grinning about?" Jeb asked as their horses picked their way in the dark.

"Nothing much."

"Don't give me 'nothing much.' Tell me."

Floyd looked over at Jeb. Now his face split in a wide grin. "It looks like Dorie is getting sweet on Muley."

"Hallelujah," Jeb exclaimed in a low tone. "I was afeared that girl would have you hitched before we reached Santa Fe."

"Had me a mite worried, too. But not anymore. I feel like a weight's been lifted from my back."

Jeb grinned back at Floyd and the two continued into the darkness, stopping every few minutes to listen. There was nothing but the normal sounds of morning life returning to the plains.

Gray spread in a line to the east, gradually widening, until light returned to start a fresh day. In the distance, a large stand of rocks jutted from the prairie. Jeb directed his horse so the two of them would pass west of the rocks, well out of rifle range. He pulled his spyglass case from his possibles bag and took the telescope from its case.

"Hold it!" he said to Floyd. The two horses and men stood, as if frozen, in the desert. Minutes passed while Jeb held his glass in one spot. Then he let out the breath he had been holding. "I swear I saw a feather, but it disappeared." He continued to glass the rocks. Satisfied, he dropped the glass in its case and slipped the case back in his bag.

"I could've sworn I saw something," he said again as they continued riding toward the rocks. "Never know about Comanches. They come out of the craziest places."

As if on cue, at least twenty or more Comanches let out whoops as their horses catapulted out of a ravine no more than thirty yards away.

Floyd reached for his rifle as Jeb yelled, "Don't shoot! Run!"

In the short tick of time, the racing horses had cut ten yards from their cushion. The two men wheeled and slapped the spurs to their surprised mounts. In two leaps the animals were at full speed, but the Indians had gained additional ground in those two leaps.

Floyd looked back. The nearest Comanche was no more than fifteen yards behind him. A dread came over Floyd he had never known before. He watched as the Indian, while leaning forward on his racing mustang's back, dropped the reins and lifted his bow.

Floyd threw himself low over Rusty's neck. Something slammed into his left arm, followed by an intense burning, and he looked down at it. An arrow had imbedded in his bicep from back to front. He urged Rusty forward. His red roan eased past Jeb's horse, and he straightened up slightly. He didn't want to leave his friend behind.

"Don't slow down!" Jeb shouted.

Floyd felt his roan driving hard, muscles rippling. He could also see that Jeb's horse was slower. In fact, the Comanches were gaining. If he stayed with Jeb, they might catch them both. Three of the Indians were slowly closing. He felt the hot breath of their horses. There was movement to his left. A glance showed Jeb pulling one of his pistols from his waistband.

Ahead, maybe a half mile, were the wagons. They were up inside the ring of wagons. At least they hadn't strung out yet.

He looked over at Jeb just as his friend twisted in the saddle. Floyd saw it all. The nearest Comanche, yelling at the top of his voice, and no more than ten yards back, had his bow and was pulling it to full draw as Jeb fired. It was almost an over-the-shoulder shot, but the ball hit the Indian in the middle of his forehead. His body went limp, and in falling he fell into the feet of the horse nearest him. In the melee, all that was visible were men and horses tangled and rolling.

Not only had the falling man taken out his companion, but

three of the Indians racing close behind. There was only one Comanche who remained close to them.

Floyd was barely able to move his arm for the pain, but he switched both reins to his left hand and reached for his only pistol. When he had it in hand, he pulled the hammer back, praying that the wind wouldn't blow all the powder out of the pan. He twisted to his left, and there was the big Comanche, not five yards behind Jeb. If the pistol fired, he couldn't miss. He pointed it at the man's chest and pulled the trigger. He heard no reassuring blast, only the scrape of flint on the frizzen. The pan must be empty.

The head of the Comanche's horse was bobbing next to Jeb's horse's right hip. Floyd slowed Rusty just a whit, causing him to drop back within reach. He grabbed his pistol by the barrel, no small feat, turned and, with all of his strength, drove the round butt of the pistol into the forehead of the racing horse. The animal staggered, and Floyd turned forward, kicking Rusty and hanging on. Minutes later he and Jeb watched as the men in the wagon train moved a wagon back just far enough for them to dash into the circle.

As soon as they passed, guns roared. Floyd jumped off Rusty to hand the reins to whoever would take them. With his rifle, he dashed to a wagon, taking aim at a Comanche as he came leaping over the wagon tongue. The .54-caliber rifle roared, and the brave rolled over and off his horse, to lie still across the wagon tongue.

Dust flew in the direction they had come, as the remaining Comanches raced to get out of range. Floyd was reloading when Salty strode up to him and took his rifle.

"I'll take that. You go sit over there and let's get rid of your arrow."

"But the Indians, Salty. We need every gun."

"Right you are, but you ain't gonna be good for nothin' if you ain't patched up, and soon. Anyways, they're gone for now, short a few Injuns."

Jeb walked up and gave Floyd a hard stare. "I told you to ride."

Pain was shooting up Floyd's arm, and the pain shortened whatever patience the boy might have had. "You're welcome. If I hadn't pitched in, you'd be minus a scalp right now."

People had gathered around the two men. Hugh walked up with his medicine kit. He had more experience with gunshot and arrow wounds than all the rest of the company combined. He stepped between the two scouts. "Let me see your arm, Floyd."

15

The arrow had sliced through the boy's jacket, shirt, and long johns. The head and shaft extended at least a foot. Hugh looked at the bleeding wound for a few seconds and said to Floyd, "This will hurt, son."

"Get it done, Mr. Brennan, and try not to ruin my clothes any more than they all ready are."

Hugh nodded, grasped the shaft behind the head and snapped it, throwing the arrowhead and attached portion of the shaft to the ground. Next, grasping the fletched end of the arrow, he squeezed Floyd's arm and yanked. Floyd winced, but that was all.

"Get the jacket, shirt, and long johns off your arm and I'll clean it up. How are you feeling?"

"I'm all right," Floyd said, though his complexion was pale.

Jeb had left and was organizing the men, preparing them for another attack.

Salty had retrieved a box from one of the wagons. He placed it on the ground behind Floyd and said, "Sit."

Floyd protested, but his legs gave out on him and he dropped to the box. He gave an embarrassed grin to Salty. "Thanks."

Once he got Floyd's bicep exposed, Hugh started cleaning the hole. "Now this will hurt, boy. Just hang on. It won't last long."

Taking the remnant of an old ramrod, which he carried in his bag for this purpose, he tied a clean cloth to the end and doused it with alcohol. Next, holding Floyd's elbow, he pushed the ramrod through the hole.

Beads of sweat popped out on Floyd's forehead while he battled with the pain, concentrating on keeping his mouth closed and his eyes open. A short distance outside the wagon ring stood a big bull buffalo, still and watching. *He's watching me,* Floyd thought. *He knows what I'm feeling.*

The buffalo bull continued to watch Floyd, and he kept his eyes on the bull. The pain melted away, and he pictured himself running with the buffalo across rolling hills and through green valleys. Soft puffy clouds floated by as the thundering herd ran, now through the mountains. They came to a wide canyon and leaped across, floating with the clouds until they landed on the far side. He wanted to stay with the buffalo and see the mountains.

"All right, son, I'm finished."

Floyd looked up at Hugh. The man was vaguely familiar. He blinked his eyes and looked around at Eleanor and Dorie Ryland. He knew them. Then his mind clicked back to the present. He was light-headed, but his arm wasn't hurting as bad.

"Thanks, Hugh."

"You did fine, Floyd." Hugh showed him some torn pieces of his jacket and long johns. "This is what we got out of your arm. If that had stayed in, it would have festered, and you might have lost your arm. You'll be fine now. Sore for a few days, but before long it'll be just like new."

"Where's Jeb?"

"He's making sure everyone and everything is ready. He believes those Indians will be back, so we'd best be prepared." Hugh packed up the case and headed back for his wagon.

The activity had died down from what it was when they rode in. Now it was quiet, everyone waiting, hopefully prepared.

Salty, after wandering off to check the mules and horses, walked up. "I'm here to tell you the gospel, boy. It's a good thing you fellers rode in when you did. If you'd waited another ten minutes, we woulda been strung out. We'd a been easy pickings."

The old wrangler chuckled. "You sure coldcocked that big Injun's horse. Reckon in all my borned days, I ain't never seen such a thing. Saw you slow ole Rusty so you could get a swing. Impressive, mighty impressive. That was quick thinking, boy. If you ain't done that, Jeb yonder would have his hair stretched on that Comanche's lance. As it is, that Injun feller's probably recovering from a bad headache, if he didn't get a broke neck.

"How you feeling, boy? I swear, I don't rightly know if you got the best luck in the world or the worst. Howsomever, you're here walkin' around, and there's some Comanche boys what are now checkin' out their happy huntin' grounds." He shook his head. "You shore you're only sixteen? Floyd, you are a caution, yes siree, a real dyed-in-the-wool caution."

"Salty, I'd better get out there and help," Floyd said, starting to stand, but his legs betrayed him, giving way and dropping him back on the box.

"Reckon you ain't about to help anyone, young feller, 'ceptin' yoreself." He grasped Floyd under his right arm and lifted. "Lean on me, boy. I'll get you to your wagon. You can stretch out fer a spell. Won't take long, and you'll be feelin' a lot better."

Floyd stood, leaning on the older man's shoulder, surprised at the solid strength. "Thanks, Salty. A brief rest and I'll be fine."

The two of them walked to the back of the wagon, where Muley was standing with his rifle.

"Help me get him in," Salty said.

Muley opened the back and hastened to clear a space, then slid Floyd in. Salty pulled Floyd's pistol from his waistband and noted no powder in the pan. From his powder horn he poured a little in and checked the flint. Once satisfied, he laid the rifle and pistol next to Floyd and climbed out.

As Floyd was fading out, he felt the tailgate being closed and heard Salty say to Muley, "He'll be fine. I s'pect when he wakes up, he'll be hungry and rarin' to go."

His eyes closed, and he heard and saw nothing—until the scream and the sound of gunfire ripped the sleep from his eyes. He snapped awake. A face, black war paint covering the lower half with dark, malevolent eyes, stared at him over the tailgate. The mouth opened, let out a blood-chilling war cry, and the Indian leaped over the tailgate.

Floyd's rifle lay under his right hand. Muley or Salty must have laid it next to him before closing the tailgate. Handling the rifle like a pistol, he only had time to raise the muzzle and thumb the hammer back. Already in his leap, the Comanche tried to move aside, hoping to have the ball miss him. Unfortunately for him, Floyd moved the muzzle ever so slightly, tracking the Indian, and pulled the trigger.

The rifle recoiled, and immediately after, the jolt of what was left of the man's neck slammed against the muzzle. The .54-caliber round ball had torn through the Indian's throat, and chunks of backbone mixed with fine red spray blew out the back of the wagon. Floyd jumped to his feet, guiding the fall of the Indian to his right with the muzzle of the rifle.

Next to him were his pistol and his old flintlock rifle. He checked that both were primed, shoved the pistol behind his waistband, and with all three weapons, jumped from the wagon. A few of the Comanches had made it inside the circled wagon train, and several men were engaged in a death dance with their opponents.

With one hand gripping the forearm, Floyd swung one of the rifles, the heavy barrel hitting an Indian in the head. He dropped the tomahawk he was about to smash into the collapsed driver he was kneeling over. The man, wide-eyed but unharmed, nodded and scrambled to his feet with his rifle. Floyd looked for Dorie and Eleanor. They were only two wagons from where he had been. There was a man, he assumed Oliver, on the ground, and the two women were bending over him. An Indian was lying dead on the ground close by.

Floyd strode over to the two women to make sure they were safe. Taking a quick look around, he saw Jeb as, with a long powerful thrust, the mountain man shoved his knife deep into the chest of a Comanche. Blood was on the arms of Jeb and the dying Indian. Charging toward him, from behind, was a Comanche hell-bent on splitting Jeb's skull with his tomahawk.

Floyd released his grip on the empty caplock and brought the flintlock to his shoulder. The front sight found the Indian's ear, moved along with him for only a split second, and Floyd pulled the trigger. He watched the Indian only long enough to ensure he was dead, dropped the fired rifle, and picked up the caplock. With a practiced motion, he began reloading while he nodded in response to Jeb's wave. He pulled out a cap, pushed it on the nipple, and pulled the hammer to full cock. Quiet rolled over the campground, broken only by several low moans. The Indians had disappeared. Still working quickly, he laid the caplock down and reloaded the flintlock. All weapons were ready.

Now there was time to see how Oliver Ryland was doing. When he walked the short distance to where he was able to make out who the injured man was, he halted in surprise. It was Muley.

"Muley!" Floyd said. He gazed at his friend, who had an arrow protruding from his chest.

Flecks of pink froth bubbled from the boy's mouth. His self-deprecating grin covered the bloody face. He coughed, coughed again, and whispered, "Sorry, Floyd. Looks like you might have to drive a wagon for a while. I'm sure sorry."

"Don't talk, Muley," Floyd said. "You need to rest up so you can get back to driving real soon." He looked across at Eleanor Ryland.

She shook her head. Hugh and Oliver had walked over, each from a different direction.

"Floyd's right, Muley," Hugh chimed in. "I need him out scouting, not driving your wagon while you laze around in the sun."

Muley looked up at Hugh. "Mr. Brennan, I want you to know that I sure appreciate you hiring me on, first at the livery in Independence, then as a driver." He stopped, a fit of coughing overcoming his weakening body, while Eleanor wiped the foamy blood from his mouth. His coughing slowed, and he continued. "I imagine I've been more pleasured out here on these plains, drivin' yore wagons, than most any other time in my life. It's been right fun."

"You've been a superior employee, Muley," Hugh said. "I'm proud to say I've known you."

"Thank you, Mr. Brennan. Sir, would you do something for me?"

"If it's at all possible, Muley, I'd be glad to."

"Whatever pay I've got coming, would you give it to Floyd?"

Floyd's head jerked as if to say something, but Hugh motioned him to silence.

"That's something within my power, Muley. I will abide by your wishes."

"Good. Floyd's gonna need money for traps and gear." His breathing was growing more labored with each breath. "He'll need it, and my pa would just send it down a bottle."

Muley drifted off for what seemed like a full minute. Suddenly his body jerked, and his eyes opened wide. "Dorie? Dorie, are you here?"

Dorie was kneeling opposite her mother. She lifted his big calloused hand in hers. "I'm here, Muley. I'm right here."

Coughing again racked his body. When it ceased, he said, "I'm right glad I met you, Dorie."

Tears were streaming from her eyes. She leaned forward and,

with her left hand, caressed his stubbled cheek. "I'm glad I met you too, Muley. You've been a really superb friend."

This time a small weak smile graced the man's face. "I'm glad, Dorie. Maybe, when I get better, you and I—"

The boy started coughing again. He made several gasps, reaching for air that was being replaced with blood in his lungs. Suddenly he stopped, his body relaxed, and he was gazing at the sky, past everyone. "Mama, is that you? It's really good to see you."

What little air he had remaining in his lungs flowed in a smooth stream from his body. His eyes remained open, as if he was seeing something only for him. He died with a smile on his face.

Dorie broke down. Her sobs carried around the wagon circle. The drivers and helpers, rough men all, pulled hats from their heads. Several took a handkerchief from a jacket pocket and wiped their eyes or blew their noses, for Muley was liked by all. Other than those sounds, a reverent silence filled the circle.

Hugh cleared his throat and looked around. "All right, men. This is a sad day. We've lost some good folks, but we can't be thinking about them now. We have to prepare for the return of those Indians. If we aren't ready, we'll all be going where Muley is now."

Salty shook his head. "He was a fine feller. Reckon there'll be danged few of this bunch, includin' me, what'll be going where Muley went." He turned and headed back to the remuda.

Hugh nodded. "I imagine you're right, Salty." He helped Dorie up while Oliver helped Eleanor to her feet.

Dorie looked across Muley's still form to her father. Tears still streaming down her face, she said, "He saved me, Papa. That horrible Indian jumped his horse across the wagon tongue and had his bow pulled back, pointed right at me. If Muley hadn't jumped in front of me, I'd be the one on the ground and not him."

Oliver stepped around Muley's body and took his daughter in his arms. "He did it because he is a good man, sugar. If you notice, Muley very seldom thought of himself. He was always doing for others."

Floyd listened to Oliver's statement, and his mind started working, going back over the dealings he'd had with Muley. Ryland was correct. *I don't know what his ma taught him,* Floyd thought, *but he sure took hold of it.*

"Floyd," Hugh called, "are you up to driving the wagon? If so, I need you there, at least until you're sure Billy can handle it."

Floyd moved his left arm. Pain slashed through his bicep, but it would get better. He'd worked injured before. "Sure, Hugh, I can do it." He turned to see Jeb headed for Hugh. Turning on his heel, he headed toward the wagon. He didn't want to be anywhere around for that discussion. He reached the wagon and checked the wagon box. They were still out there. He was sure they were.

Billy was prone on the ground behind the front wheel, his rifle pointed out to the plains. *Good,* Floyd thought, *he's ready and is in a good location. Looks like he's a sharp kid.*

"See anything, Billy?"

"Nope, nothing. Reckon they lit a shuck out of here. We oughta get goin' while we can."

Maybe not that sharp. "What if they're still out there?" Floyd said.

"We'll shoot 'em. Us, with all these guns, why, I bet we can hold off two or three hundert, at least."

Looks like I may be driving all the way to Santa Fe. "So how many times do you figure you can fire that rifle of yours, say, in a minute?"

Billy looked at him like he had just proposed an impossible-to-answer question. "I guess I don't know. Two or three times."

Floyd monitored the prairie. "All right, let's say you're really good and can do five reloads. Now we know that number is almost impossible under the best conditions, but let's use it.

"What if the Comanches attacked right now? How many times, in a minute, do you suppose one of those Comanche braves might be able to fire an arrow? Ten? More?"

Now Billy was frowning as he tried to compute the shots.

"We'll make him slow," Floyd said. "Say he can only fire one arrow every six seconds. That's ten a minute. Why, even for a slow Indian, he's twice as fast as we are with a rifle, but say he's pretty good and can fire an arrow every four seconds. Now he's shooting fifteen arrows to our two or three or maybe five shots.

"So, Billy, are you still comfortable saying we could beat two or three hundred Indians?"

Billy stared out at the plains. "Guess we're in trouble, huh?"

"Yep. That's the right answer. Now, keep an eye out. I'm stepping back to the Rylands' wagon for a minute. If you see anything, let out a yell."

"I sure will."

Oliver looked up from the back of his wagon when Floyd walked up.

"I guess Muley gave it all for your daughter."

"Yeah," Oliver said. "You are right. I am so thankful that Dorie is alive, but I find it difficult to accept the cost for her life."

"Mr. Ryland, I'm only a boy, but my pa says that you do your best and put regrets behind you. You can't ride a horse forward by watching where you've been. Be thankful Muley was such an unselfish man willing to give his life to save Dorie's. Remember him, thank him, but move forward. That ain't me talking, but my pa."

"Sounds like you have a smart pa, Floyd."

"Yes, sir, I do. I just wish I had let him know I felt like that when I was home," he said. "But there I go doing exactly what I'm saying don't do. Life's a real hoot.

"Now, Mr. Ryland, I've got a question for you."

Oliver nodded.

"Is it possible to turn my pistol into a caplock?"

"I saw what happened today when the wind blew the powder out of your pistol's pan. It's a splendid thing you had the presence of mind to do what you did, but to answer your question, yes. I can convert your pistol, and it doesn't take long to do, for I have locks that will fit it. All I have to do is a little drilling, unscrew yours and screw in the new one."

"How much?"

"For you, free."

Floyd shook his head. "I appreciate that, but I won't accept it if I don't pay for it."

"In that case, five dollars, and for another five dollars I'll convert your flintlock rifle."

There was no decision for Floyd to make. His escapade today had proven the superiority of the caplock. "As soon as we're through this Indian problem, I'll have them done."

"Bring them when you're ready."

Floyd spun around at Jeb's cry, "Here they come!"

16

Floyd raced to his wagon. The Comanches, it looked like around fifty of them, came on, riding hard. He leveled on a black-painted brave in the front of the hard-charging Indians. Though he figured those men were dead set on killing everyone in the wagon train, he couldn't help admiring them on horseback, dashing fearlessly toward the wagons. They were magnificent. If they were wearing armor instead of war paint, they'd be right out of one of Ma's books about the old country.

"Hold fire, hold fire!"

Floyd spun around to see Jeb yelling and pointing to the west. From the west came another group of Indians, galloping hard. The leader wore a magnificent headdress that flowed out behind him over his horse's rump. Several of the men wore such finery. There were at least two hundred in the group.

They neared, and Floyd recognized Standing Wolf of the Cheyenne, and Long Arm, headdresses sweeping behind them, glistening in the sun. The Cheyenne were riding to cut off the Comanche.

The drivers and helpers were murmuring and complaining about not firing.

Jeb ran to the center of the circle. "Any man who fires his weapon, I will shoot, right here, right now. Do you all understand me?"

Though some were not happy, none wanted to go up against him. Shouts of, "Yes, sir," and, "Hold fire," ran around the wagons.

Floyd's wagon faced where the two tribes would come together. Jeb ran forward to stand by Floyd.

"What," Floyd said, "is going on?"

Jeb shook his head as Hugh strode up to watch.

"I ain't got even the tiniest idea of what's happenin' here. If they get together, we're all dead or captive, but I've just got a feelin' the Cheyenne are interfering on our behalf. With what we did for Long Arm and his people after the fire, ole Standing Wolf might feel beholden. I danged sure hope so. Like I've said, they're notional. Long Arm may have put up a big argument for us." He shrugged. "That's my thoughts, but I ain't positive.

"The Cheyenne and Comanche have a peace treaty of sorts. I wouldn't say they're the best of friends, but they don't raid each other." He stood there watching the two tribes.

Hugh spoke up. "I'm glad you boys helped those Cheyenne after the fire. That may have been the deciding factor. Standing Wolf knows me, but I wouldn't think that would be enough for him to step in front of a Comanche war party."

Floyd watched the Comanche chief gesticulating, and Standing Wolf calmly pointing to his larger group of warriors and speaking, what appeared to be, in a more relaxed manner.

It went on for at least half an hour. At last, the Comanche chief pointed a finger at himself and two of his subchiefs, then at Standing Wolf, Long Arm, and one other Cheyenne chief. He then pointed toward the wagon train.

The six Indians started walking their horses toward the wagon train. Jeb and Hugh, still holding their rifles in the crook of their arms, stepped outside the protecting wagons and walked forward a short distance.

Hugh turned and said, "You join us, Floyd."

Floyd, thinking, *I'm not sure if this is an honor or a sacrifice,* stepped out onto the prairie to join Floyd and Hugh. As the Indians drew closer, Floyd recognized the third Cheyenne chief, *Thirsty Knife.*

Drawing their horses up, the six Indians looked over the three white men, then scrutinized the wagons and people. Finally the Comanche chief pointed to Floyd and in English said, "Today, you hit horse in head with your pistol?"

Floyd, surprised, kept his face blank and nodded his head, saying, "I did."

"And you kill Pawnee with knife?"

Floyd said, "Yes."

He looked Floyd over and spoke. "Where knife?"

Floyd pulled the knife from his scabbard and held it up. The Indian extended his hand.

Neither looking left nor right, Floyd stepped forward to the Comanche and, unexpectedly, flipped the knife, grabbing it by the blade. It surprised all the Indians. They didn't move, nor did their expressions change, but Floyd could swear the Comanche smiled. He laid the hilt of the knife in the Indian's hand.

The man took it, hefted it and looked at the shining blade. He leaned forward, stretching his arm, and, with the tip, lightly traced the nearly healed scar. Then he leaned back, only to lean forward again, as if to give it back. As Floyd extended his hand, the Indian did the same thing he had, flipping the knife in the air and grabbing it by the blade. Floyd's hand remained steady as a rock, his eyes locked on the Comanche.

The chief laid the hilt in Floyd's hand and said, "You are only boy."

Floyd nodded, paused for a moment, and then said, "Maybe those Pawnee thought the same thing just before I killed them."

The eyes of five of the Indians wrinkled in humor. Thirsty Knife was the exception.

"You fight like Comanche. You need Comanche name." He slapped his chest. "I am chief of the Comancia. I am Black Hand. I say you will be forever known as Pawnee Killer." Then his eyes lifted. "Because of friendship with Cheyenne, and because you, Pawnee Killer, are here, all will have safe passage through Comancheria."

He spun his horse and his two chiefs followed. The three men galloped south, followed by their braves, yelling and whooping.

Once they were gone, Hugh looked at Long Arm and Standing Wolf. "Thank you. We will have a feast in your honor."

Standing Wolf shook his head. "Not this day. We still have many buffalo to kill, and winter is coming soon." Then he looked at Floyd. "You are a brave man. Along with Jeb Campbell and Hugh Brennan, I, Standing Wolf, say you will now be welcome in the Cheyenne camp." He looked back at Hugh. "We must go. You will have no problem with the Comanche for the rest of your trip, but you must keep watch for the Apache. I hear they are killing whites."

With his last statement, he turned his horse, Long Arm on one side and Thirsty Knife the other. As they were turning, Thirsty Knife turned his head so his cold eyes stayed on Floyd. Standing Wolf said something, and Thirsty Knife jerked his head forward. They put their horses into a lope, returning in the same direction, and their braves joined them.

Hugh took a deep breath. "I wouldn't have believed it if I hadn't seen it."

Jeb shook his head. "I knew we were dead when I saw those Comanches coming. They were out for blood."

"Thanks to what you did after the fire," Hugh said, "and what this young fellow did with his Pawnee attackers, I think we've got a safe road ahead, except for the Apache."

Entering the circle of wagons, Hugh's face turned somber. "It's time we get Muley buried and be on our way. He was a fine young man."

Floyd cradled his rifle in the crook of his arm as the three of them walked toward the still form on the ground. Someone earlier must have covered his body, and Dorie sat beside him. *Death*, Floyd thought, *isn't particular. It takes the good and the bad, the sick and healthy, but Muley, he died saving a life. Hugh is right. Muley was a good man.*

∼

TWO WEEKS HAD PASSED since the Comanche attack back at the Arkansas. Though a hard worker, it was quickly obvious Billy wasn't up to driving the wagon. Hugh assigned another helper, who had driving experience, relieved Floyd of his driving duties, and turned him loose to scout.

The days had turned gloomy. Clouds hung over the plains, dropping rain in spots, only to be quickly absorbed into the thirsty earth. The temperature was colder. Floyd had taken to wearing the coat his ma and the girls had made for him. It was long and warm, extending over Rusty's sides, covering a portion of his hips and flanks. The red roan was frisky in this frosty weather. He pranced as he walked.

But Floyd's mood matched the weather. He took Muley's death hard. He had seen people die before, but he'd never seen a young man his age, a friend, die like Muley. Some of his thoughts were about his own mortality, others about Muley's heroism. Often, he wondered if he would have the courage to jump in front of an arrow for someone else.

He remained alert, even as his mind rested on bleak things. The terrain was changing, the land gradually rising. Until now, a near mesa was only visible when the low clouds drifted clear. Dark green trees held to the steep hillsides of the mesa. Jeb said they were juniper, with a few piñons.

The two men drifted along, searching for a sign of Indians or of the Flagan wagon train.

"Why do you think we haven't caught up with them?" Floyd asked.

Jeb's mind must have been on the same thing, for he answered quickly, "I ain't got the shadiest idea. I figgered we would've found them by now. I can't imagine Porter waiting so long, but I can assure you he's worse than the average thief. He'll kill you just for fun, and with those women along . . ." His voice trailed off, as gloomy as Floyd felt.

Guess these clouds and cold must be getting to Jeb, too, he thought.

They came to a ridgeline and Jeb didn't hesitate, but rode straight up the ridge, not even stopping to look. Floyd's mood was low, but he'd never ride straight up to a ridge and highlight himself.

"You looking for trouble?"

Jeb didn't turn. "I'm danged tired of these clouds and the cold. It ain't supposed to be bone-chilling cold this early. A fight might warm us up."

"Count me out. I don't need warming that bad."

Jeb was looking up at the clouds as Floyd started to ride on. "Hold up, Floyd." Jeb was grinning.

"Hold up? You want to sit up here in the open? I don't want those Comanches to spot us and change their mind." He looked at Jeb's face, the grin. "What's wrong with you? You losing your mind?"

"Well, now, there's some what'll say I lost that tool a long time ago, but no, my young and gloomy friend. Don't you want to see the mountains?"

Two days earlier, Jeb had told Floyd they had drawn close enough to see the crags of the Rockies, but they were behind the clouds. Having that piece of information soured Floyd's attitude even more.

Floyd pulled in Rusty and sat, looking at the clouds. "So how you planning on me seeing them. You going to part the clouds?" Then he saw what Jeb was talking about. Breaks were showing.

Streaks of sunlight reached and illuminated the ground. Large sections of cloud started separating. It was like an enormous hand wiped the clouds in the west. They moved, opening blue sky, and in that blue sky he saw the reason for his traveling so far. Pointing their majestic, white-capped heads high into the deep blue were the mountains. Mountains like he had never seen before.

He turned to Jeb. "They're huge."

"Yes, they are. What you're looking at is the southern end of the Rocky Mountains. These be the Sangre de Cristo range. Down farther south is where we'll cross Glorieta Pass. Beginning here"—Jeb pointed at the south end of the mountains—"that there is Baldy, it's the farthest south peak in those Rockies, just a little northwest of Santa Fe. Then they extend clean up into Canada, and there's beaver all the way."

Floyd sat Rusty, unmoving, mouth open. Then he said, "Ain't those about the most beautiful things you've ever seen."

"Well, I ain't sure if they're the most beautiful thing these peepers have landed on, but they are mighty fine."

"How far?"

"Sixty miles, I'd say. We're already running into canyon country. When all these clouds break, you'll see the mesas we've been passing, and get a clearer look at Baldy. There's a few piñons around here now and some of them scrub pines. I find one up ahead that's got nuts, we'll eat a few. You'll like 'em. They're small but mighty good."

"I've eaten pine nuts back home. Can't say they suit me, but I will eat 'em when I have to."

"Ain't the same. You'll like these. They're sweeter, almost buttery, and they don't have the piney bite those pine nuts do."

Of the same mind, the two men started their horses forward. It was hard for Floyd to keep his eyes off the mountains. In not too many days, they'd be there.

They rode for two more hours, the terrain getting rougher.

They were descending now, the green of the juniper, piñons, and pine contrasting with the yellow and reds of the broken rocks and hillsides.

"'Nother mile or so, and we'll be at the Canadian. Nice rocky crossing." In front and to his right, high canyon walls rose. It was hard for Floyd to contain his excitement. He'd heard of the Canadian River and the Pecos River, which Jeb had also told him about.

"Hold up!" Jeb said, and he stepped down from his horse. "Looky here. Flagan's wagons turned off. Looks like they be headed up that canyon. There ain't no outlet except the way they're goin' in, and the only tracks coming out are horses, more than went in." He straightened up. "That ain't good, Floyd."

The light mood Floyd had been feeling disappeared, replaced by foreboding. "Maybe they just pulled into the canyon to camp and rest. That could be it, couldn't it, Jeb?" Even as he said it, he realized how foolish it sounded. He had learned that no sane man would camp wagons in a dead-end canyon.

Jeb shook his head, but said, "Reckon that's possible, Floyd, but if you knowed that was a dead end, would you take our wagons up it?"

"No, not unless we needed protection from Indians chasing us."

"These wagons weren't chased. They wuz rolling along just nice and easy. I'm afeared of what we'll find."

In the time since Oliver gave Floyd his new rifle, he had made a scabbard for it. He didn't want his Ryland Rifle scabbard on the right side, where his other rifle was slung, so he slung it on the left. The muzzle pointed back, with the stock facing forward, and it rode under his left stirrup. His pistol was slung, in one of the holsters Owen had given him, from the saddle horn, hanging on the right side.

He tried the arrangement several times. If there was plenty of time, he could pull the rifle out with his left hand and transfer it to his right. But if he was rushed, he would cross draw the weapon. With his long arms it was easy to grab the rifle by the small of the stock and slide it out. Jeb approved of his setup.

The canyon narrowed, the sides growing steeper. It was impossible for a wagon to make it up either side. *In fact,* Floyd thought, *a man would have to be afoot to get up the sides with so many loose rocks. No way a horse could climb those steep walls.*

As the canyon narrowed, Jeb signaled single file. So Floyd dropped back in position. He didn't like riding like this. It was difficult for him to see directly in front of Jeb.

Riding around a bend in the canyon, Jeb jerked his horse to a stop and said, "Ain't that a shame." He sat there shaking his head.

Floyd rode out from behind him to see where Jeb was looking. For a moment, he wished he hadn't. There in front of them, no more than fifty yards, sat Flagan's wagons. The canvas was gone, burned off, and the wagons looked like black skeletons haunting this narrow canyon.

Tall grass waved in this portion of the canyon, competing with the juniper and cactus. A laced shoe protruded from the grass into a bare spot. Only a portion of the calf was visible from the grass, and it was bruised and bloody.

Floyd leaned to Rusty's side and threw up. Jeb climbed down from his horse and handed the reins to Floyd. Then he trudged to the woman and squatted by her side.

He started cursing as he walked to the next corpse, and the next. Slow, low, well-enunciated curses rolled across the canyon. Floyd, still on Rusty, followed his partner, walking from one corpse to the next. At last Jeb turned to Floyd.

"Guess they killed them all. It took more men than the three Porter had with him. From all the boot tracks, I'd say an additional ten men waited up here in these rocks. Waited hidden until the folks circled and started preparing for supper.

"Been no more than three days. They knew we were closing

behind 'em. They tried to wipe out the wagon tracks back at the trail, but they didn't try too hard, because they just don't care.

"We're dealing with some mighty evil folks here. Looks like they took their way with the women before they killed them. These folks are bloated a little, but it's been so cold, they're pretty much recognizable. Not that I knew many of them, but Albert Jensen was a friend. He was a hardworking, honest man. Always fair in his dealings. He'd never do any man harm what didn't deserve it. They shot him, cut his throat, and scalped him."

Jeb shook his head again. "There's gonna be some settling up done. That's for damn sure."

Floyd had been watching the wagons, keeping his eyes off the dead on purpose. When Jeb made his last statement, Floyd turned his head to look at him. Out of the corner of his eye he caught a flash of movement from a wagon in the back of the circle.

17

"Jeb! There's something moving back there." He tossed Jeb's reins to him, drew his pistol, and dashed toward the movement. To his surprise, a young boy dashed out from behind a juniper and raced toward the wall of the canyon.

"Hold up, boy," he called. "We're friends. We're not gonna hurt you."

The young fella didn't slow down.

Jeb walked his horse forward.

Floyd tossed Jeb a questioning look.

Jeb said, "The boy's scared. I imagine he saw or heard his family and everyone else killed by people supposed to be friends. You think he's gonna trust the likes of us? Look at us."

Floyd glanced down at his dirty boots and trousers. His wool coat was covered in dust and grime. He sat silent, waiting, watching.

He had seen the boy jump behind a boulder resting at the foot of the canyon wall.

"Boy, my name's Jeb Campbell. You might have heard of me back in Independence. Mr. Jenson was a friend of mine. We mean you no harm. We will find the animals that did this, and I promise you, they'll be punished."

From behind the rock, a small angry voice called, "You gonna hang 'em, mister?"

Jeb nodded. "Yep, on the tallest tree we can find, those that give themselves up. Them that don't, we'll just have to settle with shooting 'em. Would that be all right with you?"

The boy, about nine years old, stepped out from behind the rock. "It sure would, Mr. Campbell. They killed my folks and my sister, Annie."

"I'm right sorry about that. We'll make them pay. You take my word on it. I think we need to meet each other. You can call me Jeb, boy. What's your name?"

"Names Ezekiel Wilson, but my friends call me Zeke. You can if you want."

The boy had made a few tentative steps toward them.

"Thank you, Zeke. This feller with me, he's Floyd Logan."

"That's right. Call me Floyd. Can I call you Zeke?"

"Yes, sir, that'd be just fine."

"You hungry, Zeke?" Jeb asked.

"Nope, there's a bunch of them seal-tights in those wagons. I just used my Barlow to cut them open. I been eatin' mighty good."

"Well, good for you. What about water?"

"Several barrels still hold water. Most of the barrels didn't burn when the wagons burned."

"It sounds like you've done a fine job of takin' care of yourself, Zeke. Is there anything in these wagons that belongs to you?"

Zeke had continued down from the rocks. He was now right in front of them. He pointed to one of the burned-out hulks. "That's my wagon. Most of my stuff burned up. I found some blankets in the other wagons. They helped keep me warm. It gets mighty cold out here."

"Yes, it does, Zeke. Let's find your things, and Floyd can take you to our wagons. There's a nice lady there who I bet will be thrilled to have you stay with them."

"Can I get Pa's strongbox? It's kind of heavy."

"Sure," Jeb said, "you bring it right along."

"I can't get it myself. It's at the bottom of the water barrel."

"Fine," Jeb said, "you get your clothes and wrap them in your blankets, and I'll get your strongbox."

Jeb lifted the nearly empty water barrel from the wagon, poured the water out, and, holding the barrel where the sunlight would shine in, he looked at the bottom. Sure enough, there was a latch. Using the butt of his pistol, he hammered it until it unlatched. He lifted the now unlocked cover and pulled the box out. It was heavy. There was no key, just a whittled-to-size wooden pin inserted in the metal loop, holding the hasp in place.

After removing the pin and slipping the hasp off the loop, he lifted the top. The box was full of gold coins. This must have been to buy a store in Santa Fe.

The boy was back with his few clothes and the two blankets.

"Tell you what we're gonna do, Zeke. Floyd here is goin' to take you back to the wagons. We've got a lot of work around here, so he'll bring some men back to help with it. You'll like Mrs. Ryland, and I bet she might have some cookies. How does that sound to you?"

"That sounds real fine, Jeb. I wish Annie were here. She liked cookies, a lot."

"I do too, Zeke, I surely do," Jeb said. "Now let's get you back to the wagon train."

He put his hands under Zeke's armpits and put him on behind Floyd. Then he handed Zeke his blanket and clothes and his strongbox. Zeke set it on top of his clothes.

"Wagons should be getting to the turnoff soon," Jeb said to Floyd. "Tell Hugh what's happened, and let him know we need about ten men to do the burying. I'd suggest they just camp right there for tonight. We'll be at the Canadian soon after we pull out in the morning. Animals can water then.

"Not much else I can say." Jeb stepped back and waved.

Floyd and Zeke waved. Floyd pointed Rusty back toward the trail and put him into a lope. He felt Zeke hanging on tight. "We'll be there in no time."

Back at the trail, Floyd saw the tops of wagons stopped ahead. Before he reached them, he saw Hugh and Salty riding toward him. He slowed Rusty, and upon reaching him, the two men stopped.

"Zeke," Floyd said, "the man on the left is the wagon master, Mr. Hugh Brennan. The other one is Salty Dickens. And this is Ezekiel Wilson, but goes by Zeke to his friends. Zeke, you think you might figure on Mr. Brennan and Salty being your friends?"

"I think so, Floyd. They look all right."

"Well, Zeke, it's mighty nice to meet you," Salty said.

"Yes," Hugh said, "it is a pleasure to meet you."

Hugh cast a questioning glance at Floyd.

"Zeke," Floyd said, "how about if I take you over to Mrs. Ryland? You can meet her and her husband. They have a daughter who's about my age."

Zeke leaned out and peered up at Floyd. "She's as old as you are and still living at home?"

Floyd couldn't come up with an answer to Zeke's question. He heard Salty's cackle and Hugh's chuckle. He grinned to himself. *Guess I am looking older.*

He rode to the Ryland wagon. The three Rylands were there. Mrs. Ryland smiled at the boy.

"Well, hello, Floyd. It's a little early for supper."

"Yes, ma'am. Jeb asked if you wouldn't mind taking care of Zeke here for a while. He likes cookies."

Dorie spoke up. "Oh, that's great. We have some cookies we only made yesterday. How does that sound, Zeke?"

"That sounds fine, ma'am," Zeke said as he slid to the ground from behind Floyd.

Dorie held out her hand. "Come on. Let's go find those cookies."

Zeke took her hand and walked away with her toward the Ryland wagon. As if suddenly remembering, he turned and called, "Thanks, Floyd."

Floyd waved to him. Oliver and Eleanor came up close to Rusty and looked up.

Floyd gave them a brief description of what had happened. "I've got to get over to Hugh. I'm sure he'll tell everyone this evening. Thanks for your help."

He ran Rusty back to Hugh and Salty and told them everything.

Hugh turned to Salty. "Go get ten strong backs from the helpers. Bring shovels and picks and meet us in the canyon."

Turning, they galloped back up the canyon.

Arriving at the gruesome scene, they saw Jeb digging a wide grave. Floyd and Hugh ground hitched their horses and walked to Jeb, who was leaning on his shovel, taking a break.

"Mighty hard ground," he said.

Hugh looked around at the destruction and death that filled the canyon. "This is even worse than I expected from Porter. He seems to have outdone himself.

"Porter's a marked man, now. He and his bunch. They may have gotten by with the robberies and killings they've done to this point. But I'll guarantee you. Every man in the west, when he hears of this, will want to kill 'em. They may not know it yet, but they're dead men."

Men on a mix of horses and mules rode into the head of the canyon. At the sight of the massacre, several lost their dinners.

Salty walked up. "I've seen a lot in my years, and I've found that, as brutal as the red man can be, us white men can be worse. You got to wonder what gets into grown men to do what those men have done. I just hope I can get my hands on the rope that's stretching Porter's neck. It will give me no end of satisfaction."

Everyone in earshot nodded agreement.

"All right, men," Hugh said, "we've a lot of work to do here today. This ground is rocky and hard, and it's possible we may hit a volcanic level close to the surface. So we will bury families together. Make the grave wide and as near six feet as you can get. We don't have the time or the manpower to do otherwise."

The men nodded and set to work. Everyone on the Flagan train was known by at least one member of the Hugh Brennan wagon train. Their information helped with marking the graves. There were sufficient timbers in the wagon to make markers. Three men set to constructing and labeling the markers while the rest moved the dead bodies near a central site for each family and began the digging.

Floyd saw Hugh going from wagon to wagon, making notes in his notebook. Once Hugh had finished, and the graves were dug, the bodies were wrapped in what clothing survived the fires, and lowered into their respective graves. Hugh stepped up to the nearest grave and removed his hat. Every man followed suit.

"Lord, this is a sad day. A man filled with greed led these poor folks into this calamity. Flagan, like all of those he led, paid for that folly with his life. We know this is a hard land that sometimes demands the ultimate payment, but Porter's gang took these folks' lives in a most brutal way. Open your arms and bring these poor souls to the comfort of thy breast. And, Lord, we have one more request. Wherever those men are, right now, send a chill on their body, with the knowledge that retribution is in their future. Amen.

"Fill up them graves, boys. Let's get back to our wagons."

A voice spoke up. "Mr. Brennan, some of those goods are still useable."

Hugh looked at the men. "True, some supplies are viable. But taking things that once belonged to these good people seems a terrible violation. Push their wagons together and leave them for others to see what the Trace Porter gang has done. Now, put your backs to it." To emphasize his order, Hugh Brennan had stepped to a shovel and began filling one of the graves.

No word was uttered. The only sounds were the slide and slice of the shovels and then the rattle of dirt striking the bodies of the innocent victims in the graves. Hot tears rolled down Floyd's face, but he felt no embarrassment. As he looked around, many of the strongest men also had tears cutting through the dust on their faces, for few had ever seen such cruelty.

Once finished, the fire used to heat the irons used on the markers was extinguished to prevent another prairie fire. The day was drawing to a close. Before they left, each man filed by the front wagon that was turned sideways toward the canyon mouth. On the side was written: *Site of the Trace Porter gang massacre of the Edward Flagan wagon train bound for Santa Fe. All were killed, men, women, and children. The killers involved Trace Porter, Grif Pike, Mather Boswell, Wedge Titus, and others unknown.*

∽

FLOYD PULLED UP THE BUCKSKIN. Jeb had disappeared into the mountains yesterday, leaving him the lone scout, with all of the responsibility, but he felt more than responsibility.

Though he didn't know the folks on the Flagan wagon train, his mind had been concentrating on them. Why were they attacked and murdered, some heinously, and his train allowed to survive? He had dwelled on that thought and the boy, Zeke Wilson, since they had found the massacre. That boy was more than all-fired lucky. He'd been watched over. All those men, and at least some of them mountain men. How had they not seen him?

Bless that little boy, though, he'd taken a shine to the Rylands and, of all people, Hugh Brennan. He spent almost as much time riding with Hugh as Hugh spent riding. Those two had hit it off. *It still has to be hard for the boy,* he thought. *Seeing your folks and your sister murdered like they'd been could scar a person for life.*

Floyd looked back on his trip. Almost three months ago he'd left the hardwood country of home. He rubbed his scar along his left cheek. It had healed. There was still a twinge if he pushed on it near his ear, but he figured the key to that was to not push on it. His Ryland, that's what he'd taken to calling his rifle, lay comfortably across his legs, ready for action.

He reached across to his left bicep and squeezed it. Why, it didn't hurt a bit. It had sure hurt when Hugh shoved that rod through it, but he'd learned something from Hugh with that move. You'd best get a wound cleaned out as fast as possible. No telling what kind of trash or dirty shirt might get pushed into it. If it's left, the wound could fester, turn to gangrene, and kill a fellow.

Three months passed and I've already picked up a few scars. Why, I'll be a cut-up whittling stick by the time my folks see me again. He chuckled at the thought. His eyes covered every approach, every wash, juniper, or piñon in sight, looking for something out of place or a flash of movement.

Jeb had been teaching him well, and he appreciated it. But Pa had already plowed a lot of that ground. Pa, he grew up in those eastern mountains, when the Cherokee and the Shawnee weren't as friendly as they were today. He had experience a man got by surviving, and by having it passed on from his pa.

The brilliant red of cliffs and bluffs that jutted from uneven ground were lit by the morning sun. The warmth felt good on his back. Five mule deer walked from one of the canyons out into the small sagebrush valley. They were relaxed, nibbling at the sage as they walked.

I'm in the mountains where I've always wanted to be. I've seen Indians, heck, I've even fought Indians, and I've survived . . . So far. Pa's words slipped into his mind. "Keep your eyes moving, boy. Watch for something that doesn't belong, the color, the texture, or the slightest movement. That's how you'll spot a squirrel or a deer, or an Indian, before they spot you." That was the same thing Jeb said.

So while his mind wandered, his eyes traveled. He turned in his saddle as the wagons made their laborious way up the long slope. They had been climbing since crossing the Canadian. Well, he admitted, that wasn't exactly true. Yes, the land had continued to rise, but they had been following the trail that Salty swore was up, up, up, and up, then down, then up again. All that up was due to their now being in the mountains. The mules were tired, and so were the people. Everyone had lost weight, including the mules and horses.

One of their stops was where the Mora and the Sapello Rivers joined. It was a pretty little valley, perfect for running cows, Floyd had thought, if he were interested in cows.

The next stop was just after the Gallinas crossing. A beautiful place, tall pines in one direction, juniper and piñon in the other. If he had doubted he was in the mountains, the Gallinas crossing would have proved it.

The nights were downright cold. They were in the second week of October and the temperature was dropping. Hugh had a thermometer in his bag, and the night they stayed at the Gallinas crossing, the temperature dropped almost to freezing. Floyd could have used some of Ma's potato soup that night, though Eleanor was doing her best to keep them fed.

Their last stop had been the most entertaining. It was the village of San Miguel del Vado. Hugh knew many of the people. The townsfolk put on a fiesta, and many of the men and women on the train tried Mexican food for the first time.

Though Floyd liked, and was grateful to, Eleanor and Dorie Ryland for their cooking, he found he loved Mexican food. It was the first he had ever eaten, and though it was spicy, he figured it was winning the race to favorite.

He had turned from watching the wagons back to his front just as the mule deer's heads jerked up. They were looking toward the canyon out of which they had just come. Floyd held his position. He and the buckskin were well hidden behind a piñon. He waited.

Whatever it might be, it was getting too close for the deer. A flick of their tails, and they were off in their peculiar bounce. Jeb had called it stotting. It looked like they kept their legs stiff and bounced off the ground like a ball. The funny thing about that was they were fast. They'd give a horse a good run for his money.

Floyd gazed toward the canyon mouth as the mule deer disappeared from view. Sure enough, a single rider came from the canyon. Upon reaching the mouth, and while still in the shade, he stopped his horse. Floyd wished for Jeb's glass. That'd tell him what the man was. He was way too far to tell otherwise.

Floyd waited, stationary, behind the piñon. He didn't know who or what the rider was, but he knew that the rider would move first. Suddenly a bright flash of light came from the man, startling Floyd.

18

Floyd continued to watch the rider, when the man turned his horse and put him into a gallop toward Floyd. Caution was becoming second nature. He reached down and checked the rifle to make sure a cap was in place, and also his pistol, tucked at the ready in the holster. He'd almost lost it twice when riding over rough country, so he had cut a buckskin string, formed it into a loop, and sewn it to the holster. Now, when he didn't need the pistol, he pulled the loop over the hammer, securing the weapon in the holster.

He had finished checking both weapons, when he relaxed, slid the loop over the hammer of his pistol, and lowered the hammer of his rifle to half cock. He would recognize Jeb's relaxed manner in the saddle anywhere. It surprised him he hadn't realized who it was when he first rode into the valley.

Jeb slowed his horse, saving him from a sustained run up the hill. At these altitudes, it was tough on man and beast. Neither lasted a long time running. Floyd had found that out. Right after they had crossed the Gallinas River, he had jogged from the last wagon to the first and found himself out of breath. That was extremely unusual for him. He had run all over the Tennessee and Georgia hills with nary a problem. Hugh explained it had to do with the altitude. He figured, for some reason, there wasn't as much air up here.

"Howdy," Floyd said.

"Howdy, yoreself," Jeb replied, pulling his horse up next to Floyd. "Nice hiding spot."

"Thanks."

"But too thin. Through the spyglass, I made out the outline of the buckskin."

"You're funning me."

"Nope, gospel truth. If the piñon was a mite bushier or you was ridin' ole Rusty, I'd a never seen you."

Floyd grinned. "I saw your spyglass flash."

Jeb shook his head. "Dang. I held my hand out over the top of it, but I guess the sun weren't high enough. Well, shame on both of us. So, how's everything going?"

"Fine. Had no problems. I killed two mule deer yesterday. People were glad to get 'em. They're still some mighty dispirited folks. I'm thinking they haven't gotten over the Flagan train yet."

"It's a sad thing. How you doing?"

"I'm fine. I've thought about it a bunch, but I've concluded that when it's your day, you're gonna go, don't matter who or where you are."

"That's right smart, Floyd. If you can hold on to that, you'll do well in these mountains, 'cause many men die just for bein' in the wrong place."

Jeb watched the wagons labor up the slope. "Hard work on the mules. Have you seen anything worth mentioning?"

"I'm glad to say I ain't seen nothing besides the mule deer and a noisy gray bird that keeps hanging around."

Jeb laughed. "That's one of them camp robber jays. You watch that little feller. He'll come right into yore camp and steal the food, slick as can be. He's a natural thief, though mighty pretty."

"You see anything, Jeb?"

"Seen a griz. Left him alone, and seen some elk grazing nice and pretty. Other than that, nothing. Course when you're not seeing Injuns, that's when you'd best be on the lookout. Let's go check on Hugh and find out how them mules are holdin' up."

Hugh and Salty were riding toward the front of the train when Floyd and Jeb rode up. The two scouts reined their horses in, alongside the two older men.

"See anything?" Hugh asked.

"Griz," Jeb said.

"Keep your eyes open," Hugh said. "We're entering Apache country, and they're a lot better at hiding themselves and surprising a person than any Indian I've seen. Jeb, how long to Santa Fe?"

The mountain man didn't look toward Hugh. He said, "How's the stock?"

Salty spoke. "Them mules is doin' fine. They've lost a little weight, but they're pullin' right along."

"Good," Jeb said. "If you'll change out the mules before we start down, I'd say we'll make Santa Fe today, late."

"That's what I wanted to hear. Salty, change out the mules after we're done climbing here, and on a level spot. Jeb, why don't you and Floyd tell the drivers. I bet they'll be glad to hear this."

Floyd rode to the last wagon, and Jeb started at the front. It just so happened that the Ryland wagon was at the back of the train. When Floyd rode up, he saw Eleanor lean back and say something. Almost immediately, Dorie's head popped up, her hair a little rumpled.

"Howdy, folks, howdy, Dorie." He nodded to Eleanor. "Hi, Eleanor."

All three chimed in, "Hi, Floyd." They all laughed at saying it in unison. It was the first laugh Floyd had heard since the massacre.

"Would you folks like some good news?"

"Yes!" Dorie yelled.

"Good, when we level off at the top, we're going to change teams."

All three faces fell. This was not what they were hoping to hear. Another team change never rated as fun.

"Now just wait," he said. "We're changing teams because we have some down work to do—" he paused for effect "—and Mr. Brennan wants them fresh to enter Santa Fe."

"You mean we'll be there today?" Oliver asked, keeping his eyes on the mules and guiding them in the same tracks as the wagon ahead.

"Yes, sir. I sure do."

Dorie let out a scream and started clapping. "We'll be there today. I'm so tired of sitting in this wagon. Finally. Oh, thank you, Floyd."

"Don't thank me. All that sitting time you did is what got us here." He bumped the buckskin and waved as he moved ahead to the next wagon. "See you in Santa Fe."

Each driver and helper gave much the same reaction. Though these men were experienced at what they did, and sat in wagons long hours every day of their life, they enjoyed getting to their destination.

Floyd was grinning when he rode back up with Hugh and Salty.

"Nobody complaining?" Hugh asked.

"No, sir. You've got a bunch of cheerful people."

"Good," Hugh said. "Salty, why don't you grab Jeb, take him back to the remuda, and get him a change of horses. I'll be sending Floyd along in a minute."

Salty nodded, then looked past Hugh at Floyd. "You want Rusty?"

"Yes, sir. I'd be obliged."

Salty turned his horse and loped back to grab Jeb and head for the remuda, while Hugh and Floyd kept walking theirs ahead of the wagons.

"I wanted to talk to you, Floyd," Hugh said. "You've had plenty of time to think about what you'd like to do. I'd like an answer now, before we get to Santa Fe. That way I'll be able to tell my family when we arrive."

"Hugh, I've thought about it, and for me, there are plusses both ways. I want you to know that I am grateful to you for hiring me for this trip. I'm also grateful you didn't make me babysit Billy hardly at all."

"From the first," Hugh said, "you have shown me what a smart decision I made in Limerick. As for the second, Billy wasn't ready to drive one of these wagons, and frankly, my head scout would have revolted if I had left you driving too long. We have plenty of outstanding men who could step up to the ribbons, so don't mention it. Now, how about an answer?"

Floyd grinned at Hugh's impatience. That was certainly not something a person saw often. In his business dealings, Floyd had learned, Hugh Brennan was a most patient man, waiting for the right moment to strike a deal.

"Well, sir, like I said, I've thought on it quite a bit, and I've decided, if you'll still have me, I'll be staying."

At the pleasure and excitement in Hugh's face, Floyd rushed to add the caveat, "But understand, Mr. Brennan, I'm staying only until spring, and then I'll be heading out to join Jeb."

Hugh nodded emphatically. "I understand, Floyd. As long as you are here, you will live in my home and will be under my employ as an assistant buyer. For that, you will make one hundred dollars a month, plus a three percent commission on all furs you bring in. I will pay the commission based on the current price in St. Louis. Is that agreeable to you?"

Floyd's jaw had dropped. "Hugh, I'm satisfied with keeping my current salary and having a place to stay. I sure don't want to put you or your family out by staying in your home."

"Nonsense. That's what I pay all of my fur buyers. You will be no different, and you will earn it. Can you cypher?"

"Yes, sir. Both my ma and pa could, and they insisted on us kids learning."

"Very good. Every time you tell me more about your folks, my respect for them increases. You are very fortunate."

"I am."

"How much money do you have?"

The question surprised Floyd. Men did not inquire of another's wealth or lack, but it was Hugh, and he'd done so much for him.

"Well, I've got about two hundred and twenty-five dollars. That's money I made trapping in Tennessee over the past two years. Plus my three months' salary, when I'm paid, I'll have over three hundred dollars."

"Good," Hugh said as Jeb came riding up on a new mount.

"Floyd," Jeb said, "you'd better go get Rusty. Salty's already cut him out."

"We'll talk later, Floyd," Hugh said.

Floyd waved and rode back to the remuda. The mount change didn't take five minutes, and he was soon back with Jeb and Hugh.

Jeb turned to Floyd. "Let's go make sure the trail's clear to Santa Fe." With that, the two scouts galloped out ahead, as the wagons stopped on the summit of Glorieta Pass to change teams.

∽

FLOYD, eyes wide at his first sight of Santa Fe, felt a slight twinge of disappointment. The sound of the musical name had intrigued him for years. It was one of those western cities that he had always known he would see. And now, here he was. It wasn't as big as he expected, and the buildings were mostly red-brown dirt, adobe.

Jeb looked at the disappointment on the boy's face.

"I have to say, for a man that wanted to go to the Far West, you look a mite let down. Look at all these mountains we come out of, boy. And there are mountains way to the west. You can join those mountains and follow 'em north forever. It ain't about the town, which is fine, as town's go, it's the mountains."

Floyd pulled his eyes up and scanned the snowcapped peaks behind him, and the distant mountains to the west. He grinned at Jeb. "You're right. Look at those mountains. My folks would give anything to have a place out here."

"Yeah, it's mighty pretty, but let me tell you, don't you be disappointed in that there town. Santa Fe packs more'n enough excitement and pretty girls for any man, and you're about to meet some of 'em. Come on."

They rode through the town, and Floyd heard music, laughing, and singing coming from all directions. Maybe this town was better than his first impression.

They rode up to an enormous home. Eight-foot adobe walls surrounded it. A gate opened to a wide veranda, and hanging to one side of the gate was a brass bell. Floyd, amazed, watched Jeb ride right up and ring that bell.

"Do you know who lives here?" Floyd asked in a voice so low, it was almost a whisper.

Jeb grinned. "Reckon I do, and so do you."

Floyd, puzzlement on his face, heard footsteps coming down the lengthy walk from the house. The person arrived to the gate. A rather stocky man, a Mexican, opened the gate and stepped out. The man, though stocky, had wide shoulders filling his embroidered white shirt. His trousers were black with small silver conchos down the side. In his black boots, Floyd figured the man to be about eight inches over five feet.

He stepped out of the courtyard. There was a frown on his face until he recognized Jeb. A huge grin broke out and the man said, "Señor Jeb, how are you? It has been many months since you have graced this home."

He looked over at Floyd, calmly sizing up the young man.

"This is a friend of yours, Señor Jeb?"

"I reckon he is. He goes by Floyd Logan. Floyd, this here is Juan Antonio Ortega Caldron."

Floyd nodded. "Nice to meet you, Señor Ortega."

The man flashed a quick smile. "It is my pleasure, but please call me Juan."

"Thanks," Floyd said, "I answer real well to Floyd."

Before Juan responded, Jeb jumped in. "He's also a friend of yore boss."

"Ahh, I thought as much. You are the scouts for Señor Brennan. Please get down and come in. Señora Moreno will be *muy contenta* to know of her husband."

"We'd love to, Juan," Jeb said, "but we need to get back. The wagons ain't far behind. I wanted to let the señora and all those girls know Hugh's gettin' close. Figger they might want to freshen up a bit."

"Ah, señor, for your young age, you are wise in the ways of a woman."

Jeb grinned. "Juan, any man that thinks he's wise in the ways of women is settin' himself up for a big fall.

"The wagons will arrive in two hours. I'm sure as shootin' Hugh won't be much longer." With that, he glanced at Floyd. "Let's head on back.

"*Adios*, Juan."

Floyd nodded to Juan and joined Jeb as they rode back up the trail to the wagons.

"Guess I'll be leavin' in a couple of days," Jeb said, nearing the wagons.

"So soon?" Floyd asked.

"Yep. Need to get back to them mountains and plant some traps fore the streams freeze up. Figure if I'm lucky, I'll have a month, but you never know about that mountain weather. Good thing I already laid in a big supply of hay and wood. Without 'em, I'd be in a pack of trouble."

Floyd had a wave of loneliness wash over him. In two days, he'd be here by himself, in a city, and not even knowing the language. His mind struggled with the thought of Jeb leaving. Then he relaxed. He was planning on living in these mountains for the rest of his life. Much of that time, he was sure he'd be by himself. *Get used to it,* he thought. Also, it wasn't the first time he'd been alone. Why, when he slipped off to Georgia, he'd been all by himself. No different here. He took a deep breath and looked off into the darkness. He was a Logan and could face anything.

∽

LIGHTS TWINKLED across the valley as the wagons rolled into Santa Fe. The people were out in the streets, waving to Hugh and the drivers. Hugh had sent Salty on ahead with the horses and mules. By the time the wagons arrived, they were watered, fed and released into the corral at the Brennan Livery.

Hugh had a standing agreement with the government that allowed him to park the wagons in the plaza. It cost him, but was worth the expense. The wagons would be guarded, and the hotel where the drivers and owners would stay for the night was near. After that, he would have the drivers paid, and it would be up to them to provide their own housing.

Floyd rode up with Jeb, who said, "What's your plans?"

"To get home as quick as I can. I imagine Lucia and the girls have two surprises coming to them."

Floyd knew he was one of those surprises, and figured Zeke was the other, at least until the boy's relatives might be located, if they could. Zeke had been spending his days in the saddle with Hugh, returning to the Ryland's only to eat and sleep. It looked like the two had hit it off. *And why not?* Floyd thought. *Hugh Brennan is an exemplary man, and any boy would be lucky to call him pa.*

Hugh, Jeb, and Floyd rode over to the Ryland wagon. "Oliver,"

Hugh said, "let Salty put up your mules with the rest of them. He'll take them to the stable and they'll get fed and watered along with mine. Salty will take good care of them until you decide what you'd like to do."

"Thanks, Hugh. I'll be looking around tomorrow. We may sink some roots right here in Santa Fe."

"Good. Now is Zeke ready?"

The boy bounced around the wagon, holding Dorie's hand. "I sure am, Mr. Brennan."

Floyd saw the tears in Eleanor's eyes. Over the past days, the family had grown close to Zeke. The boy hugged Dorie, then shook hands with Oliver. He saved Eleanor for last. She scooped him up in her arms and squeezed him close. He hugged her neck tight and kissed her on the cheek. Finally she leaned over and set him on the ground.

"We'll miss you, Zeke."

Zeke snuffled a little while saying, "Me too. Goodbye."

He turned and, with the little bag that Eleanor made for him, marched over to Hugh.

"Don't worry about him," Hugh said. "We'll provide excellent care for him while we're looking for any relatives. If you folks stay in town, you will see him often." He leaned down and scooped the boy up, lifting him and sliding back so Zeke could sit in the front of the saddle.

"Also, Oliver," Hugh continued, "I have space across the plaza that would make an excellent gun shop, if you're interested."

Oliver looked at his daughter and wife, then turned to Hugh. "Thanks, I'm definitely interested."

"Good, we'll talk tomorrow. Goodnight, folks." Hugh turned his horse and headed home, Jeb by his side. Floyd waited a moment.

He looked at the three Rylands. "Thanks for all you've done. I'll see you tomorrow." He turned and followed the other two horses into the black night.

19

Floyd turned the white fox fur back and looked at the underside. The trapper who had brought them into Brennan Furrier was watching him expectantly. Floyd had already tossed over half of the man's furs into a discard pile because of the damage. It appeared the man knew little about skinning fur.

Sure enough, the hide was cut just behind the neck. He kept looking and found another cut by the front leg and one by the opposite back leg. Floyd rose from the table and tossed the fox into the pile.

The trapper exploded. "Boy, *you* throw another of my hides in that there pile, and I'll skin you."

Floyd had listened to this kind or similar rant since he'd started in Hugh's fur-grading shed two months earlier. He looked at the trapper. "Where'd you learn to skin? I was able to skin better than this by the time I was knee high to a mink."

The man gave Floyd a hard look. "Nobody else complains about my furs."

"Then I guess you must be selling them to a blind man."

He bent back over and pulled a beaver from the pile. The

smell hit him like a sledgehammer. He didn't even stop to look at the hide, but threw it against the wall, well away from the other furs.

"Wait a minute, boy. You ain't even looked at that plew."

"No, I didn't, because the hide is rotten."

He walked to the hide and picked the beaver pelt up, turning and thrusting it under the man's nose. Even as filthy as the trapper was, he jumped back from the hide, knocking it away.

"All right," the trapper said, "what'll you pay for my hides?"

Floyd continued to check the pelts. Once finished, he picked up his tally book, did a little figuring, and said, "I'll give you seventy-five dollars for the good ones."

The pile of acceptable hides was distressingly small. The trapper stared at the high pile of discarded furs. "Can't I get anything for those?"

"Well," Floyd said, "they're not much use to anyone, but I'll give you thirty dollars for the lot. That'll be a total of one hundred and five dollars."

The man began cursing. Moments passed, and he finally stuck his hand out and said, "I'll take it."

Floyd pulled out a roll of money that he only carried in the fur house, and counted the money into the trapper's hand. Finished, he looked the man square in the eyes.

"Job, if you'll come around here early in the morning, I'll show you how to skin an animal where you get most of the meat without cutting the hide. I'll charge you nothing."

Job eyeballed Floyd for a moment. "Why would you do that?"

"It's good business. All those hides were good." He pointed to the discard pile. "Well, not counting that rotten beaver you tried to slip in on us. You would have gotten five times what I'm paying you if your hides were undamaged. We want those good hides, so if I show you, maybe the next time your hides will be in better shape."

Job rolled the money he had received and turned for the door.

"No snot-nosed kid's gonna show me up. Mind yore own business."

Hugh stepped in from the back as the trapper was closing the front door. "Your failing is your youth, but it's also to your benefit. That was a splendid job. A legitimate trapper would never try to bring a rotten hide to sell. Only these two-by-twice newcomers to the mountains would try something like that."

Floyd shrugged, turned, and started gathering the discarded fur. "Leave those," Hugh said. "It's almost time for Lontac.

"So how are you enjoying your winter here?"

"Probably better than Jeb is right now. As cold as it is here, it must be miserable in the mountains."

"True. It won't be long and, until after spring trapping, all the fur we see will be that trapped in the low areas. Every high-country creek and stream is frozen over, and it's only the middle of December. I'm sure Jeb is curled up in his cabin, trying to stay warm.

"How are your Spanish lessons progressing?"

Floyd commented on the vagaries of the weather in Spanish.

Hugh smiled. "Son, you are a quick study. You've been here less than three months and you're almost fluent. It took me several years."

"Ma always said I had a knack for languages." He pulled the roll of bills from his pocket, tore off the tally sheet, and handed them both to Hugh. He walked to the rack where his wool coat hung. Taking it from the rack, he slipped it on.

"What's on the agenda for today?" Hugh asked.

"Training with Lontac."

"Do you think you're learning much?"

Floyd grinned at Hugh. "I hope I am. If I'm not, all these bruises aren't worth it. I don't know how you persuaded him to train me, but I thank you. After fighting the Pawnee and winning, I thought I was pretty good. Lontac has shown me I know nothing. I think I could train with him for years and never exhaust his knowledge or ability."

Hugh smiled. "I have known that gentleman since he arrived in the country. He is an outstanding man to have as your friend."

"Does he have another name?" Floyd asked.

"Lontac is what he was called when he arrived here years ago, and I have heard nothing different.

"Will you be home in time for dinner?"

"Yep, I should. See you then."

Floyd turned and, holding tight to the door, unlatched it and stepped outside. The frigid northwest wind cut into him as he came around the end of the building. It would be a cold walk to his teacher's small home.

The frozen snow crunched under his boots, and the wind bit into every inch of exposed skin. The day had turned clear, and Baldy was visible in the northeast. A steady stream of white cascaded from the top like a white ribbon swirling from Blanca's hair. Blanca, Hugh's middle daughter, was a beauty with long black hair and dark entrancing eyes.

He tucked his chin down into his wool collar. Before he headed for the mountains, he must get a buffalo coat. He had tried several, and they blocked the wind much better than wool. *What am I doing thinking about Blanca?* he thought. *She is Hugh's daughter. What about Dawn Light?* His heart leaped when he thought about her, but he also liked Blanca. He shook his head, knowing that he had better get his mind on what was coming. For if he didn't, he'd pay for it.

Floyd stopped at the tall gate attached to the high adobe wall surrounding a small home built using the same materials. He felt in his pockets to make sure he had his moccasins with him and breathed a sigh of relief when his fingers touched the reassuring leather. He walked across the courtyard, up the step, and onto the veranda, stopped at the heavy wooden door, and rapped on the door with his gloved knuckles once.

The door opened and a dark, wrinkled man of indeterminate age said, "Come in, quickly. The warmth escapes."

The man's speech had a slight accent. Not over five and a half feet tall and slim, he was almost skinny. But his strength was impressive. His arms lacked the bulky muscles carried by most Americans. That didn't mean he had none. They were lean, long and tight. The old skin was loose around them, giving the false impression of weakness.

Prior to his first visit, Hugh had warned Floyd not to underestimate the little man. In his baggy clothes, he looked old and as worn as the clothes, but he had amazing strength and leverage.

Floyd closed the door and glanced around the spartan room. As always, no pictures of homeland or trinkets were visible. The furniture was as plain as the room. Cut from pine, and seasoned long, to purge out the sap, each piece had been shaped and assembled by a true craftsman. The table had been hand rubbed for hours using an oil Floyd was unfamiliar with, but left a soft sheen emphasizing the intricate movement in the wood. Four chairs were in the room, two at the table and two against the wall. Through his conversations, Floyd had learned that Lontac had made all the furniture in his home, each piece with the same care and attention he used in training Floyd. He thought back again to his first introduction to this man he respected so much.

Evidently Hugh had filled in Lontac on Floyd prior to his first visit. When he arrived for his lesson, he had unfastened the belt Owen had made him, which held his knife. He looked around the room to find a spot for his gear. Lontac stepped forward, took it, and hung it all on a peg on the wall. He unfastened the leather loop securing the knife and pulled it from the scabbard.

Holding the knife, the little man hefted it, and so quick Floyd hardly saw the movement, he threw it at the wall behind him. It drove deep into the board that showed gouges where other blades had struck home.

"It is a good knife," Lontac said. "Well balanced, but in town, you should not have the knife locked down. From your scabbard, it will not fall, and you never know when you might need it. The few seconds it takes to unlatch could be your end."

Lontac pulled the knife from the board and, in one quick motion, spun and tossed the knife gently to Floyd. He had not expected the move, but deftly caught the big knife by the hilt and turned to put it back in the scabbard.

"Wait," Lontac said. "You kill man with this knife?"

"Nothing I'm proud of, but yes, I did. A Pawnee who was trying to kill me."

"Then you are good with knife," Lontac said, more in a statement than a question. His dark brown eyes looked almost black in the dimly lit house.

Floyd hadn't expected the question. He wasn't proud of killing the man, but he had to admit that he was proud of his performance. He fixed the little man with his deep blue eyes and said, "I was good enough to win the fight with the Indian. I'm not sure if that makes me good, but I ain't dead."

He could have sworn he saw a glint of humor in Lontac's eyes.

"You are big for your age." Another statement.

"All the Logan clan runs to big. My brothers are a good couple of inches over six feet, and all broad men. Course, my ma stands five feet and seven inches in her stocking feet. My folks on her side, the Tilmans, all tend to a big size themselves."

Lontac nodded. "I am five feet and five inches—" he paused before continuing "—in my stocking feet."

Floyd wasn't sure if the little man was mocking him, but his temper rising, he said nothing.

"Take your *big* knife and stick me. Stick me right here."

It shocked Floyd. He stood, shaking his head, with the knife hanging loosely from his right hand. "No, sir. I can't do that. I have nothing against you, and if I did, I wouldn't try to attack you with my knife."

"Oh," Lontac said, "you would only attack me with your hands?"

Floyd was really embarrassed now. He had nothing against this little man and no desire to harm him. All he wanted to do was get out of here. He was angry, but he'd never kill or hurt a man for such a small infraction.

"No, sir, I won't attack you. I don't have any reason to attack you, especially since you're so . . ." He realized at the last minute what he was about to say was an insult to this man.

"Especially since I'm so small? Is that what you were about to say?"

"Mr. Lontac, I should go. It doesn't appear this is going anywhere but an argument. I've no cause to argue with you."

"It is Lontac. Only Lontac. No mister. Now, let me be clear. I am not angry, and I am not arguing, I am only telling a big, strong, clumsy boy to stab me, right here." He lifted his right hand and placed his pointer finger directly over his heart.

Now Floyd was getting angry. *I may not be seventeen yet,* Floyd thought, *but I will be soon, and this little man is calling me a clumsy boy. That's still no reason to stab him.*

"Lontac, I think this was a mistake. I should just leave."

Lontac shook his head. "Boy, your father should have taught you a problem cannot be resolved by running from it."

Floyd was almost beside himself. He swung around and stabbed his knife into the scabbard, but did not flip the leather loop over it.

Before he strapped his belt around his waist, Lontac said, "Take this."

He looked over his shoulder and it was a wooden replica of a bowie knife. It was thick and dull. It would hurt no one, except leave a bruise if the man wielding it used enough force.

He took the wooden knife and hefted it. It had weight to it. *It'd make a good club,* he thought.

"All right, boy, use your wooden toy and stab me right here." The little man again pointed to his chest.

Floyd, burning with anger and with lightning speed, stepped forward and thrust hard toward Lontac's chest. But it was no longer there. It was as if the little man had wished himself someplace else and was whisked away. But the grip on his forearm was no wish. A deep pain shot from his forearm to his hand, which involuntarily sprang open. But it still wasn't over. He watched the knife fall into Lontac's grip. For a moment, Floyd felt himself floating in the air. Then he slammed hard on the solid pine floor, driving the air from his lungs.

He lay there gasping to get his breath, while aware of the wooden knife blade resting lightly at his neck. Lontac waited until Floyd had regained his breath, then stood and extended his hand. Floyd took it and felt the strength in the hand and arm as Lontac pulled him from the floor, then motioned to the table.

"For American man, you are quick. I am sure your speed surprised the Pawnee. But Floyd, understand, you are very slow to me. I see your movements as if you are walking in mud. Before you are close to me, I know where you are going, where your knife or fist is going, and all I must do is lean slightly, and you miss."

"I'm not sure if I understand. You can see my movements and see where they are going?"

"Not just yours, but many others. It takes years to learn this skill, but Mr. Brennan tells me we have only six months. He also tells me you have bad temper and have difficulty controlling it. I see that today. It slows your movements."

Floyd was at a loss for words. His temper made him slower? He didn't understand that at all, but the proof of it was him lying on the floor with a knife at his throat, and all by a little man.

When there was no response, Lontac continued. "You are a kind man. You did not want to hurt me, and I was unable to goad you into doing so. That shows that you can control yourself.

However, for you to be my student, you must do exactly as I say. Realize that even after six months, you will not be able to hurt me. If I tell you to use a knife, do it. If you refuse again, you will no longer be my student. Do you understand?"

Floyd nodded and Lontac continued. "If you are willing, be here tomorrow, same time. We will work every day. You will learn to fight, and your temper will become your friend."

Floyd nodded. "I'll be here."

"No matter what. Friend hurt, you sick, you be here."

"I'll be here."

"Good, we are done."

Floyd expected to start training. "That's all for today?"

Lontac had given him no answer, just a long look.

He nodded quickly and said, "I'll be here tomorrow at the same time."

And that was his first meeting with Lontac. In their conversations before or after training sessions, Floyd had learned his teacher was from the Philippines. So far, that had been all he shared about himself.

Floyd quickly pulled his boots from his feet and slipped on his moccasins.

Today, he shed his coat and hat, hanging them on a peg. Then he looked over to Lontac. "The belt and knife?"

"Yes, you may take it off. You will not need it. Today, we will deal with *Buno*, one of the Philippine arts that deal with wrestling and throws. To begin, though, I would have you attack me using whatever methods you have learned to this point."

Floyd stepped into the middle of the room and made a slight bow to Lontac, which he returned. Even before the teacher was completely vertical, Floyd launched a series of attacks using *Mano Mano,* a technique that incorporated the use of all the body's extremities. His first blow was a finger-strike, using three stiff fingers of his left hand. He had planned the move this morning. He faked a punch with his right fist, sure Lontac would move inside his right, exposing his opponent's solar plexus.

With a nod of satisfaction, and a level instructing voice, while countering Floyd's attempted blows, he said, "Excellent move. But you must be careful not to transmit your plan to your opponent. For if he knows, he might do this."

Lontac glided outside Floyd's attack, guiding the bigger man's right hand higher, and striking him, using the fingers of his left hand, in the solar plexus.

Floyd dropped his hands to his knees and bent over, gasping for air.

20

Always teaching, Lontac said, "Do not bend over to find your air. With practice, you will learn, though you are struck in the chest, your solar plexus is deep within your body. You will not die. In fact, you can still breathe if you have hardened your stomach and chest before being hit."

He grasped Floyd's shoulders and brought him vertical. "Breathe. You can."

Floyd concentrated on taking a breath and did. It wasn't deep, but it was a breath, and in a fight it would sustain him.

"Another thing," his teacher said, "if you are bent over, you have given your back, neck, and head to your opponent for him to do with as he desires. If you are standing, you can see and protect yourself."

Floyd nodded, realizing he had learned an important lesson. Only three minutes into the training today. "Thank you," he managed as his breathing smoothed out.

Businesslike, Lontac nodded. "Now, you will learn Buno."

The teacher and the student fought, fell, rolled, kicked, and fell again. Sweat covered Floyd's body. Over the past month, his pants had gotten looser while his shirts were becoming taut around his chest and arms. But his body also carried many bruises, and his muscles were sore like they had never been when working with Pa. Today he felt he had spent most of his time either on his back or stomach, or twisted in one of the several locks Lontac taught him.

"You have done well. Come, I will make us tea."

This also was a ritual, and while the little man methodically made his tea, he talked. "You can become a marvelous man, Floyd." The old man smiled at him. "Yes, you are still a boy. You must face that. It is a fact of nature you should accept with gladness. You have many years ahead to be a man."

While the tea steeped, Lontac placed the pot on the tray with two cups and brought it to the table, setting it down between them. He sat and looked up at Floyd. "You have the potential to be the best of my students. I am most proud of you in the control of your temper. You are becoming much better at seeing past the anger when I goad you."

The tea was ready. Floyd picked up the dainty teapot in his large hand, first pouring tea for his teacher and then for himself. Knowing that in the west, men did not inquire of another man's past, he couldn't resist asking, "Lontac, can you tell me how you came to Santa Fe?"

Lontac's wrinkled hands did not look strong, but Floyd had just finished fighting him and was well aware of the strength in those fingers. The grizzled head gazed serenely into his teacup, swirling the golden fluid. After a few moments of contemplation, he said, "I will make the story short. I killed the wrong man. For me, he was the right man, but the government placed high value on him, making him the wrong man.

"He was a very handsome man who drew women to him. My sister was drawn to him. An occurrence that saddened my heart, for I knew him as dishonest and a cheater on his bride-to-be. Many times I tried to talk to my sister, but she would not listen to me. One evening he took her to a wine shop and plied her with wine. She became very drunk, for my sister never drank, and he took her to a room in the shop, for he was good friends with the owner. There he had his way with her. When he finished, he further disgraced her and our family by dragging her, with her pleading her love for him, outside, and dumped her into the gutter in front of the shop."

Floyd was sorry he had asked. He had learned his teacher's expressions, and though to the average person, Lontac appeared calm and peaceful, Floyd saw the pain he suffered by reliving the incident.

Lontac continued. "She came home, crying, took a talibong, it is a long, sharp knife we will fight with soon. Then she went into the pen where my parents kept their chickens at night to protect them from marauders, and stabbed herself in the heart—a most difficult thing to do."

The teacher stopped speaking, refilled first Floyd's cup and then his, and continued his story. "At the time I instructed for the army, doing what I do for you. When word reached me, I went to the home of my broken-hearted parents, took the talibong she had used, and traveled to the man's office.

"He sat behind his desk, like the very important man he believed himself to be. He even gave me a smile and stood. In fact, that smile remained on his face when his head rolled to the floor. I never saw my family again. A ship's captain, a friend, sailed to Los Angeles and hid me on his ship. I spent many years in Los Angeles. Having never married, when I heard of a group of men going east, I joined up with them." He held up his hands and shrugged his shoulders. "So, I am here."

Floyd sipped the last of his tea, then said, "And you have never seen your family?"

The little man slowly shook his head. "That is the only result of my actions I regret." He sighed. "But life brings both heartache and happiness. It is not for us to choose when each shall arrive."

Lontac stood. "I am an old man and have burdened you with long-past problems of my life. I will see you tomorrow."

After collecting his gear, Floyd stepped through the open door, which quickly closed behind him, and into the northwest wind. The cold hit him with a vengeance. He turned his back to it and headed for home, his mind going over all he had learned today.

Floyd, with his back to the wind, tramped in the cold toward home. He thought of it as home, for he enjoyed the warmth and hospitality. That four pretty women waited for him, and often on him, provided extra incentive to hurry. Ana Maria, Blanca, and Gloria, all daughters of Hugh and Señora Moreno, were each beautiful in their own way. Ana Maria was almost three years older than him, Blanca was his age, and Gloria was only ten, but a pretty ten, who had her father completely under her spell. Señora Lucia Moreno, Hugh's wife and the mother of those three lovely daughters, was still very attractive and very regal.

All of them had welcomed a big dirty Tennessee boy into their home with enthusiasm. Floyd suspected with a little too much enthusiasm from the señora and Hugh. He wasn't aware of what they had in mind, but they were cooking up something between themselves.

Of all the women, Floyd found Blanca, the one his age, the most attractive, and he would have to say she seemed the kindest. She'd taken to Zeke like he was her long-lost brother. The other two were kind and accepting, but Blanca took him in like a mother hen. She showed him his room, sat on the bed with him, walked him through the house, and introduced him to the servants in the kitchen. It looked like Zeke had for sure found a home.

He turned up the street that would take him to the Brennan home, and his step picked up. *I like Blanca,* he thought, *but I still can't get Dawn Light out of my mind.* He shook his head, as if to toss the picture from his mind, and in the process glimpsed someone suspicious in the alley he had just passed.

Though his mind froze for a second, his step never faltered, something he was learning from Lontac. Never allow an opponent knowledge of what you are thinking. He ambled over to the next building. As he passed the corner, he nonchalantly stepped into the alley. Once there, he ran to the opposite end, stopped, examining all the places that might hide a man. Once sure there was no one, he dashed back to the opposite end of the alley where he had seen the man. Again he stopped and peered around the corner. Nothing.

Floyd examined the ground and saw a boot track. A track he would recognize for the rest of his life, at least until the man no longer made tracks—Grif Pike, one of Porter's henchmen. The track of the man who so wanted to kill him was now imbedded in his brain forever. He had seen it again at the massacre, along with Porter's, near several of the women.

"Is Trace Porter and his bunch in town?" he asked out loud.

After further examination of the alley, he found nothing and returned to the tracks where they exited the alley. He checked his pistol, insured the cap was in place and dry, and started trailing the man. The tracks traveled over to and up the next alley and disappeared at a short boardwalk. He strode to the end, expecting them to continue, but they were gone. The boardwalk was streaked with many wet tracks going into the Santa Fe Cantina. Floyd checked the horses, seeing none he recognized.

He opened the door and stepped into the saloon. The heavy odor of man sweat mixed with horse smell and cigarette smoke was almost overwhelming. He scanned the crowd, seeing a few folks he recognized, but no Pike or Porter, or any of the members of Porter's gang he would recognize. After waving to several of the men, he turned and exited the cantina, headed for the Casa de Brennan. If he saw nothing else, he would at least let Hugh know. Those men deserved capture and hanging.

The nearer home, the more he questioned if he had actually seen Pike. It didn't seem possible the man would be so bold as to come into Santa Fe.

At his arrival, Zeke's voice reverberated through the house. "Floyd's home!" The small moccasined feet slapping the tile floor echoed through the house as the boy ran to greet him, sliding to a halt and staring up at him. "You're late, Floyd."

Floyd tousled the boy's thick blond hair and said, in a low conspiratorial voice, "You're right, Zeke, but don't tell the women."

"You're too late, Floyd. They've already been talking. I think you're in trouble."

Floyd walked on into the large house with the welcoming smells of food and leather and women's perfume. After hanging his wool coat on the tree along with his hat, he stepped over to the blazing fireplace. Hugh sat in an enormous leather chair, his sock feet resting on an elk-hide footstool.

Zeke looked at the two men, surmised this would be a boring conversation, and dashed for the kitchen.

Without wasting a moment, Floyd said, "On the way home, I saw Griffith Pike, one of Porter's gang."

Hugh's feet hit the tile floor as he sat up. "Grif Pike?"

"That's the one. I doubled back to catch, or at least follow him, but I never saw him again. His tracks led to the boardwalk in front of the Santa Fe Cantina, but no Pike, at least not where I could see him."

Hugh shook his head. "You've got to be careful, Floyd. That cantina is a dangerous place. Those coyotes run in packs. Where there's one, it's likely you'll find others. You could be hurt or worse."

Floyd nodded. "I understand, but I only spent a few minutes inside and saw nothing. No Porter, or any of his men. At least none I recognized."

Hugh started to stretch his legs out again, when Juan Antonio came into the room. "Is not time for you to get comfortable, Señor Brennan. It is time to eat."

"*Gracias*, Juan, we'll be right there."

Juan smiled at Floyd. "Good evening. You look tired and excited."

"Very accurate, Señor Ortega. I am tired from dealing with traders and Lontac, and excited from seeing an old acquaintance."

"Ah," Juan said. "I hope your acquaintance is doing well."

"Better than me," Floyd said, watching the confused expression on Juan's face. He added, "An enemy."

"Ah, yes. Well, it is time for *la cena*."

Hugh stood and turned toward the dining room. "Suppertime, with all the family." He ushered Floyd into the dining room. "A favorite time for me."

Faces turned to them as they entered the dining room. The din of chatter subsided. Hugh moved to his place at the head of the table, Lucia not yet seated, but she would sit at the opposite end. With all the leaves in place, the table would seat twenty people, but it contained only three, to provide a more intimate setting for the family of seven.

Lucia along with the cook, Sofia, was bringing loaded platters of food to the table. Lucia spoke sharply. "Hugh, Floyd, sit down. It is time to eat before this delicious food Sofia has prepared grows cold."

"Yes, ma'am," Hugh said, smiling at his wife.

When she looked up, Floyd saw Hugh wink at her, and caught her quick look at him. *Like my folks,* Floyd thought, feeling a slight twinge.

"Come sit, Floyd," Blanca called, patting the chair next to her. Zeke sat on her other side. As he lowered himself into the chair, he could smell the faint fragrance of perfume drifting from her jet-black hair, and inhaled deeply. *She sure looks good tonight.* He looked up and caught Lucia looking at Hugh, a faint, knowing smile spreading her lips.

"Blanca, could you say grace tonight?"

"Yes, Papa."

Everyone bowed their heads and her sweet voice offered the blessing over the food, followed by the obligatory, "Amen, dive in," from Hugh, and the frown from Lucia.

An immediate rush of conversation came from all three girls and Zeke at one time. Floyd stayed out of it unless asked a question, and concentrated on the fry bread and pinto beans.

The beans were cooked in a red-pepper sauce made from the red peppers grown in the fields around Santa Fe. The first time he had put a spoonful in his mouth, he thought it would burn through his tongue and fall out his lower jaw. But now he had grown to like them, if he also had fry bread.

The *carne adovada* smelled delicious as he placed a sizable piece of the pork on his plate. He had gotten used to the sweating caused by the fiery spices. It seemed they cooked every meal with either red or green chiles. He had learned to love it, and for supper, Sofia always made a dessert. Sopapillas rated high on his list of favorites.

The meal lasted almost an hour. Each member of the family discussed where they had gone and what they'd done through the day. Much laughter from the girls, with Zeke often contributing, accompanied the conversation.

Floyd glanced at Hugh, who was watching the younger boy. Hugh cast Floyd a small smile. *Zeke's adjusting well,* Floyd thought. *He likes it here.*

With everyone finished, they were about to retire to the parlor when there was a knock at the door. Urgent voices carried into the dining room, followed by Juan Ortega.

"Señor," he said, addressing Hugh, "there are men at the door. There has been a killing." The girls gasped and looked at their father.

Hugh said, "That's not unusual in Santa Fe, Juan."

"No, señor, it is not. Except this time Señor Castillo, the banker, on the way home after closing the bank, was killed. But Capitan Rivera awaits you, señor."

"Yes, of course," Hugh said, standing. "Floyd, why don't you accompany me."

"Sure," Floyd replied, slid his chair back, and inadvertently touched Blanca's hand. He felt and heard the snap as the spark jumped from his hand to hers.

"Oh," she said, and rubbed her hand. Then she smiled up at him with those exciting dark eyes and whispered, "We are magnetic."

He grinned back. "Guess we'd better be careful."

Floyd glanced up the table to Señora Moreno. "Excuse me, ma'am. I've got to go."

She smiled and nodded her consent and said, "You had better be careful who you strike sparks with, Floyd."

"Yes, ma'am," Floyd said, pivoting and exiting the room to a chorus of giggles, while hiding his brick-red face. He stepped up to the captain, nodded, and asked him, in Spanish, how he was this cold evening. The captain, arrogant as always, replied positively about his health, but turned back to Hugh without inquiring of Floyd's.

"How was he killed?" Hugh asked.

"By the knife. They stabbed him many times. There was more than one, a senseless killing. If they wanted money, they should have robbed the bank, not the man. Señor Castillo never carried much money, only enough to buy something for his wife, on occasion.

"I come to you because you are friends with the Castillos. Also, with your fur buying from the Yankees, you are familiar with much of the unsavory element in our village."

Floyd caught the veiled insult, but noticed Hugh let it pass. "There is no one who trades with me who might have done this awful thing." He nodded at Floyd and said, "However, my young friend believes he may have seen Griffith Pike this evening."

"And who is this Griffith Pike?" Rivera's words stabbed at Floyd, followed up quickly, not giving Floyd a chance to draw a breath to answer. "Speak up. I do not have all evening."

Floyd found himself calm. He even saw some humor in Rivera's demeanor. The man had given several indications of his interest in Blanca and had been politely but firmly rebuffed by her mother. He must have seen the exchange between Blanca and Floyd through the wide dining room doors and heard the giggles of the girls. He caught Hugh's eye as Hugh was about to rebuff Rivera for his rudeness and gave a quick shake of his head. Then he looked down at Rivera.

21

In a pleasant voice, one that future enemies would learn to fear, Floyd answered the man. "Señor Rivera, the name you mentioned belongs to a member of a gang led by Trace Porter."

"And who is that?"

Floyd gave the man a surprised look. "You don't know? Why, I was under the impression, mistakenly I see now, that all the marshals were familiar with this man and his gang of evildoers."

At the mention of marshals, Rivera's chest came out and his shoulders snapped back. His black eyes glinted like wet obsidian. "I am no marshal. I am a captain leading thirty deadly lancers. I am only doing this because the comandante asked me to assist."

Floyd estimated the man's age to be approaching thirty. He had no idea, but thought he would give it a shot. "I would expect a much younger man in charge of lancers. You know, one who could keep up."

Rivera's face took on a tinge of red. "Because you are a child, I will let you get away with your remark. Had you been older, you would answer to me, Logan, and that would be deadly for you."

Hugh stepped in. "We must get to the Castillos'. Floyd, would you ask Lucia to come? She will be a comfort to Señora Castillo, and tell her to dress warm, it is cold out there."

Floyd strode to the dining room, explained quickly, and Señora Brennan was on her way. She gave Rivera a cool greeting and said to Hugh, "Gabriella will need me. Shall we go?"

Not knowing Lucia well, Captain Rivera was unprepared for her quick response. He recovered and was the first to grasp the door latch. He opened it with a slight bow. Hugh and Floyd followed her out, leaving Rivera with the door. Ortega was sitting at the front of the house with a carriage.

Floyd helped Lucia into the carriage, waited for Hugh to board, and climbed in after them.

Hugh first laid a heavy buffalo blanket over his wife's legs to insure she was warm, then leaned forward and said, "The Castillos', Juan. After paying our respects to Señora Moreno, Floyd and I will go on to where he was murdered."

Juan popped the reins, and the pair of blacks stepped out together, eager to move in the wintry night air. Rivera had to run out to his horse, tied in the front of the Brennans' entrance, and was just swinging on board as the carriage passed him. He jerked his horse around and jabbed it viciously with his spurs.

Neither Floyd nor Hugh failed to catch the vicious move of Rivera. The man's mount had done nothing to warrant such treatment. Floyd looked at the man and shook his head with disgust. Rivera's face tightened in the moonlight. *He saw my reaction,* Floyd thought, *but who cares.* Then his thoughts went to Blanca. *Sweet, kind Blanca. It makes me sick to think you might be this animal's wife. It's a good thing you have such excellent parents.*

After dropping off Lucia and paying their respects, they were on their way to where the stabbing had occurred. Upon arriving, the two men walked to the spot where the victim had fallen. Floyd immediately registered the chopped-up ground. Boot tracks were everywhere. Any sign would be destroyed.

He began walking in a circle, starting where the assault

occurred, and gradually widening. He noticed Hugh examining something on the ground, but turned his attention back to the surface in front of him. At last he saw it, a boot track. Kneeling, though it wasn't necessary, for it was the same track he had seen in the alley. Pike and other members of the Porter gang did this, and for nothing. The banker had no money with him.

Seeing Floyd squat down, Hugh stood and walked over. "Find something?"

"I did. I had to get out of the chopped-up ground, but here it is." He pointed to Pike's track. "That's the same track I saw in the alley, and check out this one. That's Boswell or Titus. I'm not sure which. I didn't see who was making them, back home, but I saw those boot prints again at the massacre."

"Do you think Porter is behind this?" Hugh asked.

"Not a chance," Floyd said. "I saw no sign of him at the scene of the murder, nor have I seen or heard of him in town. Probably, his boys just wanted a little drinking money and spotted a well-to-do fellow walking around and killed him. It was unplanned, just a spur-of-the-moment attack."

Rivera was listening to the conversation. "You don't think? What does an inexperienced boy know about how a killer thinks?"

Floyd looked up at Rivera. His eyes drifted to the blood dripping from the sides of the man's horse. His anger was rising, but at almost the same time, he heard Lontac tell him, "Channel your anger. Use it to your benefit, not your enemy's."

"Captain, these same men attacked me in Tennessee just before I headed west. I know them. They are worthless vermin who would kill their own mother for a dollar, but their leader is smarter than this. He would never have ordered a killing where he made nothing."

Hugh nodded. "I can attest to the veracity of his assessment. Members of the Trace Porter gang did this, but Porter did not order it done."

"You are positive this Trace Porter was not involved? If he is such a criminal, as you say, this would be a perfect opportunity to hang him."

Floyd could hear the frustration in the captain's voice.

Irritated, Rivera continued. "You will attest to Porter not being involved in court?"

"I will," Hugh said. "But it still remains that he and his gang were involved in the Flagan Massacre." He turned to Floyd. "Let's go back to help Lucia." The two men returned to the coach and, sitting under the buffalo robe, rode back to the home of the deceased, leaving Captain Rivera at the crime scene.

∼

WITH THE MEN OFF TO work, the women sat in the atrium, soaking up the warmth of the Santa Fe sun. The girls, like many children around the world, were busy quizzing their mother on what their Christmas gifts might be. With smiles and occasional laughter, she repelled their probing questions. When her daughters resorted to pleading, she changed the subject to their papi.

"Oh, Mami," Ana Maria said, "I'm making him a muffler for his neck. You know how cold his neck gets in the winter."

Lucia turned to her middle daughter. "What do you think about your papa's cold neck, Blanca?"

The girl had been staring out the window. "What?" With a blank face, she looked around at her sisters and then her mother. "Why, yes, Mami, I agree."

Lucia shook her head. "Daughter, where is your mind? It is definitely not on your papi's cold neck."

Blanca dropped her face to stare at her hands in her lap. She was sad. Floyd seemed to like her, but nothing ever happened beyond smiling or occasionally touching her hand. Did he not care about her?

"Mami, do you think Floyd likes me?"

The other two sisters looked at each other, eyes wide. Lucia stopped her sewing and placed her hands in her lap. "My little Blanca, do you find him difficult to understand?"

"Oh, yes, Mami. I don't understand him at all. I dress nice for him, wear what I think is his favorite perfume, even..."

Lucia's voice became stern. "Even what, Blanca?"

The girl looked at her mother, her eyes brimming. "I even bite my lips sometimes to make them appear redder. Is that awful, Mami? Must I go to confession?"

"First, and this applies to all of you, you must go to confession when you feel the need. Now, nothing you have done is bad, but, my dear girl, I must tell you, it is very hard to understand a man in most things. Some, yes, most, no."

Blanca took a deep breath, held it for a moment, and slowly let it out. "That is no help."

Lucia nodded. "Yes, I am sorry you find this quiet boy with the long scar attractive—"

"But I do, Mami, I really do."

"I understand, daughter, but do not interrupt me. The boy or man you have chosen..." Here Lucia looked out the window as if she were hunting for the right words.

"He is a mountain man. You have seen them in your papa's store. They are a wild lot. I believe they have but one love, and that is the mountains, the faraway. I am sure they like the wildness, the danger, and they must like the loneliness. Look at your uncle Jeb. We would have gladly welcomed him into our beautiful home for the winter, but what does he do? He rides to the mountains, to risk his life, maybe freeze to death or be killed by a grizzly, and live in a little one-room shack."

Ana Maria, the oldest sister, looked inquiringly at her mother. "Have you seen his house in the mountains?"

Lucia shook her head. "No, I haven't, but I have been around these mountain men for many years. They have no care for their possessions. As long as they have traps, a horse, a rifle, and a knife, they are satisfied."

Blanca turned pleading eyes on her mother. "But Papi married you, and he was a mountain man."

Lucia leaned forward and spoke in low tones. "I want each of you to promise me you will never repeat to your papi what I am about to tell you. Do you promise?"

They all three nodded their heads.

"Not good enough. I want each of you to say I promise."

Each girl did as asked.

Lucia looked around, as if to make sure no one else was listening, and motioned for the girls to lean closer. When they had, she said, "He was not a mountain man."

Blanca was astonished. She looked at her sisters, and they were as surprised as she. "But Mami, Papi says he was a mountain man."

"Yes, Blanca, he says that. He says it because he believes it, but tell me, have you ever seen him staring at the mountains as if he longs to return?"

Blanca thought for a few moments. "No, I never have."

Each of her sisters answered in the same way.

"Now, Blanca, I want you to think before you answer. Have you ever seen Floyd staring at the mountains as if he had lost something in them?"

Blanca peered at her mother for what seemed like minutes. Then recognition flooded her eyes. She leaned to her lap, her hands closed tight around her face.

"Yes," Lucia said, "he stares at them every day. I am sorry, Blanca, but you must face reality. Your Floyd will not be staying. He will leave, and if he comes back, he will leave again. Enjoy your time with him, for he is a splendid boy, but realize he is already married. He is married to the mountains."

Lucia watched, her heart torn asunder, for a moment hating Floyd for what he had unknowingly done to her daughter, as her sweet Blanca sobbed into her dainty hands. Hands any sane man would move a mountain to hold. Then, shocking her other two daughters, Lucia said, "Married to those damned mountains!"

∼

Floyd had learned much. He had become one of the best of Hugh's fur buyers, with an eye for fur and a nose for rot. It was possible for him to smell a hide even if it was only a little off, and he worked hard at everything. He was speaking Spanish like a native and continued to impress Lontac.

His days were full, and through his hard work for Hugh, he had made an impressive amount of money. He used part of it to buy himself a coat made from buffalo hide. Not just any coat. He wanted a coat that would button, with the back split like his wool coat Ma and the girls had made him. There were warm, special pockets made into each side of the coat above waist level.

He had also been busy with Oliver Ryland. With what little extra time he had, he spent it in Ryland Guns and Repairs, learning how to work on his and other weapons. He had swapped out his Virginia 2nd long rifle for another Ryland rifle. Now he had two, plus three more caplock pistols.

Floyd's brother Owen could work magic with leather. The holsters he had made Floyd were not only pretty, but functional, the way they hung over the saddle horn—one on each side. They were always ready. While examining them, he had an idea and made two more holsters, but these attached to his belt. He also had a flap fixed in his buffalo coat pocket that allowed him to reach all the way through and draw a pistol from either holster. He had practiced with the coat on and found he could get either pistol into action fast.

Floyd looked out the office window. Two trappers were bringing in fur. He looked around. He was the only buyer in the office, so he stepped up to the counter. The two men came in and dropped their bundles on the long counter.

"Good morning," Floyd said. "Looks like you fellers are planning to sell your fur."

One was nodding good-naturedly when the other spoke up. "We aim to. You got a man around here we could deal with? This ain't a kid's job."

Floyd had learned much from Lontac and recognized much about this man. First, he was a bully. The type who might be dangerous if he thought he had the advantage. He'd also learned control.

"Well, gents, if you'd like to come back after lunch, there will be other buyers here. I'm sure they'll be glad to help you. Have a good day." Floyd turned and headed back to the desk where he had been working.

"Hold up there, kid," the gruff one said. "I ain't through talkin' to you."

Floyd turned around and his voice became softer. He exercised the control that Lontac had taught him. "Then go right ahead, Mister..."

"That's better. My pard here is Jesse King, and I be the one and onliest Van McMillan."

"How do you do, gentlemen," Floyd said. "Now, if you don't want to sell your furs, what can I do for you?"

"Howdy," Jesse said. "Van, why don't you let this feller grade our furs and pay us. Hugh Brennan has an excellent reputation. For sure he ain't gonna hire no one that was bad."

"Shut up, Jesse. Don't give me no lip." McMillan turned to Floyd. "Boy, you trot yore little be-hind outta here and find us a buyer. We ain't waitin'."

"Well, Van, you have several choices. You can trade with me, or you can wait, or you are free to go somewhere else."

Van exploded. "Boy, don't you back talk me! Now you git out

there and find us a buyer." With his last word, he reached across the wide counter to grab Floyd by the front of his shirt.

It wasn't difficult. Floyd remembered what Lontac said when they had first met about him being so slow. He saw McMillan's intention before he ever started moving, and when he did, the arm seemed to move so slowly. Floyd slid easily out of the man's way, and the big fellow stumbled, falling against the desk.

Befuddled, he straightened up, looked at his partner, and then at Floyd. "Boy, you trying to make a fool out of me?"

"No, sir," Floyd said, "looks like you're doing a fine job of that all by yourself."

"Boy, you shouldn't oughta done that. Now, I'm gonna hurt you bad." McMillan turned toward the end of the counter and the pass-through. Floyd reached under the counter where a company shotgun was kept, just in case. The man stopped when he heard the deadly sound of hammers being eared back. He turned to find the gaping holes of the muzzle staring into his face. Both of his hands shot up.

"Count me out of this," Jesse said. He took one pack of furs and slid them down the counter toward Floyd. "I'd like to trade with you, friend." He looked back at McMillan. "You can join me or leave, but don't mess with me."

"I was just funnin', boy. I ain't meant no harm."

Floyd gave the man a cold smile. "I'm sure you didn't, but why don't you take your furs and get out."

McMillan said nothing. He picked up his bundle of furs, stopped to say something to Jesse, considered, and stepped out the door.

"Whew," Jesse said. "Yore almighty quick. I figured he had you for sure, but let me tell you, he's a grudge-holder. He'll try to jump you when you ain't looking, so keep an eye out for him."

"Thank you for the information," Floyd said. "Now, let's take a look at your furs and get some money in your pockets."

Jesse gave a single vigorous nod. "Yes, sir. That sounds good to me."

Floyd was grading the furs when Hugh walked in. He saw Jesse and said, "How are you? Looks like you've got some good pelts there."

"Yep, I reckon I do. Learned how to take care of a hide by my pappy back in Virginny. He shore knowed how to do it."

Floyd grinned up at him from the pelts. "He must have, for he taught you well. These are some of the nicest looking furs I've seen." He slid the last one onto the pile beside him and pulled out his tally book. After figuring for a moment, he looked up at Jesse and said, "How does six hundred and twenty-two dollars suit you?"

Jesse leaned back his head and let out a whoop. "Whoo-ee, why, I reckon this ole hound would be pure tickled with that much money. Are you sure?"

"Well," Floyd said, looking at Hugh, "this is the owner, Mr. Hugh Brennan. He can do a recount if you'd like."

Jesse shook his head several times. "No, sir. If you're happy, so am I."

Hugh grinned, waved, and walked to the back while Floyd counted out Jesse's money.

After Floyd paid him, the man divided the money into three piles. One pile was stashed in each boot, while the remaining money went into his hat brim. His face turned serious, and he leaned on the counter. "You strike me as a fine feller. I wasn't funnin' when I said McMillan will try to jump you when you ain't looking. He figures you for a boy that he can whip, but I'm thinkin' he best bring a lunch for that task. Good day to ya." Jesse doffed his hat and went out the door.

22

Before Jesse stepped out the door, Floyd's mind was again on the murder. If Pike was in town, he might be found in one of the saloons on Burro Alley. Gambling and prostitution in Santa Fe were confined to that area. For the citizens it was difficult, because this was also where wood was sold. It was hauled in on burros, hence the street name.

I should go look around for Pike, Floyd thought while continuing to finish up the paperwork he was taking care of when Jesse and McMillan came in. *He'd tell me where Porter is hiding out. He and his entire gang need to be captured, tried, and hung.*

"Floyd," Hugh called from the back.

He pulled out his pocket watch, another convenience he had purchased for himself, checked the time, stood, and walked into the back of the trading center. Hugh was looking through a stack of hides and making notes. He stopped, put his notepad down, and turned to Floyd.

"You called?"

"Yes. I wanted to find out when you plan on leaving us for the San Juans?"

Floyd ran his hand over the soft beaver pelt lying on the table. "Hugh, I haven't decided. I had hoped to leave next month, but the trappers I talk to say it has been a hard winter, and they're expecting a late thaw."

"Based on that, May might even be too early."

Floyd shook his head. "It'll take me at least three weeks, maybe more, to get to Jeb's cabin. Plus, I'll be leading two packhorses, so I'd expect to spend five weeks to get there."

Hugh nodded. "That sounds about right."

"If I figure five weeks, I should leave either the second week of next month, or April, depending on when I'm expecting the thaw."

"April will be soon enough, Floyd. You leave earlier than that, some adventuresome soul will find your bones, because you will definitely freeze. I've been in that country. It's rough, broken, and cold. You'll hit spots where the snow will be so deep your horses won't make it and they'll die. Without horses, this time of year, you'll be dead. Stay here until April. You'll have more time with Lontac, you'll be able to put away more money from here, and you will be safer."

Floyd shook his head. "Hugh, I feel like I'm imposing on you and your family. I appreciate all you've done for me. Just learning Spanish is more than I can ever repay you for, but add on staying in your home, and Lontac. I never realized how much I didn't know about fighting until I met him."

Hugh motioned toward several chairs. "Let's sit. We're by ourselves. No one will hear us."

The two men walked over to the chairs and sat, facing each other.

Hugh continued. "I can tell you he's taught you much more than how to fight. You have calmed down tremendously. If someone isn't familiar with you, it would be impossible for them to tell if you are angry, a huge improvement."

"He has shown me so much. My pa and brothers taught me how to fight, but that only goes so far. At my age I don't have much experience to fall back on."

Hugh grinned at the last statement. "Before Lontac you would have never made that statement, and you would have been angry if someone suggested you were young."

"Yeah, but it's true. I've got to face it and learn while I can. Lontac has taught me patience and how to channel my anger. I also learned how to use my knife. I was very lucky in besting that Pawnee, but now I am much better, and I have learned so much more. His training has been priceless, and he won't take a cent."

"Yes, that's Lontac. He wouldn't promise me he would take you, only that he would meet you. I guess he liked you."

"Speaking of Lontac," Floyd said, rising from his chair, "I'd best be on my way."

Hugh stood. "Think about what we were talking about. April will be soon enough. Don't leave next month. It will devastate the family to find out your departure is so close."

Floyd recognized both the sincerity and concern in the older man's face. "Hugh, I'll wait till April. I can't begin to explain how much it means to me the way your family welcomed me into your home. I will always be in your debt. Plus the things I've learned here are priceless."

"Lucia and all the girls love you, and you are the older brother Zeke needed to help him through this crisis. He is adjusting very well, and you have helped him immensely. We still have found no signs of relatives. If we cannot, Lucia wants to adopt him."

Floyd smiled at the suggestion that Lucia wanted to adopt Zeke. He knew it was Hugh's idea from the time he let the boy ride with him on the trail. The family would be good for Zeke.

"Hugh, I've got to be going. Lontac demands timeliness."

"Yes, go," Hugh said, his arm over the boy's shoulder as he walked him to the door. "I'll see you at supper."

Floyd left, hurrying toward Lontac's adobe. He glimpsed two men standing across the street talking, but thought nothing of it. Today was a warmer day, and people were out, enjoying the warmth while it lasted.

They had been working for no more than thirty minutes when someone began banging on the front door.

Floyd stepped back while Lontac strode to the door. Floyd had learned he did not like interruptions, so he knew his teacher was not happy, though his features reflected nothing. He opened the door, and Juan Ortega was standing there.

Juan saw Floyd at the same time. "Come, Mr. Brennan has been shot."

Floyd was shocked only for a moment. Then he was galvanized into movement. He grabbed his hat and swung his gun belt around his waist, yanked off his moccasins, shoved them into his pocket, and slammed his boots on. Nodding to Lontac, he dashed out the door. Juan had a buggy. The two of them leaped in, and Juan guided the racing horses to the Brennan home.

Before the buggy came to a stop, Floyd leaped out and raced to the door. It swung open as he reached for the latch. Blanca was standing there, looking beautiful. Her big brown eyes were wide with tears, black hair cascading over her shoulders.

"How is he? Where is he?" Floyd asked in a harsh voice.

Lucia appeared at the head of the stair. "Come, Floyd, he is up here."

Floyd took the stairs four at a time. Lucia stepped back, allowing him entrance to the bedroom, and there he lay.

Floyd was shocked. This was the man who had offered him the opportunity to head west, the man who guided the wagon train through rivers, bandits, and Indians. Why, only thirty minutes ago, Hugh had his arm around him. Now he lay in the big four-poster bed, looking as white as the sheets he lay between. The doctor sat at his bedside, listening to his chest with a device.

A momentary sense of relief washed over him. Hugh's chest and shoulders were uncovered. He had a visible wound above his shoulder, but the hole was so high it amounted to only a flesh wound. Then the doctor pulled the sheets back to expose a wound in his left side. It was anybody's guess with a bullet strike in that location. It might pass through causing no fatal damage, or hit a gut, in which case Hugh would die.

Zeke stood at the end of the bed. No tears fell and he was silent.

Floyd put his arm around Lucia's shoulders. She seemed so small. "How is he?"

"The doctor says he has a chance, but he's most worried about the head wound."

Floyd looked puzzled at her statement, for there was no visible head wound.

"He was first hit in the back of his head with a pistol butt. Then the two men shot him while he was on the floor."

Floyd felt his anger growing. He held it in rein, but it was there, smoldering and intense.

The doctor called to Lucia. She moved to the opposite side of the bed, leaned over her husband, and kissed him on the forehead. Then she began helping the doctor wrap a lengthy piece of linen around Hugh's head.

Blanca came up the stairs and moved next to Floyd. Instinctively, he wrapped his arms around her and held her while she sobbed. Her tears lasted only a few moments. She pulled away, looked up at Floyd, and said, "Will Papi die?"

Without hesitation, Floyd said, "Not a chance. He's too tough to die. He'll be back at his office in no time."

All the servants had gathered around the walls of the room, many with tears in their eyes. Juan eased next to Floyd. "Señor Logan, may I speak with you in the hallway?"

Floyd looked at Blanca. She had turned and was intent on

watching her papi. Ana Maria stood with her arm around her youngest sister, Gloria Petra. "Give me just a moment."

He stepped to Zeke and knelt next to him. "How are you doing?"

Zeke turned dry eyes to Floyd. "Is he gonna die? Most people I know die."

"Believe me, Zeke, you had nothing to do with this, and he will not die."

Zeke looked away. Floyd took the boy by the arms. "Look at me, Zeke." Slowly, Zeke turned his head back to face Floyd. "Since you've known me, I've not lied to you. I never will. In my heart, I know that Hugh will not die."

Zeke's eyes showed some hope. "I sure want you to be right."

"I wouldn't steer you wrong."

Lucia, who was working on her husband, had heard the conversation taking place at the foot of the bed. She turned and locked Floyd with stern dark eyes. He held her gaze until she turned back.

"I've got to go for a while, Zeke, but I'll be back."

The boy nodded and turned back to watch what was happening with Hugh. Floyd stood and followed Juan out the door.

"Señor Logan, it was two men. I was going to the shop to pick up Señor Brennan. I must have just missed them. A lady passing by the office witnessed everything through the front window. When Señor Brennan turned to go to the money drawer, the tall one hit him on the head with his pistol. He collapsed, and while he lay on the floor, helpless, they shot him."

"Did she see which way they headed?"

"*Si*, toward Las Vegas."

"Is Rivera going after them?"

"He is not in town. He took a patrol out to look for Indians."

"All right, would you get Rusty ready to ride? Have Sofia put together enough for three days. I'll grab some clothes and be on my way."

"Señor, do not throw reason to the wind. That will get you killed."

"Don't worry, Juan, I'm cool as ice. I'll be fine."

"I wish it was possible for me to accompany you, but my duty is to protect this family . . ."

"Don't concern yourself, Juan. Your job is here. Would you get word to Lontac, so I can continue with him when I get back?"

Juan nodded. "I will."

With that, Floyd turned and raced up the stairs, already going over weapons and supply needs. Five minutes later he came out of his room with his saddlebags, rifles, powder, lead, caps, and clothing. Lucia stepped out of the bedroom as Floyd turned down the stairs.

"Floyd, do you know what you are doing?"

Floyd looked at the wife of his benefactor and said, "Yes. I've been long taught by my pa, my brothers, Jeb Campbell, and Lontac. Do not worry about me."

"Then find the men who did this and kill them. They should not be walking the same earth as Hugh Brennan."

"I'll do it, ma'am."

He turned, rushed down the stairs and out the door.

Juan had Rusty ready along with the familiar buckskin.

"It would be better if you took two. They are both saddled. This will save you time. Your food and supplies are on the buckskin. Also, the bedroll on Rusty is yours, and the one on the buckskin is two thick blankets for the horses."

Juan had tied the stirrups of the spare saddle to the saddle horn so they did not bounce against the horse. Floyd examined his mounts, hung two of the holsters across his saddle, and slid the two rifles into their respective scabbards. He mounted Rusty.

"Juan, the description."

"Yes, two men. One is about average with a fat belly and dirty beard. His coat was open, and she saw the red sash he was wearing. The other one is tall and thin, with a scraggly beard. She heard the tall one call the other man Pike."

Floyd nodded and, leading the buckskin, turned Rusty down the street to Hugh's office. If there hadn't been much traffic, he wanted to see the horses' hoofprints and the boot tracks for himself.

He pulled up across from the office and a few yards down from the hitching rail. After looping the buckskin's reins around his saddle horn, he stepped down and ground hitched Rusty. It only took him a few moments to find the boot prints that belonged to the man in the alley and the man who had killed Castillo. In fact, the other boot print gave him a match of the two killers involved in Castillo's murder. He studied the horses' hoofprints only for a moment, then swung back into the saddle, heading out on the road to Las Vegas.

The men had no more than a two-hour lead on him, but it was getting late. He couldn't take the chance of losing them in the dark, so as much as he itched to continue, he started looking for a camping spot. Spotting the banks of a draw only a hundred yards from the road, he guided Rusty toward it. A convenient game trail led down into the arroyo's bottom, and he pointed Rusty toward the trail. The red roan didn't hesitate, dropping off the bank and into the draw, with the buckskin following. There wasn't much grass, but Juan had put some oats in a tow sack and wrapped it in their blankets.

Floyd unsaddled both animals, and though he would have preferred to stake them out on a long lead, he had some pieces of short rope with which he made hobbles. After gathering enough dried cedar for the night, he built his fire. It would be cold, but at least the draw would keep them out of the wind as it whipped around the huge red boulders surrounding the arroyo.

He started his fire, fed the animals, covered them with their blankets, and crawled under his. He was exhausted. It had been a long day, and his training with Lontac, even though it was cut short, had drained the energy from his body. The draw blocked him from the sight of others, and with the buffalo robe and blankets, he'd stay warm. He'd take his chance with a flash flood. His eyes slammed shut, and he slept.

He was dreaming about the mountains with Jeb, but Jeb was talking louder than normal. That wasn't like him. He was most always quiet and never whiney. But now he was loud and—

"Well, would you look at this? This feller is all wrapped up and snug as a bug in a buffalo rug."

Floyd willed himself not to move. Fortunately, both of his hands were already in his buffalo coat, and he could feel his pistols.

"Howdy, boy. It's been a while since ole Trace beat the snot out of you, now ain't it?"

"Howdy, Pike," Floyd said, working his hands to his pistols. "You're uglier than I remember."

Pike's partner let out a howl of laughter. "He's got you pegged, ain't he, Pike."

Pike was sitting near enough to Floyd to kick him, and he did. "Watch yore tone, boy, or I'll whip you within an inch of your life." He turned to his partner. "That ain't funny, Lester."

"Seemed mighty funny to me." The man continued to chuckle.

Floyd was calm and in control. He laid out his plan. He would shoot Lester, because he was too far to do anything else, but he wanted to give Pike a chance to administer the whipping he had threatened him with.

"Boys," Floyd said, "I'll give you one chance to surrender. You can do that now, and I'll take you back to Santa Fe. Turn me down, and you won't like the results."

Pike cackled and slapped his knee. "Boy, I will say you are funny. Trace's gonna be sorry he missed this. I might just truss you up and haul you in on one of them fine horses." He thought about his idea for a minute. "No, ain't a good plan. Trace would have all the fun with you. I'll do it for him, just what he promised you. I'm gonna whip you within an inch of yore life, and then I'll gut you from belly to gullet."

23

The world won't miss trash like you, Floyd thought.

"Then," Pike continued, "while yore still kickin' and screamin' like that old banker did, I'm gonna cut them guts out and hang 'em on a tree, just like Trace said. Now ain't that poetic, boy?"

"Shore sounds like poetry to me," Lester said.

Floyd shook his head. "I gave you a chance. Too bad you didn't take it." When he finished, he threw back the blanket, shoved the pistol out from behind his coat, and pulled the trigger. Both of his horses startled and tried to buck, but gave up quickly with the hobbles on. The thieves' horses took off into the night, but Floyd could hear them. They ran only a short distance.

The bullet doubled Lester over. He sat down hard on the rocks and was now moaning and holding his belly. Pike had leaned his rifle against a small boulder and, at the gunshot, grabbed for it and missed, knocking the rifle to the ground. After a brief scramble, he clamped his shaky fingers on it and looked toward Floyd, only to stare into the gaping maw of Floyd's remaining pistol.

He froze and gave Floyd a sickly grin. "Boy, you know I was

only funnin' you. Why, while you was sleepin', I was tellin' Lester over there how much I like you."

Floyd nodded. "I'm sure you were, Pike. Tell me, why did you kill Señor Castillo?"

"Why, we needed some drinkin' money, and here comes this old Mex strollin' down the street toward us, and he come out of the bank. We was only goin' to rough him up a bit, but he started fightin' us, and we had to defend ourselves."

Floyd felt the anger, but it was different. It was more cold than hot, not the uncontrollable anger he'd had before Lontac. "Kinda like you had to defend yourselves against Hugh Brennan?"

Floyd thought Pike was looking at him differently. Maybe fear was edging itself into the man's thinking.

"I didn't want to do that. If he had given us the money, wouldn't nothing have happened."

"You mean before or after you hit him from behind and shot him while he was out."

"'Tweren't me, boy. That was all Lester. I tried to stop him, but he weren't havin' none of it."

"So Lester shot him twice?"

At his name, Lester called out, "Help me, Pike. I'm hurtin' bad. I'm thinkin' this boy done killed me."

"Shut up, Lester," Pike snapped. "I'm busy."

"Hang on, Lester," Floyd said. "Pike may beat you to where you're headed."

Now, Floyd saw the bare fear in Pike's eyes.

"You can't shoot me, boy. That wouldn't be legal."

"Oh, Pike, I'm not going to shoot you. I want you to pick up all the guns and move them over here and lay them on the blankets."

When Pike heard he wasn't in for the same pain Lester was suffering, Floyd watched the relief flood over him.

"Why, sure, boy, I'll be glad to help."

Floyd watched as Pike gathered all the weapons and laid

them across the blanket. He motioned his weapon toward the pistol behind Pike's sash, resting under his coat. The man reluctantly pulled it out, putting it with the others.

"Now, turn around and keep your hands up."

"Don't shoot me, boy."

"I told you, I will not shoot you."

Relaxed now, the man turned, and Floyd searched him from head to foot, checking under his shirt and in his boots, nothing except the knife still under the coat.

"Now pull that knife out."

Slowly, Pike pulled the knife from its scabbard and looked at it longingly as he moved to put it in the pile.

"No, you hang on to your knife."

Pike looked up and stared at Floyd. A smile creased his face. "You want some of me, don't you, boy?"

Floyd removed his coat, and without it, the cold cut deep, but he did not want it hampering his movement. He looked Pike over one more time and laid his pistol on the blankets along with the other weapons.

Pike said, "Boy, you done made the biggest and last mistake of yore life."

Floyd smiled at Pike. "What are you gonna do, Pike, talk me to death?"

His enemy's face took on an evil grin, and he ambled toward Floyd. "You're fightin' on my turf, now, and young-un, you'll be sorry." With his last word, he lunged at Floyd, coming in low with a feint, followed by an upward thrust with his knife.

Two things happened. First, Floyd recognized the move as the same one the Pawnee had used when he ripped his face. The second was how slow the man appeared to be moving. His shoulders, his arms, even his head had telegraphed this move. Floyd saw it coming from its inception.

He slid his body only a touch to his right, came in over Pike's left arm, nicking him under the chin, and then tripped him.

Pike sprawled in the dry creek bed, grabbing at his neck. His hand came away bloody. He lunged to his feet and spun around to meet Floyd's charge. But there was none.

Floyd was standing, his hands at his sides, smiling. "Not as easy to gut this boy as you thought, is it, Pike?"

"Lucky," Pike grunted.

"If you say so."

Pike eyed the guns lying on the blankets.

Floyd watched him and said nonchalantly, "You'd be dead before you reached them."

Pike turned his attention back to his opponent. Floyd could tell the man was desperate but determined. Moving fast, Floyd whipped in, sliced the razor-sharp knife across the woman-killer's belly from left to right, only deep enough to draw blood. He stepped back, out of range, before Pike made a move.

Pain now showed in Pike's face, and the fear returned.

"How about that, Pike. Things aren't always as they seem, are they?" Thoughts of the massacred wagon train flooded Floyd's mind. The women and little girls.

"I'm not a little girl, Pike. I can defend myself."

He drove straight for Pike's face. When the man's knife moved to block him, Floyd's point dropped and entered Pike's belly an inch above his navel. Floyd ripped up hard, throwing his back and shoulders into the stroke, as Lontac had taught him, ripping through muscle, cartilage, and bone. He yanked the knife out and stepped back.

Pike stood, wobbling on his feet, and looked down at the blood pouring from his body. His knife dropped to the ground only moments before he fell to his knees, hands flying to his stomach and chest. Eyes wide with horror, he grasped the slash, trying to hold it closed and stop the bleeding. "Yore just a *kid*," he gasped, and toppled forward, face-first into the sand.

Floyd stood for a while, looking down on Pike's body. He felt no pleasure in the killing of this man, as he thought he would. He moved up the arroyo a ways and threw up, heaving for almost a minute. He felt some better. His hands were shaking, and though it was freezing cold, sweat covered his arms and head. After wiping his mouth with his sleeve, he turned back to the two dead men.

He glanced at Lester. The man had died while the fight was still going on. He lay on his back, eyes open, staring at the stars he would never see again. Floyd squatted down next to Pike and cleaned his knife on the man's trousers.

His mind was churning. What would his ma think of her son killing a man in a knife fight? What about Pa? *They would be fine with it,* he thought, *especially if they knew about the massacre in the canyon.* His ma and pa both came from frontier stock.

He was thankful for the training with Lontac. It had saved him tonight, and he was sure it would do so again. He took a deep breath and looked around the dry creek bed. A pair of coyotes, not far away, tuned up to serenade the stars, ending with a few rapid barks. Something shuffled under a bush nearby, probably a porcupine. The stars continued their trek across the sky.

He noticed he was cold and put on his coat. It was heavy, but the warmth felt good. Moving over to the fire, he poked it to rejuvenate the flames and tossed more sticks atop the few remaining. Shortly it was cracking with enthusiasm.

Thanks to Pike and Lester, it had been a short chase. When daylight arrived, he collected the bandits' horses, as they had remained near the reassuring fire. Once the horses were in hand, he loaded the two killers to take back to the sergeant. He figured Rivera would be unhappy on two counts. First, he had returned and, second, had taken care of the killers. He dug in his saddlebags and found that the killers had eaten most of the food. After searching deeper, by the flickering light of the fire, he found the sopapillas. *How had they missed these?* he thought.

THE MORNING WAS active in the square as he rode in, but all activity stopped at the sight of the two dead men tied across their saddles. As he passed, people followed. His first stop was the Brennan Furrier.

Salty walked out on the boardwalk. "Looks like you collected two varmints, boy." He walked to each one, grabbed hair and pulled the head up, exposing each face. "Well, I'll be doggone, you done catched yoreself two wooly wildcats. This one be Grif Pike, and I ain't seen this other one in a coon's age. He's Lester Porter."

Salty looked up at Floyd. "He's a cousin to Trace. That feller ain't gonna be too happy."

Floyd climbed down from Rusty, trailing the reins, and walked back to the horse Pike was draped over. He untied and pulled the saddlebags from the animal and tossed them to Salty. "That's the money they stole from Hugh. I doubt they had time to spend any of it. How's Hugh doing?"

Salty caught the saddlebags and watched the tall young man walk back to and climb on Rusty. "He's woke up. Doc says he's got an excellent chance of makin' it if those wounds don't sour. Lookee here, boy. You hear what I said about Lester and Trace?"

A flood of relief washed over him. "That's really good news. I oughta get up there, and yes, I heard, Salty. But I can't imagine it makes much difference. Porter's already promised to hang my guts on a tree limb when he sees me. He can't do it but once. Now, should I take these vermin to the fort or leave them here?"

"I will take them."

Floyd looked around to find the speaker, and recognized Alcalde Ortiz, in the street with the rest of the crowd. "Thank you, Alcalde. These two jumped me at my camp. I had to kill them both."

The mayor turned to a man next to him and pointed to the two horses. The man jumped toward them, taking the reins of both horses from Floyd.

Before speaking, he looked at the two dead men and turned to the boy in wonder, then said, "I am glad you were not injured, Señor Logan. Captain Rivera may visit you."

"I'm heading on up to the house. Tell him I'll be around." With that, he waved and trotted the horses toward the house.

People had gathered around the two bodies. Floyd heard Salty say, "Would you look at this? Pike's been gutted like a fish."

Floyd stopped by Lontac's adobe, dismounted, tied the horses, and walked to the door. He had raised his hand to knock when the Filipino swung the door open.

Lontac looked him up and down and said, "You caught the outlaws?"

Floyd nodded. "I did."

"Are *they* injured?"

"Dead."

"But you are not."

"No, thanks to you. One man I shot. The other, I killed with a knife."

"Ahh, yes. Come in."

Floyd stepped into the warm house. He indicated the coat. "May I?"

Lontac gave a short nod. "Come sit."

Floyd hung the coat on a peg, pulled out a chair, and sat.

"Tell me all of it."

Floyd did, leaving nothing out, including the outlaws finding him and building his fire back up while he slept. Lontac said nothing until he had finished.

With a concerned face, he said, "You were very lucky they did not shoot you where they found you."

"Yes," Floyd said, "I grew up in the woods. My pa drilled into all of us boys to sleep light. I didn't. The only reason I'm talking to you is the coat and the holsters I made. They saved my life."

"You have learned a valuable lesson. I think it impossible you will ever sleep so soundly that someone can move upon you. But there is another lesson here. A positive lesson. Planning ahead. You made those holsters, and you had the buffalo coat tailored so you could reach your weapons. Because of that, you were prepared. Many times, previous planning can offset one mistake. Keep that in mind."

Floyd leaned back in the sturdy chair. "I hadn't thought of that. I considered myself lucky."

"No luck, planning."

"One thing I must tell you," Floyd said. "Do you remember when I first came here, and you told me I could not move fast enough to harm you?"

The teacher nodded. An ever so faint smile pulled at his lips.

"I couldn't believe that I knew what Pike would do with his knife before he ever twitched. It was uncanny, kind of like reading his mind."

"Yes, as you develop, this will happen more and more. I have seen demonstrations where masters fight six, seven, even eight people, and no one can touch them. That takes years of work and dedication, which you do not have. But, Floyd, you have a little time left, and we will spend that time developing what you have learned.

"Now, since you are back. Get some rest, for we have a lesson this evening."

∽

DAYS PROGRESSED. Hugh healed, and Floyd felt the pull of the mountains. He continued to work hard for Hugh and Lontac. He no longer took Spanish lessons, since his teacher had told him he had progressed past needing a teacher.

Hugh was up and around. He was still weak, but getting stronger by the day. The fur business had slacked off for several weeks, but now the weather was warming, it was picking up again. Trappers were telling Floyd that in the near mountains, ice was breaking and they were setting traps in the lower streams.

Each day he grew more anxious. He also felt Blanca no longer cared for him as she had. She still liked him, but the looks with those big brown eyes she used to give him were no longer there. He mulled it over in his mind. After examining her actions, he thought, *I know nothing about women, but I bet it happened after I killed those two men, especially Pike. Word got around about how he was cut up. And not only her, but other people look at me differently.* To make matters worse, nowadays Captain Rivera was walking her out, and it seemed like Lucia approved. He shook his head. "I'll never figure them out."

"Figure what out?" an older buyer who had worked for Hugh for several years said.

"Women."

"Ha," the man replied, "after being married to one for ten years, I love her to death, but she puzzles me every day."

Floyd went back to work when a trapper walked in. It didn't take him long. The man's furs were prime. He paid him and had finished logging the purchase and checking the calendar as Hugh walked through the door.

"Well, look at you," Floyd said. "The way you're getting around, it'd be hard to guess you were shot."

"I'm good, but all that resting in a house full of women is driving me crazy. They won't let me do anything. It's like they think I might break. I had to get out."

Hugh followed where Floyd's eyes had been when he opened the door. "Looks like I'm not the only one needing to get out."

"It's that time. I'd be lying if I said I wasn't eager to go. Those mountains are calling, Hugh, and Jeb needs my help. So, if you're up and about enough for me to hit the trail, I'll be out of here bright and early in the morning."

Hugh shook his head. "I wish I hadn't walked down here today, if this is the result." He recanted, saying, "I'm only kidding,

Floyd, but I'd be lying if I said I won't be sorry for you to go. It'll be hard on the family, too, especially Zeke and Blanca."

Floyd grinned. "I've got Zeke taken care of. I promised I'd bring him a bear claw necklace when I came back. Now, he's raring for me to go get his necklace." Floyd shot Hugh a sly glance and said, "It doesn't appear you'll have to worry about Blanca. Seems like Captain Rivera has latched onto her interest pretty fierce."

Hugh shook his head and grimaced. "I've seen that. Lucia seems fine with it. Maybe she knows something I don't. I hope she does. Rivera's family is in Spain. If that union happens, I hope he treats her well and doesn't take my little girl across the ocean. I'd hate to not be able to see her." Then his face brightened.

"That's enough of that. We need to have a fiesta to celebrate your departure." He grinned at his last statement. "Maybe I should say celebrate your adventure, because we all hate for you to leave, except for Captain Rivera."

The man and the man-boy laughed together, enjoying each other's company. They talked for a time, took care of a customer, and both left together. Hugh on the way home, and Floyd stopping at Lontac's.

Floyd knocked, and Lontac stepped outside. The day was warm, and the old man had a talibong in his hand.

"You leave tomorrow."

Puzzled, Floyd said, "How did you know?"

"Your knock, it was different. It was final. Anyway, this is the end of April. You said you would leave after April."

"True, I did. No practice today?"

"No, you do not need it." He waved his hand like a falling bird. "Oh, if you were going to become a master, you would need to work for years, but you want to defend yourself. You know much more than most men you will meet, but be cautious. There is always someone better."

Wasting no time, Lontac said, "I have a gift for you. It is a prized gift. It has been in my family for many generations. I had planned on giving it to my son."

The old man paused, looking at Floyd with those hard obsidian-colored eyes, but they were not hard today. "For me, you are as close as any will ever be."

Ceremoniously, Lontac offered the blade and scabbard to Floyd.

Amazed, but realizing he could not refuse this supreme gift from Lontac, he bowed at the waist and accepted it with both hands.

"Thank you, Lontac. This is a great honor. I am not worthy, but very grateful."

A glint of humor in his eyes, Lontac said, "Worthiness is not a requirement for a gift."

A boyish grin broke out on Floyd's face. "That's good." Then he became serious. "I have brought you no gift, except my deep gratitude for all that you have taught me."

Lontac again made the falling bird wave. "That is more than enough for a teacher. Travel in safety, Floyd." He extended his hand, the two men shook, and he disappeared inside his adobe.

Floyd stood for a moment, replaying the days of the past six months. Lontac had been hard. He had worked Floyd rigorously, removing whatever excess weight might have been on him. Standing on the veranda, his shoulders were wider, and his waist was smaller, and he could kill a man with hands, knife, or spear.

Slowly he turned, slid the talibong back into its wooden holster, and walked to the Brennan home.

24

Floyd walked Rusty up the main street of Santa Fe, then north toward the shining mountains. He led the buckskin; he had named him Buck. The name was no more imaginative than Rusty, but it fit, and the dark brown mule, he named Browny. The additional horse and the mule were loaded with supplies, powder and lead, caps, and traps for whatever the mountains held in store. The castoreum, for the beaver sets, was in a glass bottle, wrapped and padded, on Browny's back.

It had been difficult saying goodbye to everyone. Zeke, a while back, had been promised, by Floyd, a bear-claw necklace when he returned. Now the boy seemed torn whether he wanted Floyd to leave or stay.

Blanca had been cool and reserved, giving him a peck on his cheek much like her sisters. Floyd couldn't help but notice, no longer captain, but Major Rivera in the Brennan's sitting room much more often. Now, his even more superior smile was present any time the two men met.

The difficulty was with Lucia and Hugh. He hadn't realized how fond he had grown of the couple. Lucia watched over him constantly. Her attention had increased since he had avenged

Hugh, but even without her attention, he would have missed the lovely, caring woman.

Leaving Hugh had been almost like leaving his own father. The man paid him handsomely for the time he was employed, gave him the two horses and mule, and tried to give him the traps and gear. Floyd had objected, trying to pay him for the animals, saddles, and all the equipment.

When Hugh would not even consider accepting payment, Floyd finally agreed, except for the traps. He threatened to go to a competitor if Hugh would not accept payment. Hugh laughed and gave him a ridiculously low price. Floyd counted out twice as much, refusing to accept any money in return.

Now they were all behind him. He had passed Lontac's house, watching for his friend and teacher, but the door remained closed, and he saw nothing. *Well,* he thought, *we already said the words. I reckon he likes goodbyes about as much as I do.*

The bustle of Santa Fe faded behind him. He was about to put the animals into a lope when he heard a fast-approaching horse. He turned and grinned, watching the still-visible streets. Chickens raced from the street, cackling at their near brush with death. At the last minute, a piglet that had been rolling in the street's dust, seeing the horse and rider bearing down on him, dashed clear, squealing.

Salty, slowing for nothing or no one, rode at breakneck speed through the streets of Santa Fe, leaning low over his horse's neck. Catching Floyd, he slowed his horse and pulled up beside him. "I'll be danged, boy. I was workin' on a stubborn wagon axle when Hugh walked in and said you'd headed out. Whatsa matter with you, not stoppin' by the stable?"

Floyd, now embarrassed for not stopping, said, "Sorry, Salty, I just figured you ain't much for goodbyes."

"Yore sure right, exceptin' good friends. Mind if I ride along with you to La Vega de los Vigiles? Got some folks up there I might pick up a wagon from. They been wantin' me to fix it up."

"I appreciate the company. I figured since this is the first day, I'd make it an easy ride for the stock. Should be no problem, but it'll give me a chance to look for irritation or rubbing from the packs."

"Good idea. So, you spending the night?"

"Reckon. Last chance for a warm bed for a while."

Salty nodded as he said, "A long while. It'll be cold in them mountains. Nighttime stays cold year-round, mostly. Folks think with the cold nights, there ain't no mosquitoes up there 'cause they're so high up. I guess I ain't seen me mosquitoes like they can be up there, and I seen mosquitoes most everywhere, even on them ocean sides."

"Seen 'em in the Tennessee mountains," Floyd said as they rode at a comfortable walk. "Don't think I'll like 'em any better out here."

The two men rode through the valley in silence, with Baldy and Truchas peaks rising to the east. They crossed a dry spot on the Rio Tesuque creek. Water was held, for now, in the deeper holes along the creek.

The day passed easily, the sun warming the two men. Salty glanced at the long holsters hanging from Floyd's saddle horn, and then at the additional holsters on each hip. "Two rifles, four pistols, you planning on starting a war, boy?"

"Nope, but I'm sure aiming on stopping it. Porter's gang has already ambushed me twice. If it hadn't been for these holsters"—he patted his right one—"I wouldn't be enjoying this pretty ride."

"You sure got a point. Man can't have too many guns. I just wish that a man would invent an easy-to-shoot weapon what would hold three or four cartridges. Now that'd be something."

Floyd nodded. "I expect it'll come along. Pa always said that when a new something was needed, along comes an inventor to make it happen."

"Hope you're right."

After crossing the Pojoaque River, they found themselves in farmland that stretched well past La Vega de los Vigiles. Floyd's farmer side interest piqued. From horseback, he could see men all around him working on their irrigation systems. "It sure makes a lot of difference when you have water."

"Yep," Salty said. "Look at those crops. In each little field, they're all the same height and color. A dry-land farmer's would be all uneven. Where the crop had about the right amount of rain, it would be nice and green and full. Then you'd have a part of the field where it ran off before it could soak in good. That'd be spindly and thin and yellow. Course, there'd be the low part, where much of the rain ran to and stood. That'd be barren, all the crop drowned out, but this irrigation, that for sure is the way to go."

"Yes, sir," Floyd said. "Notice that corn, already getting tall. Just from sitting here, I see peas and onions and melons, and, of course, *chiles*."

They both laughed, and Salty pointed along the river. "And look at them orchards. Why, I'm guessin' they got about any kind of fruit a man could want." He swung his arm to point ahead. "There's los Vigiles."

Floyd had enjoyed the ride. He was sure the horses and mule had as well. They continued on the road toward the river.

"Got themselves a crossing up ahead. The Rio Grande spreads out pretty good, for now, so it ain't too deep. Shouldn't even get your boots wet. Give it another month, though, with all that snow melt, and you'll need a ferry boat, which they have, to get you across."

"You spending the night, Salty?"

"Oh yeah, these horses ain't the onliest ones what enjoy a short ride. I'm gettin' to the age where it really feels good to get in the saddle, and it really feels good to get out."

Floyd laughed. The sun was drifting lower in the west. It wouldn't be long before it reached the mountaintops and disappeared. While it was high overhead, the day had been warm, but now it was getting chilly. He reached behind for his coat and slid it on. He wasn't so cold yet that he needed it, but it helped to hide the guns on his hips.

"You know this place well enough to know where to eat and stay?" Floyd asked Salty.

"As a matter of fact, I shorely do. Only one place I'd eat at, if they ain't changed the cook, and that's the Rio Cantina. Man and wife own the place. Their daughters help. Only problems they have are from the gringos. She cooks real good, and he makes excellent beer. As far as a place to stay, I always stay at Juanita's."

Salty grinned and ran his tongue over his lips. "She always has clean rooms, and she's a good-lookin' woman. Plenty of meat on her bones. We're friends. Too old for you."

Floyd let his remark pass and said, "Good stable?"

"You bet. It's run by a younger feller, leastwise, he's younger than me. Names Arturo Ruiz. You can leave a money bag with him and it'd be safe. Good man."

They had ridden straight through, without stopping to eat, since it was only about twenty-five miles. Now Floyd's belly was talking up a storm. As they pitched over the riverbank, it let out a particularly loud growl.

Salty turned in the saddle. "Boy, if you don't get something in that thing quick, it's liable to eat its way out."

Floyd grinned, raising his voice because of the splashing noises the horses were making in the water. "Why don't we get the horses put up and then take care of my problem."

The two men drew up on the far side of the river, just before they came out, and let the animals drink. Then they rode on into town.

It was like Santa Fe but much smaller, with many open-air stands for the farmers to display their wares. Shadows were spreading, and those who had anything to sell were picking up their goods or covering them. The adobe buildings glowed red in the slanted sunlight. Salty led the two of them into the thick-walled adobe stable.

"Señor Salty," a voice called from the back. A tall middle-aged man, wearing a heavy wool poncho and a big black sombrero, walked to the front. "Get down, let me take care of your fine animals."

"Arturo, how are you, my friend?" Salty said, swinging a leg over the saddle. "This is my amigo Floyd Logan. Please take care of him as well as you do me."

"Of course. Señor Logan, it is nice to meet you."

"And you, Señor Ruiz." Floyd swung down from Rusty.

"Please, señor, call me Arturo."

"Only if you call me Floyd."

The tall man smiled, nodding his head. "*Si*, Floyd, *gracias*." He had collected the reins from Salty and reached out for the three sets from Floyd.

Keeping the reins and lead ropes, Floyd canted his head slightly. "My animals are used to me taking care of them."

"Floyd," Arturo said, with a slight head bow, "I understand, but I have never found a four-legged creature that did not like my attention. Two-legged, especially the señoritas, that is a different matter."

Salty chuckled. "Let him have 'em. He'll take good care of those nags for you, boy."

Reluctantly, Floyd handed the lines over. "We're heading into the mountains tomorrow. If you've got some oats or corn . . ."

"*Si*, Floyd. I'll take excellent care of them and anything you'd like to leave, including your weapons and saddlebags. Nothing disappears from Arturo's stable. You are going to the mountains? It will still be cold there."

Floyd released the talibong from the tie on the back of his saddle and fastened it to the right side of his belt, just in front of the pistol scabbard. Then he removed one of his pistols from the saddle, slipped it behind his belt, and slid a rifle from its scabbard.

Salty had been watching him. "Floyd, you reckon you're gonna need all that?"

"Hope not, Salty. I just don't want to be ambushed and defenseless."

"Boy, I don't think you'll ever be defenseless. You learn fast, and things stick."

The two men headed for the door. "Night, Arturo. See you in the morning," Floyd said.

"What time shall I have your animals ready for you?"

"Not leaving too early, maybe five or six."

"See you tomorrow, Arturo," Salty said and waved as he led Floyd through the small door of the barn.

Salty was thrown back into Floyd as the crack of a rifle reverberated through the small town. Shouts and screams chased the rifle shot. One hand hung onto Salty while the one with the rifle slammed the door closed as Floyd jumped back into the barn. Arturo straight away dashed for his rifle.

Floyd dragged Salty to an adobe wall and laid him on the hay spread across the floor. Blood was soaking Salty's coat. Floyd pulled the coat back and saw the puncture wound just below the old man's collarbone. Blood was oozing from the hole. He pulled the man's coat off, rolled him, and found the exit wound.

Salty tried to wave him off. "I'll be all right. Give me my gun. I'll take care of them sidewinders."

"Just relax, Salty." Floyd turned to Arturo. "Arturo, do you have some rags to plug these holes? I'm going to find out who's shooting at us."

"*Si*, Señor Floyd," Arturo said, running to his office. Moments later he emerged with a clean cotton cloth. "I am sure it is those *animales* the Trace Porter gang. They have been coming and going recently. Miguel Chavez at the Rio Cantina tells me Santa Fe has gotten a little too hot for them, so they moved up here."

No sooner had Arturo spoken than a harsh voice spoke up from outside. "Floyd Logan, this here is Trace Porter. I told you what was gonna happen should you come west. Now I'm gonna show you. Come out now with yore hands in the air and we won't put any more bullets into Salty. We still might kill that Mex in there with you, but I don't imagine you'll mind that."

Floyd didn't answer. His pa had told him about men like this. They liked to hear themselves talk. So be it. Let him talk himself right into a lead ball.

Turning to Arturo, he said, "Is there another way out of here?"

"*Si*, Floyd. This building backs up against my home. It is all adobe. None of those bullets will make it through that wall."

Floyd looked down at Salty. The man was pale and barely able to keep his eyes open.

He showed a weak grin to Floyd and croaked, almost in a whisper, "Do what you gotta do, and by all means, kill that lowlife."

Floyd nodded to Salty, turned and ran to his saddle, withdrawing the other pistol and rifle. He checked them both to make sure caps were in place, and went through the back door into Arturo's home. A determined-looking woman with a butcher knife in her hand stood just inside the door.

"Pardon, señora," Floyd said. "I must find the shooters."

She pulled a son to her, who looked to be almost twelve years old. "Juan, you stick with this man. Show him where those *animales* are hiding. Hurry! They are trying to kill your papi."

Floyd didn't argue. Right now he needed a guide, and this boy was plenty old enough. The two of them dashed out the door with Floyd right on Juan's heels. Floyd laid a hand on Juan's shoulder. "Go at least two blocks. We want to make sure they don't see us when we cross." Three more shots rang out, and he heard a horse scream. *Whoever did that will pay,* he thought.

The boy looked down the street and pointed. Floyd looked where the boy was pointing and saw Wedge Titus tilt a bottle, taking several pulls. He shoved the Ryland Rifle against the corner of the building and sent a .54-caliber lead ball toward Titus. It hit the drinking man where Floyd had held the sights, in the right temple. Wedge Titus released the bottle, and the two of them hit the floor at the same time. The bottle broke, sending liquor all over the dead Wedge. Floyd laid the empty rifle on the ground and checked the cap on his remaining loaded Ryland.

Then he nodded to Juan. The boy looked up and down the street and dashed straight across into the opposing alley, Floyd on his heels. The boy continued to run until he reached the other end of the alley. He looked out and jerked back, turning to Floyd. Just as he did, a tall man with narrow-set, mean eyes walked around the corner and grabbed Juan. With no time to think, Floyd threw his rifle to his shoulder. His sights settled on the man's thick nose. The unbidden thought jumped into Floyd's mind. *It must have once been broken,* and he squeezed the trigger.

The man's nose disappeared, and he too fell limp to the ground. Floyd led Juan to the opposite end of the alley, pulled a pistol from his belt, eared back the hammer, and asked, "Juan, can you shoot this?"

The boy nodded, and Floyd handed it to him. Quickly he reloaded his rifle, slipped a cap on the nipple, and thumbed back the hammer. Juan motioned him to follow. They ran to an adobe building directly across from the stable. Juan held his finger up to his lips, then eased to the edge of the window, going only high enough to allow his eyes to see the interior.

He dropped back down and held up two fingers.

Floyd crawled under the window, traded his rifle for Juan's pistol, and pulled an additional pistol from his left holster. He rose to his full height and pulled the latch on the back door. Floyd thanked the owner of the house for keeping the door hinges oiled, for the door swung open silently. He stepped into the long room.

The room was not only long but also wide. He took four steps inside and stopped. Floyd knew he wasn't as good with the pistol as he was with the rifle. That was why he had been practicing, but it was too late now. He was either good enough, or he wasn't. He took a deep breath.

"You boys looking for me?"

Shocked, the two men spun around and stood there gawking at him. He held a pistol on each killer. It was their move.

The short and stocky one said, "And who might you be?"

"I be the same guy who killed your two amigos a few nights ago."

There was more silence. Then Floyd, feeling no anger, but a cold sense of justice, said, "You boys going to shoot or pee your pants?"

He watched the short one, who would be the quicker of the two, yank his rifle to his shoulder, but he was way too slow. Floyd shot, the ball driving into the short man's right eye. Shorty collapsed to the floor. The remaining man stood there watching Floyd and said the same thing Pike had said. "You're just a boy."

"Were you with Porter at the massacre?" Floyd said, his voice as cold as the snow on the mountaintops.

"I didn't want to be, mister. He made me."

Floyd hung the pistol down, muzzle pointing at the floor. "What you men did wasn't even human. I'll give you a better choice than you gave those girls. You have your rifle in your hands. I'll keep this pistol in my left hand. You shoot anytime."

"Mister," the man said, "I don't want to die."

"That's probably the same words one of those girls said to you."

Silence filled the room. A chicken cackled in the street, bragging about the egg it had just dropped. The honks of Canada geese could be heard as they headed to their nesting grounds in the north. A dog barked. The man snapped up his rifle.

He was quick. He had the hammer eared back and the butt of the stock resting against his shoulder. It looked to Floyd, though he couldn't really tell in the darkening room, that he was squeezing the trigger when Floyd fired. He had to make a quick shot, so he fired for center mass.

His pistol roared, and the man staggered back, his rifle firing into the ceiling as he fell through the front window and lay still. Acrid smoke from the gunfire filled the room. Floyd coughed, ears ringing, then turned and moved quickly through the door, again outside. Juan was standing where Floyd had left him, to one side the door, only looking into the room, his eyes the size of saucers. He handed Floyd the loaded rifle. Floyd asked, "You know where Trace Porter might be?"

The boy pointed to the next adobe building. It was cold and getting dark. Juan ran to the window to look in. Floyd grabbed him, and when he looked up, Floyd shook his head. He took off his hat, picked up a stick and placed his hat on it. Then he eased the hat above the window sill. Immediately a shot rang out, and Floyd's hat went flying into the dry brush. He grasped Juan and shoved the boy behind him. Inside, the sound of running feet carried to where he was standing with a loaded rifle in one hand and a pistol in the other.

The back door burst open and Trace Porter, with Mather Boswell, charged into the darkening night, staring where they thought Floyd's body would be, broken and bleeding.

When they were well outside the building, Floyd said, "Hello, Mr. Porter."

The two men slid to a stop, frozen, afraid to turn. Slowly, Porter turned his head toward Floyd.

"You boys reloaded? I'm sure you have, because no outlaw worth his salt would dash out here without reloading. I'm going to kill you both for what you did to the people on that wagon train, so I'd better shoot fast since I know you must have reloaded."

Trace Porter stammered, "Wait, wait, there, boy. You've no call to shoot us. We ain't had a chance to reload our rifles. Why, you might just call us helpless."

"Yes siree, Trace," Boswell said, his voice tight, "we be helpless as newborn babes. Why, we ain't got a chance against you, boy." With the last statement, Boswell brought his offhand out from behind his back. He had a pistol in it. Floyd, using those big wrists he had developed from working on the farm and being a Logan, tilted the heavy Ryland up. He fired it like a pistol and shot Boswell dead center in the stomach. The murdering outlaw dropped both of his weapons and, whining like a baby, grabbed his stomach before falling to the ground.

Without turning, Floyd asked Juan, "Are there any more?"

"No, señor, these are the last ones."

"Good, thanks for your help. You go check on your papa, and make sure he's all right. I'll be along shortly."

Boswell moaned again, and Porter turned to him. "Shut up, Mather. Take it like a man." Then he turned back to Floyd. "You been quite a burr under my saddle, boy."

Floyd said nothing. His cold blue eyes watched the killer, but he listened for other movement. Juan had said he had killed all the other outlaws in town, but he was still cautious.

"So, boy, what am I goin' to do with you? You want to join my gang? You want money? I've got money. I can give you a heap of money. All you need do is let me walk outta here, and I'll get you the money. Would you like that?"

Floyd was still silent.

Porter was sweating, though the evening was cool. Having heard nothing from Floyd, he took a tentative step, and the night was filled with the sound of a hammer going to full cock.

"Now see here, boy. You ain't got no call to shoot me. I'm just a poor man tryin' to make a dollar."

Floyd finally spoke. "Is that my rifle you're holding?"

Surprised, Porter glanced down at the rifle. "Why, yes it is. It shot so good, I started usin' it myself. You took right good care of it, boy."

"Where are my pistols?"

"Is that what this is about? Why, shoot, boy, I reckon you done followed me so far, I'll just give them back to you. They're stuck right here behind my sash."

"Lay my rifle down, gently, and the pistols next to it. Don't try anything, Porter. This pistol I have has a mighty light trigger."

"Sure, boy, sure." Porter laid the rifle gently on the ground with the two pistols beside it. "Now, there, boy, you got your guns back, why don't you just run along. We can call it even."

Floyd saw the glint of teeth when Porter gave him a sickly grin. "I thought you said you have a lot of money?"

"I do, boy, I sure do. Why, I wouldn't mind giving you a part of the money. How much would you like?"

"How much you got?"

"Boy, you can't take all my hard-earned money. You can't do that. Why, that wouldn't be Christian."

During the movement and conversation, Porter had been easing his right hand to his belt knife. It was big and sharp, a good thrower. He had killed several men with it and was confident he could do it again.

Floyd, like many of the Logans, had been blessed with superior night vision. He caught the first movement of Porter's hand. He knew the man was going for a knife and figured Porter was convinced he could pull his knife and throw it before Floyd fired. It was a big gamble, but one that, if Porter was right, would get him out of this deadly situation and allow him to build another gang. Floyd waited, pistol cocked, but hanging at his side.

Porter droned on while moving his hand back to his knife's hilt. Reaching it, he continued to talk. "Boy, you know you can't shoot me. I ain't got no gun."

He shouted his last word, and his right hand grabbed the knife haft. He was fast and confident as he lifted and began extending his arm to the rear for the power needed to sink the knife deep into Floyd's chest.

At the point where the knife arm was fully extended and ready to release the pent-up energy in the shoulder, Floyd fired. The bullet flew true, striking the outlaw leader in the third button of the greasy, cheap black linen shirt. Porter staggered and sat, leaning his left shoulder against the adobe wall.

Floyd loaded first his rifle, then his pistols, keeping a close watch on the outlaw leader. Soon, he was ready for any other surprises the Porter gang might have for him.

Boswell had stopped moaning and lay still. Floyd walked over and toed the body. Nothing, the man was dead. He continued to Porter, who was moaning almost as loud as Boswell had been.

Porter looked up, surprise on his face. "You killed me, boy."

"I have. Guess you won't have the chance to hang any of my guts on a tree. Any last thing you want to say before you go where we both know you're going?"

"I ain't a bad man. I . . ."

Floyd picked up his rifle and pistols, then turned to leave.

"Where you goin', boy? What about animals? There's wolves, coyotes, and bears around here."

Floyd started walking.

Porter raised his voice in desperation. "Wait, I mean it. You can't leave me here. Have some mercy."

Floyd stopped, but didn't turn. Looking straight ahead, he said, "I'm showing you mercy, Porter. I'm showing you more than those folks you murdered on that wagon train." He continued walking. At the side of the building, he turned to follow Juan's path. He could see people in the alley, holding torches.

"Wait," Porter screamed. "I don't want to die!"

Floyd saw Arturo in the street. "That's Porter screaming. He's shot hard. The others are scattered around, dead."

"We will take care of the bodies, and Porter." Arturo spoke rapidly to the man standing next to him. Leading the other men, the man headed to the back of the building where Porter lay. All of them had drawn machetes.

"Other than this rifle and two pistols, which he stole from me in Tennessee, all of their possessions—guns, money, horses, everything—belong to you and the town. There are others lying around. They are yours. How is Salty?"

"*Gracias*, Señor Floyd, we can use them, the powder and lead too. It is hard for farmers to afford weapons for protection and hunting. Come, I will take you to him. You can see for yourself." He chuckled.

25

Salty was propped up in bed, shirtless, with a clean bandage wrapped across his chest, covering his wound. A rather plump lady was wiping his forehead. "Howdy, Floyd. After all of that shooting, I wasn't sure what to expect."

"How are you feeling?"

The lady bumped Salty's shoulder, making him wince.

"Oh, yeah. This here is Juanita Salizar, a mighty kind hostess."

She was an attractive woman with a bright smile. Long black hair hung over one shoulder. The blouse she wore was low cut and working hard to hang on to its contents.

"I'm Floyd Logan, ma'am. Pleased to meet you."

"It is very nice to meet you, Señor Logan." She stood, gave Salty a proprietary kiss on the temple, and started from the room. "I will leave you to talk, but remember, he is hurt and he must have rest."

Floyd said, "Yes, ma'am."

Arturo shook Floyd's hand. "*Muchas gracias*, Floyd. Those were terrible men. They stole from us and would sometimes take our women. It is good they are dead."

Through the open window, the screams from Porter, which had been going on during their walk and arrival here, broke off.

"A proper ending for such an evil man. Now I too shall leave. Your horses will be ready for you in the morning."

Floyd moved to a chair by the bed and leaned his rifle in a near corner. "How are you feeling?"

"I'm fine. I'll get the gent I came up to fix the wagon for to take me back to Santa Fe tomorrow."

Floyd grinned. "Looks like you're welcome here."

"Yes and no. I can't stay around her too long fore she starts gettin' clingy. So, getting out of here tomorrow will be perfect. Now, tell me what happened."

Floyd detailed the action for Salty, giving Juan most of the credit for getting him into position. When he finished, Salty was shaking his head.

"Boy, when you're riled, you are one catamount. Remind me to stay on yore good side. Is that it?"

Floyd nodded.

"I guess you're leavin' in the morning."

Floyd nodded again.

"Well, I mean to leave you with some advice."

Floyd was tired, and he needed to leave in the morning. He had a long way to go, and he'd best get moving if he expected to do any trapping. He leaned back in the chair and said, "Shoot."

"First, you're a fine feller. If I still could, I'd ride the river with you anytime. Here's something you need to understand. I ain't no mountain man. I'm more sociable and better around people." He caught Floyd's raised eyebrows.

"All right, most of the time. Some people rub me the wrong way. Anyway, you're young and trusting. That pretty much comes from bein' young. You've got to watch that trustiness. It'll get you in big trouble. There are folks out there like Porter. They'll wait until another man has earned his keep, then they'll steal it, and they's mountain men. There's good ones and there's bad ones.

The bad ones will clean you out and most likely kill you to boot."

Salty pushed himself farther up in bed, causing a grimace from the pain, before he started again.

"Now you gotta be on the lookout. You got to understand that most folks are out for themselves, and that ain't bad. That's why they work so hard and build and grow. Those are the good folks. But the bad ones work hard to take everything you have, so mark my word, and trust no one till they earned it. That way, you'll keep yore hair.

"Floyd, I want to say one other thing. You got the look. There's a lot of those mountain men what can't stand people. That's why they stay in the mountains. There's others that are fine with folks, but they love them mountains. I reckon you fall in that second bunch. You're cut out for it, boy. You stay cautious and keep yore eyes open and clear, and you'll be in them mountains enjoyin' 'em for many a year to come. Now gimme yore hand, and git. You need to rest more than you need to listen to an old man gabbing."

Floyd shook Salty's hand, picked up his rifle, and stuck his head out the door to find Juanita. He needed a room. She was sitting in a chair next to the outside wall of the room Salty was in. As soon as she saw him, she rose.

"This way, Señor Floyd. Your room is right down here." Walking to his room, Juanita said, "Salty is a marvelous man. He must like you very much to tell you what he has."

Floyd nodded. "I like him."

She pushed a door open to let him in. He looked around. The room was small, but clean.

"Thank you," he said.

"*Si*. What time will you get up?"

He was having a hard time keeping his eyes open. "About five."

"*Bueno*, I will have breakfast for you."

She pulled the door closed.

Floyd sat on the edge of the bed and, though he was beat, checked and loaded all of his weapons, undressed and fell into bed.

~

FLOYD SAT RUSTY, the horse moving easy up Rio Chama. The sun, the town, and civilization were behind him, and the San Juans waited in front. From what Jeb had told him and the trappers he had talked to, he had little doubt he would find Jeb's cabin.

He had waited for this moment since he was a little boy. He was about to enter the mountains. Mountains with beaver, grizzly, mountain lions, and Indians.

He had been gradually climbing, the river winding but the town remaining in sight. The next turn would block any visible evidence of town or people behind him. The homemade meals, the warm beds, human contact, and other creature comforts he had grown used to would soon be far behind, and that was all right. Yes, it was comfortable where towns and people were, but those same comforts softened a man, both in body and mind.

The horses seemed excited to be out of town. Rusty was alert and smelling at every breeze, while Buck stepped high through the foothills. A few more hours, and the animals would settle down to new surroundings in the mountains.

Floyd kept a sharp lookout. This was Apache country. He had listened closely to the mountain men who brought in furs to Santa Fe, and last night listened to Salty. Many stories about the Apache suggested that if a man was careless, his hair would soon be gone.

One thing he had learned was to stay off beaten paths. He rode twenty-five to thirty yards to one side of the trail, leaving no tracks on the trail and preventing a surprise meeting. Also, he had a rifle across his legs and quick access to his pistols. His knife rode on his hip. He had tied the talibong to his saddle on his left side. He had a special plan for that knife. The weapons he had taken back from Porter were tied on the mule. Next time he was in Santa Fe, he'd have Oliver convert them to caplocks.

The land around him was becoming more vertical. He had learned that in the mountains, night came on with a vengeance. Before the sun lowered very far in the west, he found a protected campsite. It was against a bluff that had a long overhang jutting out and over the grass below.

Several blowdowns provided plenty of dry wood for a campfire, and the overhang was high enough to shelter horses. The bluff was close to seventy-five yards from the river, so Floyd led the horses to the water, letting them drink their fill. He returned and stripped the packs and tack from the horses. Staking them with sufficient rope to graze, but not enough to leave the overhang, he set to making a fire and brewing up some coffee. He had gathered dry wood, and watched it as it burned, giving off only an insignificant amount of smoke.

The last couple of days had been long and tiring. Even as young as he was, he could feel the fatigue. After the water boiled, he set the pot to the edge of the coals. It would stay hot there. He tossed in the coffee and pulled some jerky and the last two sopapillas from his saddlebags. *I'd better enjoy these,* he thought. *I fear this is the last I'll taste for a long time.* Floyd tore a section of the jerky with his teeth and settled back to wait on the coffee.

A chill wind whistled down the river, coming out of the northwest. It had been warm enough today to wear his wool coat, so he'd left his buffalo coat bundled and tied on the packhorse. *I'll switch coats tonight. It's liable to get pretty cold,* he thought. *We might even get some snow.* Floyd took a handful of cold water from another pot he had filled, and tossed it into the coffeepot to settle the grounds. Salty had shown him that trick, and it worked. He'd said he preferred to drink his coffee over chewing it. Floyd waited only a moment and poured himself a cup, leaned back against a dead stump, and took a sip of the coffee. He felt the bite and warmth all the way down to his toes.

He picked up a sopapilla and took a bite, savoring it. In the dry air, it was already a little stale, but still delicious. He lifted the pastry to take a second bite. A horse neigh blew in the brush. He pulled his rifle to his lap, completed the additional bite of the sopapilla, and waited.

"Hello the camp," came floating through the trees. "Wonder if I could come on in. I'm friendly."

"Come on," Floyd called back. "I've got something here that'll go a long way to converting you if you're not."

He heard a cackle in the brush, and a man came riding out of the trees. "That coffee smells mighty fine to this old nose."

"Light and sit," Floyd said. "I welcome company on a night like this."

The man was riding a mule and leading another. He unsaddled the one he was riding, and pulled the packs from the other, not hobbling or staking them out. He walked up with his saddlebags and rifle, laid them down, and pulled out his cup. Steam rose from the brew, the aroma filling the air around the campfire. He groaned slightly as he lowered himself to the ground. "Bit of rheumatis. Acts up when the weather's about to change."

He took a long sip of the coffee. "Mm-mm, that's mighty good. Your ma teach you how to make coffee like that, boy?"

"Nope, Salty Dickens did."

"Well, I'll be a sodbuster without a plow, how is ole Salty doing? I ain't seen him nigh on to twenty years. Don't guess I'll see him again, neither, what with him in Missouri. I been east my last time."

"If you're headed for Santa Fe, you can see him. He's working for Hugh Brennan at his livery, though he might not be there for a few days."

The older man had drained his cup and was reaching across

for the pot. He looked up at Floyd and said, almost apologetically, "I like my coffee, mind?"

"Go right ahead," Floyd said. "You didn't mention your name."

Now the man looked at him and said, "Nor you."

Floyd grinned. "You've got a point. My name's Floyd Logan."

The man jerked back with his coffee at the mention of Floyd's name. "So you be Floyd Logan?" The old man ran his finger down his jawline to his chin, mirroring Floyd's, his finger rippling the mostly gray beard. "You be that Floyd Logan."

Floyd hadn't shaved since he left Santa Fe. The beard seemed to protect his face against the chill wind and did a fair job of covering the scar. He ran his hand over his cheek. At seventeen, he had developed a fairly thick black beard. Logans not only tended to size, but the curse of a thick beard. Only a fraction of an inch of his scar was visible, if a person looked closely.

"You can tell me what you've heard, right after you tell me your name."

"Boy, yore mighty insistent. I'm known as Everlight Kensley. My given name's Dallas, but that just never seemed to stick." He glanced over at the fire, picked up some sticks, and laid them gently across the flames. "Seems I was always good at starting a fire. Folks would say, 'Let Everlight do it. He ain't ever failed to get it a-going,' and you know what? Them folks was right. Any time, any place, I can get a fire going."

The man pulled off his worn cap, scratched around his head a bit, and then stopped. He looked at the tiny bug he'd caught and smashed it between thumb and forefinger. "I hate those danged lice.

"What was I a-talking about? Oh, yeah, I stopped in with a friend of mine. Reckon he's got a cabin below the head of the Animas on Deer Park Creek. They call it that 'cause most of the year, they's deer all around, 'less you start shootin' 'em. They get scarce when that happens."

He looked at Floyd, his brows wrinkled, and a baffled look wandered across his face. "I was speakin' of what?"

Floyd moved the piece of jerky he was chewing on to the side of his mouth, and said, "Deer Park Creek."

A grin split the old man's beard. "I sometimes get a mite forgetful. Anyways, this friend looks like he's found him some fine beaver streams. I trapped that country a few years back and figured we had cleaned it out. You never know." He shook his head as if in puzzlement for a moment. "Oh yeah, his name's Jeb Campbell. Don't know if you know him or not."

"Why, I sure do. Jeb and I are partners. That's where I'm headed, for the spring trapping."

Everlight shook his shaggy head again. "Yore gonna be a mite late. That's some distant travel, and those streams will be losing ice any day now. At least they should. This here storm we got coming may cool it off and keep those beaver shut up for a couple more weeks. Though, them beaver tend to work through just about any sort of weather."

"I'm getting some more wood," Floyd said, standing and moving into the trees. There were a couple of deadfalls near the overhang. He made it to the first one. Being outside of the protecting bluff, the wind was biting, but the buffalo hide kept the cold out and the warm in. He looked it over and moved on to the farther deadfall. There was no telling how long they might be here, so he'd save the easier wood for later, if they needed it. He grabbed a dried, many-branched limb and dragged it near the camp. Floyd picked up the ax and began chopping. In no time, he had a large pile of wood.

"You had practice with that implement, I see."

Floyd looked at the ax. "Yep, I lived on a farm." With more than enough wood to make it through the night, he checked his horses and mule, talked to them, then moved back to the fire.

"While I'm up," he said to the old man, "you want me to grab your mules and bring them in with mine? Might be a little warmer, and make them less susceptible to the Indians."

Everlight, who was finishing the last of the coffee, which included the dregs, glanced up, chewing. "That'd be mighty nice there, uh..."

"Floyd."

"That's right, Floyd, reminds me, I had an uncle once, named Floyd, or was he a cousin?" He jerked his hand to his hair, scratched for a moment, and said, "Danged lice." Then he looked at Floyd. "Oh, yeah, the mules. That'd be right kind of you, Floyd, right kind. Bring 'em in close, 'cause there's a humdinger of a storm brewing, and it's liable to be here tonight."

Floyd turned and walked into the trees and grass. The mules had drifted down to the river and were drinking. Their heads popped out of the water and turned, watching him. "Easy, boys. I'm a friend. I'm here to take you where it's a little warmer." At his voice they dropped their heads back into the water and finished. He gathered the wet reins and led them back to camp. "You got some rope, Everlight?"

He glanced over at the old man and saw he was already bundled in his bedding, lying against his saddle, sound asleep. Floyd walked to the man's equipment, took out the ropes, and tied the mules out. He moved the packs and gear in closer to the fire, picking up the man's rifle. After checking the load and primer of the flintlock, he laid it next to Everlight and moved to his gear.

Both rifles he laid next to him and the two pistols from his saddle. After wiggling around, he stretched out on his bedroll and pulled a blanket over him. A soft snore came from Everlight with a little wheezing. Floyd listened for a moment more and leaned against his saddle. *The old man is probably right,* he thought, noting the dampness in the air. *Feels like cold weather is on the way.* As he slipped off to sleep, his mind wandered to

Dawn Light. He could see her dark eyes and shining hair. *I think I'll see her this summer. Maybe I'll go to her village.*

∽

THE LATE SEASON storm blew in with a vengeance, packing little snow, but high winds and plummeting temperatures. For three days the mountains were battered. Snapping and falling limbs could be heard throughout the forest, but the two men remained protected and warm thanks to the rocky ledge and abundance of wood.

The fourth morning brought clearing skies and only a faint north wind. Floyd kicked out from under his blanket, slapped his hat on his head, took off his moccasins, and pulled on his boots. Everlight was still bundled in his blankets. Floyd looked around. He had cleared a wide swath of dead trees. It was a good thing he'd left the nearer deadfall, because it had contributed to the fire yesterday and last night. He glanced over at his still-sleeping companion. *Wonder how old he is?* Floyd thought, for the old man had helped little during the storm.

Everlight squinted through one slitted eye and said, "Coffee ready?"

"Cookin' up right now," Floyd responded.

He had learned a lot from listening to Everlight over the past three days. He now knew more about the Lewis and Clark expedition than what he'd gotten from books. Floyd felt like he was on a first-name basis with Hugh Glass, George Drouillard, Manuel Lisa, and Jedidiah Smith. In a way, he regretted leaving Santa Fe. If he'd stayed, he would have had the chance to meet Jedidiah Smith. Everlight said the well-known mountain man was supposed to be bringing trading goods to the city this year. It was certain that Hugh knew him well.

There was still a lot of these original mountain men in the

mountains. He looked forward to meeting the men he'd heard and read so much about.

With a groan, Everlight threw his blankets off and surveyed the morning. "Time I was movin' on."

"Goes for both of us. I imagine Jeb's expectin' me."

"Wouldn't worry about that. Jeb's been in the mountains long enough to know that a man shows up when he shows up."

"Straight up that there Animas, boy. That's the way to go. You can rest up there for a day before tackling those San Juans. They're rough this time of year. May still be so much snow, you ain't gettin' over any pass, but come to think of it, you ain't got no passes to speak of to go over. You should be fine, barring no broke legs or Injuns."

"Thanks, Everlight," Floyd said, grinning at the old man. "I'll make sure I stay away from both of those."

"You do that. Neither them Apache or Ute would pass up a chance to get ahold of all that hair you got under yore hat. Plus, they wouldn't mind getting yore animals and supplies, specially those fancy guns, but they really like mule. They see that mule, and they'll trail you across them mountains to get a bite of him, figger mules is mighty tasty."

The two men ate and took their animals down to the river.

"Watch yoreself, Floyd. Take a second thought on following that Chama river. If you do, you got canyons you got to travel through. Heavy rains in the mountains, or sudden snow melt, could get you drowned. Some places there ain't no gettin' out."

While the animals drank, Floyd considered what Everlight was saying. He said, "Which is the quickest route?"

The older man shook his head. "Boy, it ain't about quicker, it's about gettin' there. The canyon is quickest, since I've traveled it on several occasions, but it sure ain't fun. You'll be in that thing for days, and if them Apache catch you in there, you're for sure a dead man. I'd say hold to the north side, climb them horses up on the mesa, and mosey along."

"Thanks," Floyd said, "I might do that."

Everlight squinted at him. "Boy, I hope you do, 'cause that ain't the only canyon. After Chama, there's Huckbay canyon, Mine canyon, and Dark canyon. That Dark canyon keeps on a-going. Cliffs rare up anywhere from three hundred all the way to seven, eight hundred feet or more."

Floyd swung into the saddle. "Thanks for the information. I'll be seeing you."

The old man shoved his hat back on his head and scratched at his scalp. "You got some fine country to go through afore gettin' to the Animas, but yonder is full of Injuns. You're going through the heart of 'Pache country. Once you get to the San Juan River, you'll be in Ute hunting grounds. They's both dangerous. Apaches'll leap right out of the ground at you, so you'd best be ready all the time.

"Them Ute are some fine-lookin' folks, but they figure this entire country is theirs, and they'd as soon kill a white man as look at him."

Through all the time the horses drank, Everlight kept talking. Finally, he too mounted. "Well, Floyd, it's been right nice meetin' you. I appreciate the grub. You ever get to my cabin, you help yoreself. Mind my words, boy, and watch yore hair." The two men shook hands, and Floyd turned up the Rio Chama.

∼

JEB STOOD at the door of his cabin, sipping his cup of coffee. The ice was breaking, and he had already started getting his traps ready. The snow, melted enough for a horse in most places, was still too deep for a man.

He had just gotten back from the beaver streams. He had been fortunate. Though all of the ponds were still iced over, the beaver were active, always working. Another week or so, and he'd be ready to trap.

The morning sky was clear, and the breeze cutting. At these levels, even with the tall pines and aspen breaking the wind, it was frigid. Taking another sip of coffee, he admired the solitude his cabin gave him. Here he was in the middle of the up tall mountains, and as far as the eye could see, there wasn't a soul near him. His gaze settled on the tall peaks of the Rockies, at least the ones visible from the cabin. These mountains went on forever, but rising in front of him to the east were Mount Rhoda and Whitehead. When he looked down Deer Park Creek, and across where the Animas was, to the west, there was Spencer Peak, Grand Turk, and Sultan as big as you please.

In his exploring over to the east, he'd actually found a crossing up there. Not so much a pass, but a possible route over a not-so-sharp ridge. It was high up and hard breathing for both man and horse, but it was doable, but mighty cold and windy. Today the wind was taking the snow from those peaks and dusting them like a wave across the far valley.

Taking one last look around and seeing nothing, he turned to go back inside. Movement caught his eye as the resident robber jay sailed in. The bird hopped around, occasionally stopping and cocking his head to look up at him like he expected something. Jeb shook his head and reached into his pocket. He pulled out a hard biscuit and broke off a piece, tossing it to the ground. The jay jumped on it, pecked twice, the biscuit disappeared, and the bird turned his little black eyes back up to Jeb. Jeb ripped off a larger piece of biscuit and dropped it to the ground. The gray and white jay hopped twice, reached the biscuit, and started pecking. While he was still pecking, Jeb stuck the rest of the biscuit in his mouth, lifted the latch and stepped inside.

He was proud of his cabin. He had found a shallow cave well over twelve feet tall. It maintained the height for at least twenty feet, so he'd built his cabin around it. He'd sealed the cracks where the wood joined the rock, with a mixture of rock, dirt, and water. By himself, he had split logs, built the cabin and rock fireplace, and chinked the logs to keep the heat inside. His fireplace provided enough heat for the cabin and cave so he could bring in the horses when it was too cold for them outside. He'd also built a stable outside, on the protected east wall, that would handle seven or eight horses.

He walked over to the little mountain mustang and patted him on the neck. "What do you think, Buster, how do you like yore house?"

The horse kept chewing the hay Jeb had tossed into the cave. He walked over to the mule and his other horse, patted them both and moved to his table. He placed his cooling coffee cup on the table, retrieved the pot from the fire, and topped off the cup.

Jeb placed the pot back on the edge of the fire and said, "Boys, where do you suppose Floyd is? He could've left in the middle of April, but I bet Hugh would have talked him into waiting. I sure hope he's on his way now. With his traps and mine, this spring we'll make quite a haul if'n he's already makin' tracks."

He sat at the table, gazing at the walls. Windows would've been a pleasant touch, he thought, but then shuddered. The icy winter wind would have found every crack and opening. Windows would be too cold.

"Dang it, boys, I'm tired of waiting!"

At his shout, the animals jerked their heads toward him. Then the mule turned back to the hay while the two horses stood watching. Jeb stood and started packing. It didn't take long. He saddled Buster, tied on his bedroll and saddlebags, and grabbed his rifle. His pistol was already behind his waistband, so he took the heavy buffalo coat from the peg hanger that had been driven into a log. Once he had his coat on, he swung his belt around the coat and cinched it tight. On the belt was his knife and tomahawk.

A THINNED-DOWN FLOYD LOGAN sat on Rusty. The horse's ribs were also showing. But now, here he sat, on the south side of Deer Park Creek, looking at the cabin he had labored so long to reach.

It had been a tough trip, and he didn't just mean the one from Santa Fe. His mind closed in on Limerick, the Tennessee hills, Martha his sister, Pa, and Ma.

"We've made it, Rusty. There is Jeb's cabin."

He thought of the Pawnee, and how lucky he had been to win the fight with the Indian. His seventeen-year-old mind couldn't help but think, *I've been watched over this entire trip. That Pawnee's knife blade might have found my throat. Pike should have killed me instead of waking me up so he could gloat. I might not have met Lontac and learned so much. So many things, and the list goes on.*

His thoughts again traveled back to his ma. *I know you were praying for me, Ma, and I've made it. I only wish you and Pa were able to see how beautiful this tall mountain country is. Why, it has more clear streams than I've ever seen, and I've only seen a small part of it.*

Rusty stomped his foot, and Floyd said, "Don't be impatient, boy. We're here. We've found our place."

He looked at the peak to the east. An eagle soared high and free, writing slow circles in the sky above the snow-covered peak. Across the creek, Floyd heard the cabin door open. Jeb stepped out, stared for a moment and waved.

Floyd stood in the saddle, thrusting his body as high as it would go. His arm stretched to the sky where the eagle circled, the Ryland clutched in his hand. Softly, almost reverently, he said, "I made it to the shining mountains!"

AUTHOR'S NOTE

Thank you for reading *Soul of a Mountain Man*, the first book in the Logan Mountain Man Series. The second book of the series, *Trials of a Mountain Man*, is now available. I hope you enjoy his continuing adventures.

If you have any comments, what you like or what you don't, please let me know.

You can email me at: Don@DonaldLRobertson.com, or you can use the contact form on my website.

www.DonaldLRobertson.com

I'll be looking forward to hearing from you.

BOOKS
Logan Mountain Man Series
(Prequel to Logan Family Series)

SOUL OF A MOUNTAIN MAN
TRIALS OF A MOUNTAIN MAN

Logan Family Series

LOGAN'S WORD
THE SAVAGE VALLEY
CALLUM'S MISSION
FORGOTTEN SEASON

Clay Barlow - Texas Ranger Justice Series

FORTY-FOUR CALIBER JUSTICE
LAW AND JUSTICE
LONESOME JUSTICE

NOVELLAS AND SHORT STORIES

RUSTLERS IN THE SAGE
BECAUSE OF A DOG
THE OLD RANGER